The Boy and the Beast

The Boy and the Beast

Marshal A. Garmo

VANTAGE PRESS
New York

Illustrated by David Bond

FIRST EDITION

All rights reserved, including the right of
reproduction in whole or in part in any form.

Copyright © 1996 by Marshal A. Garmo

Published by Vantage Press, Inc.
516 West 34th Street, New York, New York 10001

Manufactured in the United States of America
ISBN: 0-533-11864-6

Library of Congress Catalog Card No.: 96-90053

0 9 8 7 6 5 4 3 2 1

To Claudia, Chanel, Sean, Nicole, and Kathleen

1

Fifteen-year-old Peter's only concern was surviving the night in the wilderness. He watched with mounting fear as grayness turned into darkness, enveloping the mountainous area of western Wyoming. It was a cool September night when strong winds turned into storms and writhing fluffy clouds transformed themselves into shapeless monsters mirroring the rock formation below. Some of these rocks stood as erect as a speaker at a podium or a chimney over a barn. There were others, resembling sharks with gaping maws ready to devour the forest creatures. It was a scene that Peter would not have missed for anything. He had, however, lost interest in the vastness of nature and its beauty, for he had retreated to a cave.

His cave retreat was one of many that honey-combed the conical hills. The cave was more like a natural clay-colored tent with a semi-round dome with the look of a work of a sculptor. Peter crouched in his cave, crumpled and weary, trying to curb his continuous coughing. He squatted on the damp pebbles blanketing the floor, his back glued to a rocky wall.

As he stared at the darkness toward the cave's entrance, he watched for unwelcome creatures who might hear his coughing and come in. Everything was engulfed in silence. Nothing broke the tranquility except the sporadic grunting of bears coming from a distance and the intermittent howling of coyotes, wolves, and other unknown wild sounds, striking terror in Peter's heart.

Peter lay motionless, his hands numb with fear and the chilling night. *I will be dead any minute now*, he thought, *either as a prey to a wild beast or to the chilly weather.* He tried to take control over himself through positive thinking and kept reminding himself to be sensible and calm.

His thoughts shifted to the morning before when he'd ventured into the wilderness. He had planned to spend a few hours there and return home on the same day. It was something he had always wanted to do.

He reminded himself not to panic. He recalled reading adventure books and being greatly influenced by them. There were books that sparked his imagination like the discovery voyages to unknown places and others that plunged into the depths of the oceans. Sinbad had discovered hens that laid golden eggs and fish that metamorphosed into mermaids as they approached the coast. There were magical surroundings engulfed with thick-colored vapors where bears and mermaids swam.

The cold winds seeping into the cave brought him back to reality. He tried to go back to his thoughts and recalled watching movies whose heroes were challenged by monsters and faced death. Peter was heartened by their abilities to snatch victory from the clutches of death. These thoughts, however, provided only a little solace for his fear-paralyzed soul. The unknown, the darkness and stillness that cut through his bravado, chilled him to the bone with fear, sending his fever-wracked body into paroxysms of trembling. The thought of his certain death overwhelmed him.

His thoughts took him to the time when he had resorted to that rock tent several hours earlier. He had been wandering aimlessly in a desperate attempt to find his bicycle. He had left it that afternoon hidden near berry bushes in order to return to it later. But it had become dark and he could not find it.

I should have left for home earlier, he thought. *If I did, I would have reached home on time. Even if I didn't, I could've stayed in one of the houses by the road. It would then have been easy to find home tomorrow morning.*

The darkness inside the cave was absolute. The towering thunderheads that Peter had seen earlier had turned into thick masses of low clouds covering the entire sky, thus preventing the light otherwise reflected from the moon and the stars from reaching Peter. The only light sparkling in the sky was spawned from the sporadic lightning that illuminated the woods outside. Some of the light would reflect from the outside, intermittently revealing a grand room with a round, jagged ceiling inside Peter's cave shelter. He could see bundles of rock formations, in various sizes and shapes of lightness chandeliers, hanging from the ceiling of the cave. As more light penetrated into the place, Peter could see that some of these rocks oozed with water.

He wanted to move around to find a smoother ground to sleep on, but he was apprehensive of even making the slightest movement. He was fearful that it would trigger an onslaught by some hidden dragon or would awake a sleeping beast.

He groped the ground around him, like a blind person trying to locate his bag of food. Soon his cold fingers clasped it. He hoped that he still had something to eat. The thought of food reactivated his appetite and he felt hungry. He had forgotten about the bag. Now he would eat whatever food he had left.

When he examined the bag, he was enraged to find out that there was only an empty water bottle. There was no food. Peter was not excessively disappointed, however. An hour earlier, he was starving to the point of shaking, but later his feeling of hunger had disappeared. Now his hunger was replaced by a feeling of dizziness and fatigue.

His wracking cough had become less severe; it was mainly a dry cough. The echo of his coughing sounded throughout the grand room of the cave in consecutive waves of thundering, frightening sounds. It occurred to him that strange creatures and ferocious monsters hidden in the cave might in fact be the ones returning that echo. He shifted his glance between the cave's en-

trance and the depth of the cave, where the echo of his coughing was still roaring. He repeatedly attempted to curb the cough, but in vain.

Finally, he lay down fully clothed, wearing a sport jacket that Aunt Pauline had insisted he wear at all times and a new sweater. He was thrown there on the rocky ground, utterly spent. The full day's journey had sapped his remaining energy. He was infected with an incurable type of tuberculosis that was driving him to his grave. That was what Peter had concluded from the death of his mother, a victim of the same disease.

Peter had loved his mother and the thought of her dying a victim of this disease angered him more than the fact that he was stranded hopelessly in the middle of nowhere. She had been a kind and brave woman. *I wish I could see her now just for an hour*, he thought. *It doesn't matter if I die after that.* He tried to think of pleasant memories of her, but his mind blurred with fever and fear, leaving little room for other subjects.

He was afraid not so much of death itself but more of the unknown. What would happen, for instance, if one of the beasts showed up all of a sudden, such as a grizzly bear or a bison? He would not be able to defend himself. *Beasts are not compassionate*, he thought. They could not be persuaded to leave a prey alone, even if the prey was a human being. Only sheer force and trickery could stop them.

At this moment, lightning struck near the cave's entrance, revealing a towering rock inside the cave hanging over the entrance on his right side. The view of the pyramidal rock allayed Peter's fears somewhat. It was about ten feet high and Peter realized that he could climb up there if he was attacked.

As he was thinking about the rock that was now swallowed by darkness, he heard a coyote calling, followed by more and more calls, as though they were waiting for one of their number to start. This distracted him from his thoughts of death and fear, and he started to concentrate on the coyote's calls. But he was not alarmed by them; they would be the last animals to scare him.

He reasoned that wild animals constituted a primary threat to him. The animal kingdom, however, was different from man's domain. Whereas he might manage to handle any human being, animals were a different story. Therefore, the more he knew about animals, the greater his chances for survival. Peter had very little personal experience with wildlife. All the information that he had learned about nature stemmed from his association with Bob Jones, his neighbor, and from reading books and watching television.

"Animals have superior perception and are intelligent creatures, even more intelligent than man in certain aspects," Mr. Jones had told him. "Some animals are many times superior than man in several qualities essential for survival, such as smell, vision, and the transmission of sonic vibration. Since the principal objective of all living things is survival, animals are better at that." Peter knew that animals could survive under extreme circumstances, such as spending a night covered with layers of snow or wandering for a week without food.

Peter tried to remember some of the stories that Mr. Jones had told him about his trips in the wilderness to recall if he'd ever been in the same circumstances, but none came to mind. Peter's mind was teeming with feelings of distress and grief. He had to get ready for any attack. His body, or whatever would be left of it, would probably never be discovered for years.

In addition to wild animals, he was also concerned about the beast he had heard about. The human beast roamed these areas. According to many who had seen him or heard about him, he was a human being, but a savage one with a huge awkward body, living in isolation. This hulk, that most people hereabouts simply called the beast, assaulted and slaughtered animals as well as people. Peter feared that he would be roaming these mountains. He could be worse than all the wild beasts in the forest.

Peter heard footsteps of an animal crushing the bushes and

broken branches in the woods. The footsteps were heavy and systematic. Peter shivered and the blood froze in his veins. The footsteps were coming his way. For several long seconds, his mind went blank. All he could do was wait for the beast and offer him himself.

When he realized the gravity of the menace, his mind went to work. He remembered the rock at the cave's entrance and wondered if he really could climb it at the appropriate moment in the event he was attacked. He focused on the rock, trying to determine, in the midst of darkness, its distance and height.

What kind of animal is it? thought Peter, as the footsteps persisted. *But I won't know what to do until I know what it is.* To vanquish an enemy, one must first know who the enemy is.

Peter continued shivering as he started surveying all the large animals that he knew, recollecting their size and height to determine if the footsteps belonged to one of them. He found the task intricate as in his mind he thumbed through all the names of wild animals he had seen in the zoo or in Tarzan movies. Only Mr. Jones could probably identify a wild animal just from listening to its footsteps. *But what could the animal be?* he wondered. *It can't be a bear because I know what a bear sounds like. It can't be a coyote or even a wolf because the sound of their footsteps is light and sometimes not even audible.*

As the footsteps were almost at the cave's entrance, an idea occurred to Peter that struck horror in his heart. Could it be that human beast? It was not only possible but very likely.

Suddenly the footsteps stopped. Peter felt confused. Why had the thing stopped? Was it trying to figure out the scent it was getting from him? Perhaps it was moving toward him stealthily trying not to alert him. Could it be that smart? Peter's mind was asking questions and answering them simultaneously. *That is impossible though*, he reasoned, *because the forest floor is full of leaves and dried grass stems. I am bound to hear some sound unless the creature is flying. Besides, how will it know that I am here? I don't have any food that it can smell. If it is the human beast, he would not be able to smell my scent. So, if the thing found out about me it has to be an animal, unless the beast has developed the same acute senses as those of animals.*

It occurred to Peter to crawl outside and face the creature. It was better, he thought, to face him there, where Peter would be able to climb a tree, and not inside the cave. But the frightening scene of coming face to face with an unknown beast made him change his mind instantly. He felt safer when he remembered the rock over the entrance. He was again trying to repress his cough but was finding it increasingly difficult to do so. As an attack of coughing was over, he decided to get a look at the mysterious animal.

The tall rock by the entrance provided him with hope. *If it is a bison or another dangerous animal, I'll climb the rock. If it is the beast I'll reason with him, if he can understand me. I'll tell him that I will not make a good meal for him because I am sick and dying of a wicked disease, and if he eats me he will also die.*

Encouraged by this thought, Peter started crawling toward the entrance. Doing so, his hands came across a broken stick. He held it in his hands if for no other reason than to distract the beast. The pebbles covering the ground were piercing his chest, but they did not stop him.

He climbed over a rock at the cave's entrance and gazed at the darkness outside. The darkness was still impenetrable. Peter wished he could see his enemy; then he would feel a little better. Once an enemy was identified, Peter thought, half of the victory was achieved. The intermittent thunder was not accompanied by lightning. He strained his ears for any sound from the direction of the beast. But there was no sound. It was as though the forest had opened up and swallowed the creature.

At one point, lightning shed light at the cave's entrance. Peter was startled and felt a whisper of terror run through him. The dreadful beast was only yards from the entrance, lying over a cliff. It was not the human beast but a lion. It was a huge and long cat.

It had to be a lion, he thought, although it was different from the African lions that he had seen on television. There was slight mane around its neck and above its head. The rest of its long body was covered with a short, smooth coat of fur. Peter knew that it was not a wolf. It had to be some sort of mountain lion. Or perhaps it was a cross between an African lion escaped from a zoo and a cougar. Peter withdrew quietly inside and kept listening for any sounds, but none came.

For a long and seemingly interminable hour, the singing of the crickets and the gurgling sound, caused by water dripping inside the cave, were not disturbed. Peter started to relax. He tried to remember everything about lions that he had read or heard from Mr. Jones. He recalled reading that lions were the laziest creatures in the world. They slept most of the day. In fact, some slept twenty hours at one time. They woke up, ate, and slept again. They only ate twice a week and some even ate only once a week. How could it be that they were the kings of the forest then? *I have not seen any real kings, but I wonder if all of them spend most of their day sleeping?* Peter asked himself. *If this creature is a lion then I do not have anything to worry about for many hours as it will sleep all night.*

Peter noticed an interesting fact. He had never read of lions in North America. *I have read about the mountain lions*, he thought, *the pumas that have very short hair, and this lion has to be one of them. Perhaps, I did not take a good look at it. At any rate I wish that he would vanish and leave me alone so I can go home in the morning. I've had enough of the wilderness today, and I'm ready for life in the city. In the meantime I will try and get some sleep.*

He pulled up the zipper of his sweater and put his hands in his pockets to keep them warm. He was already less fearful. He closed his eyes, and as he was dozing off, he started blaming himself for taking that crazy trip early that morning and venturing into the heart of the untrodden wilderness. The event of the day passed through his mind like a movie reel.

2

Peter soon woke up terrified. It was another sound in the wilderness, something falling. Then silence prevailed. His mind took him to the morning of the day before.

He had awakened to the sound of Aunt Pauline, calling him to get up. The warm bed enticed him to stay in his place. The pains caused by the illness blended with the pleasant feelings brought by the warmth. This coziness gave him a comforting feeling in his limbs and his emaciated chest.

A pleasant numbness seeped through his body, allowing his thoughts to flow freely. *Even the illness sometimes goes to sleep with its victim*, he thought. *But often I get coughs that tear off my chest and crack my bones. These moments that I am enjoying now hardly visit me. I must learn how to take advantage of them. But I'm still young and in the care of my aunt. How precious these moments are when the pain and fear leave me. I feel alert and my thoughts are miraculously clear.*

I must invent special memories. And if I must perish, then it's better to perish with them. I'll imagine that I was a courageous soldier and that a beautiful princess fell in love with me. I'm worthy of her love because of my valor and my manners. I could also imagine that I was the first astronaut who stepped on the moon. My spacecraft then wandered to other planets, penetrating deeper and deeper into the far reaches of the galaxy. There I witnessed new experiences and I met strange creatures. I returned loaded with cheerful memories.

My memories should go beyond my surroundings, and further

than this because my disease has made me feel as though I am a stranger and an outcast from my friends, my neighbors, and people as a whole. My memories must stretch to the worlds of distant stars and the spirits. My memories are the foundation I'll stand on to defy disease, weakness, and hopelessness.

His aunt called him again and asked him to get out of the bed. She was coming from the kitchen, carrying a hot bowl with vapors mounting from it.

"I want you to eat all the soup in this bowl," she said. "It's good for you."

"What is this?" Peter asked grumbling.

"You ask me the same question every morning. It's a medication that clears the windpipes and enlarges them. Natural medicine is better than chemical drugs. It has been proved by experiment that boiling the buds of asparagus mixed with garlic and honey is better than all medicine to treat weak lungs."

"But I think that a few minutes of morning sleep are better than all types of medicine," he said.

"Sleeping is good, but it's not as good as medicine."

Aunt Pauline rushed to the kitchen and brought out two boiled eggs and a piece of ham and toast. She placed the food in front of him and sat next to him, watching him while he ate. Peter knew she would not be easy on him unless he finished the plate, so he went on devouring his food as he watched her piercing blue eyes. As he did that, he imagined, for a few seconds, that Pauline was, in fact, his mother. Pauline was forty, just two years older than his mother. He closed his eyes to preserve the image, but his mother was gone.

Peter turned to Pauline and asked her, "How did my mom die?"

"Your mom did not die of the disease. She could have lived many years despite her illness. But she died from too much grumbling and complaining of the disease. I think her excessive complaints caused her death and not the illness itself."

"But she wouldn't have died had she not been sick."

"I don't know. I attribute a big percentage of her death to her childish attitude and her changing mood."

"What do you mean, Auntie?"

"I mean that she did things to their fullest."

"I still don't understand."

"You'll understand when I will explain some of her attitude. She was beautiful and overly sensitive when she met your father. She loved him dearly and gave him all the money she had saved over a period of five years when she worked as a waitress in Salt Lake City. She gave him everything, although she was known to be frugal. Remember what I said, that she did things to their fullest. She was extremely frugal, but she also loved him dearly."

"What happened to her and my dad after that?"

"Your father is basically a good man who tried to influence her by changing some of her habits, but she discovered that he was an alcoholic and then she started to hate him."

"But I thought he turned to alcohol after she became sick."

"That's possible. I knew he drank before, but after he knew she was going to die, he started to abuse alcohol."

"What happened after that?"

"You know your dad left after your mother died."

"How about me?" asked Peter.

"You're under my care now."

She stood up and headed to one of the rooms, returning with bundles of wool threads and started to move her fingers with astonishing speed.

"Tomorrow I'll finish this sweater. I want you to wear it. It is very strong around the back, and it fastens from the chest. Very soon it will be cold, which might cause a relapse. Something we don't need."

"You probably want me to sleep with it, too."

"I wish you'd do that. You know how much I'm concerned about your health."

Peter examined her for a minute. She had never seemed more serious before.

"Auntie, tell me something. If a boy's mind is telling him he can do certain things, can he do them?"

Pauline stopped knitting and looked him straight in the eyes. "I would like to give you a brief lecture. You should be kind to yourself. And if you fail to do that, no force in the world can do it for you. Beware of doing things that can hurt you and harm your health. First, you've got no resistance and, second, you must know that I, your aunt, love you dearly. I don't want anything to happen to you, but whether one can do what his mind tells him he can do, I doubt that very much."

She returned to her knitting. Peter lowered his head and closed his eyes. He was disoriented and depressed.

He spent the rest of the day thinking of the big decision he had been trying to make in the last several weeks. He had become more and more convinced that the decision was right. His mind told him that he could do it, although his aunt had just told him he could not. Yes, he would head to the wilderness tomorrow. *Aunt Pauline will no doubt suffer, but a man has to do what a man has to do*, he thought. *Besides my aunt, I have no one here except Mr. Jones and Cynthia. But neither needs me.*

Peter then thought of his father. *Perhaps my mother would have been alive had he not been drinking so much. Not only that but he quit his job at the mine because of her illness.* Peter blamed his mother's death on his father, Harry's quitting his job at the mine and turning to alcohol.

That evening Peter went to the family room where his aunt was reading. He told her that he wanted to go to Denver to see his father. Her answer was that since his father was the one who left, then he should be the one to come back and that Peter ought not to go all the way to Denver to seek him there.

"But I miss my father and I want to see him," he had said.

"You don't know where he is, do you?" She had a stern look

in her eyes. "Do you know if he is in Denver itself or in one of the many towns and cities near it? Do you know where he works?"

Peter had no answer to any of her questions. He examined his aunt with a feeling of desperation. She had stubborn watchful dark blue eyes, which did not cease to gaze at his face not even for the flutter of a moment. He was unable to convince her. Then he remembered Mr. Jones

"Mr. Jones mentioned that my father works at a factory in Fort Collins. I can inquire there."

"But suppose he doesn't want to see you?"

Peter thought it was a possibility, but he wasn't about to give up and he persisted, "I know that my father loves me."

"You still say that after he abandoned you? I can't believe how he just came to me that evening and said, 'Listen, Pauline, take care of Peter. I'll go in the morning.' "

Pauline was speaking slowly, examining the ceiling of the room. When she finished, she turned to Peter. "You know, both you and your mother share this stubbornness and a desire to do crazy things."

"He had to get away for a while." Peter did not know why he defended his father.

"You can't go, Peter. Not now at least. School just started."

Peter stood up and started heading toward his room, his piercing blue eyes denoting determination and stubbornness. He stood at the door of his room and looked sharply at Pauline with a mixture of pity and challenge.

"One day, I'll just go to the next town and catch a Greyhound bus to Denver," he said, looking up fully at her eyes, then sneaked to his room without waiting for an answer from her.

Pauline did not appear to have the slightest idea about Peter's actual plan the next morning. He never intended to go to Denver. He did not want to see his father, at least not at that time. He was angry at him for leaving the house. His father had left when Peter needed him most. Peter had decided to undertake a task whose consequences remained to be seen. Peter also thought that if for any reason he did not get back home, then the Denver story would offer an explanation for his absence. Somehow the possibility that he might be out for a long time thrilled him and a feeling of glorious happiness sprung up in his heart. Was this a subconscious desire to get away from it all? He had determined to attempt something and he himself did not know why. It was prompted by his wounded pride and his feelings of inadequacy and disease.

He had started climbing the low elevations leading to the real mountains. He was ready for any contingency. He wanted to prove to the world that he was strong and not on his way to the grave to follow his mother, as many would gossip.

At first, he had followed a paved road at the edge of the mountains. It was a cool morning, so he had dressed up with a warm sport jacket and the sweater that was almost finished. He also had on a new pair of sneakers that his father had bought him just before leaving town. He'd taken some fruit, cookies, and a sandwich with him, in addition to a plastic bottle of cold water, figuring that his trip might last for more than one day.

About five miles down the paved road, he got off of it and followed a gravel trail leading directly to the mountains. The sun was shining and the autumn-colored leaves covered with a light mist glistened under the sun. Houses and barns scattered along the gravel road with their dogs barking. The area became less and less inhabited as he advanced toward the mountains. The few isolated farm houses on the side of the road disappeared from view.

As he got close to the top of the mountain range, he found himself climbing low hills, which merged into the higher elevations. The gravel trail was now a narrow dirt path littered with small pebbles. As Peter's glance followed the trail, it disappeared behind the low hills, resembling a spotted serpent from far. Once Peter was on top of the ridge, it became a smooth ride through ponderosa pine and firs. The few aspen and elm trees that dotted the low elevations had disappeared. The ground was covered with small cactus, sage, and numerous wildflowers and bushes loaded with wild tiny red and brown berries.

Peter started climbing, swerving the slender tires of the bike among the sharp pebbles. He decided to follow a path leading uphill, to take a better look at the mountains. As he continued to do that, he found it difficult to climb the hill on the bike. The persistent coughing would visit him now and then.

On the top of the first hill, the mountains loom up as jagged peaks against the azure sky. He stopped for a while and gazed with admiration at the barren peaks, which were sharpened points or rounded domes. Beneath the peaks, the pine-filled ravines dropped precipitously to the deep valley surrounded by trees whose leaves were orange, gold, and amber.

Peter continued his pedaling, heedless of the fatigue that was taking hold. By the time he reached the edge of the mountains, he was in the wilderness. The trip to the foot of the real hills took much longer than expected, but it was worth the pain, he thought. The vegetation was thick, rendering the forest impenetrable at times so that Peter had to follow numerous detours. At other times he had to move the needle-filled branches and thorny bushes out of his way to provide an easy access for his bike.

With every advance he made, he would look at the mountains and discover more details. Something in those giant ranges had attracted him since childhood. It wasn't merely their colossal size and picturesque shape that mesmerized him. It was something much more profound, going to the very core of his soul.

Peter thought of Mr. Jones. He had related to him countless stories about his wilderness adventures and Peter would sit down, his eyes glued to Mr. Jones, and listen attentively. He'd showed Peter some of the woodwork that he had invented. He used them to trick small animals. Once he'd showed Peter a special box one cubic foot large that, when he submersed it in water, produced a vibration, attracting a great number of fish to it.

There was also a trap to catch pheasants and other birds. Mr.

Jones had made a crate with a small opening on top. The crate had a door sliding down from above. Mr. Jones would tie the door with a long rope and would lie in wait, hiding by some bushes. When the bird entered the box to pick at the seeds, Mr. Jones would pull the rope and the door would slide down, trapping the bird. He would then use the opening at the top to retrieve the helpless creature.

Peter remembered last fall when Mr. Jones had brought back two deer carcasses and an elk and given away their meat to the whole village. Mr. Jones had smiled at Peter when he saw him the next morning, saying, "I've had enough of it." All that he'd kept from the three animals were their skins. In addition to their value as warm garments, they were also an important symbol to Mr. Jones as a respectable hunter.

Mr. Jones's house was like a small but complete mummified menagerie. It was filled with various stuffed wild-animal heads, horns, and skins affixed to the walls. Peter recalled that whenever he'd visited Mr. Jones's house, he would spend a good hour looking at the various animal heads on the walls. They looked so real that Peter had been afraid the first time he'd seen them. The wild animals seemed to look him straight in the eye. There were scary-looking grizzlies, red-eyed wolves, elk with gigantic, multiheaded long horns, a humongous bison with its round black head, deer, both mule buck with horns and female deer with almost no horns, different kinds of wild sheep with snow white wool, foxes with bushy tails, coyotes, a moose with a long, ugly face, and even marmots, bobcats, and squirrels. As Mr. Jones had showed him around and explained to him some facts about the animals, Peter had seen the glory and pride gleaming in his brown eyes.

In addition, there were many birds whose names he did not know, and Mr. Jones had kept repeating them to him. He could see the male and female pheasants with their beautiful multi-colored feathers, the pelican with its long yellow beak, the green-winged teal, the bald and golden eagle, and the osprey. Mr. Jones had even taught Peter the art of skinning deer. Peter recalled him saying, "Shoot the deer in the neck to preserve the skin."

Peter's dream had been to accompany Mr. Jones on one of those fantastic trips, but his mother would not allow him. She would always say, "Next year you can go." But he knew the real reason. His mother had thought he was too sick to go. He would probably not make it back from the hunting trip, she'd confided to Pauline. If Mr. Jones were with him now, Peter would not need anyone else.

Mr. Jones had told him a great deal about the mountains and its wild-animal population. He'd advised Peter that the wild animals were not evil, as many people were led to believe. "Most of them are more scared of man than people are scared of them," he had said. Even the gigantic grizzly bears would stand still gazing at him, but would not charge him. The most fierce animals would not attack their prey unless they were hungry. "Animals do not think of food and how to preserve it," he would add.

"You must remember, Pete," which is what Mr. Jones used to call him, "wolves and other wild animals are smart creatures. They can take a look at you and conclude at a flash whether you're scared or not. Don't ever give them the impression that you are afraid. That is when they are most likely to attack."

One day Peter had asked him about the monster man who roamed those areas. Mr. Jones had laughed and replied that someone had invented the story.

"But, Mr. Jones," Peter had insisted, "I heard the story from more than one person. They even provided details and a precise description of the animal man. Now why would anyone make up such a story?"

"Because they wanted to discourage other people from settling in their territories."

"But I heard that the only Indian village in the mountains moved to a new location in South Dakota after several of their children were kidnapped by the monster man."

Mr. Jones's lips had remained sealed, but his brows had knitted in a frown. Peter had gone on. "You do believe that the beast exists, don't you? Please tell me the truth."

"Maybe he does," Mr. Jones had said, "but he never scared me."

"Why didn't the police go after him? Don't tell me the police didn't believe them after the Indians lost many of their children and even some adults?"

"The Forest Service dispatched choppers to search for the creature, but they suspended the search a week before Christmas when the snow was hindering the search effort. Besides, they thought that no man, not even a beast, could survive such a cold winter."

3

Back in the cave, the sound of an object falling in the woods brought Peter back to reality. *It is probably a tree falling to its death*, he thought. That morning he had seen many fallen trees as he had continued his journey to the wilderness. The sound took him back to that journey. The fallen trees had hampered his advance. Some had stood erect like statues in an ancient Babylonian temple that he had seen in a history book. Others were like spears standing at a 45-degree angle.

Peter recalled stopping by a small lake hidden by huge fern and spruce trees. He had examined his image reflected in the water. His normal pale color had been replaced by a healthy rosy color, especially on the cheeks of his long face. Above the right eye was a deep seam that had healed. As though an invisible power was pushing him in the water, he'd walked into the lake. The water had been cool and inviting, and he'd felt like taking a dip, but he had not dared. He had never gone swimming in his life. His mother had prevented him from getting close to water.

Peter walked slowly in the crystal-clear water, but he was scared, feeling the muddy ground. The water covered his legs up to his knees when he brought out his bottle and filled it. A great desire to swim took hold of him. The more he watched the tiny harmless waves caressing his thighs, the more he wanted to swim. *How could swimming hurt me?* he reasoned. *I won't drown. I will only swim in the shallow water.*

As he advanced in the lake, the countless tiny fishes that blanketed the lake floor fled in disarray, scattering around, rushing for the depth of the lake. Suddenly he stepped into a hole and fell. The water was cold, and for a few seconds, he thought he would drown. He stood up and soon he had already adjusted to the water temperature. In no time he was enjoying himself.

Peter recalled Aunt Pauline and his mother scolding him if he undertook an activity involving physical exertion. "You can't do this. You can't do that." The phrases were still ringing in his ear like an annoying bell.

Leaving the lake, he looked above and the mountain ranges were closing on him, aided by the rippling bright clouds that were now forming. It had now become mostly cloudy, and the sun played hide-and-seek with him.

Amidst his recurring cough, the sounds of the animals and birds rose now and then. They were intermixed with the gurgling of the water and the blowing of the wind. Among the larger animals, only deer could be seen. Herds of them grazed in the valleys and over the meadows. He was able to distinguish the males from the females. The mule bucks were larger, with dotted brown colors and crooked horns. The females on the other hand had no horns.

Peter wanted to see all the wild animals, but they had become invisible. *Mr. Jones was right*, Peter thought. *They all run like a scared cat when they see a man. But am I a man? Why not?* he was thinking. *I'm fifteen now*. Peter, however, felt more like seventeen or even eighteen. In fact he was an "old" boy whose troublesome life had cast him at the threshold of manhood. He would keep reflecting, *Why did this disease choose me?* He remembered spending hours under the blanket, feigning a deep slumber, but he was reflecting on his bleak future.

Peter continued riding and passed by small peaks, some of which resembled ancient castles and gigantic pyramids. But his bike would not go any farther. He could not ascend and remain on the bike. He had to abandon the ascent or the bike. Since he was determined to go to the end, he decided to leave the bike by some bushes.

Now he was traveling upward on his feet for the first time. It was much harder. His feet became wet as a result of stepping over so many green plants and flowers. The fresh smell of broken plants was intermingled with the other odors emanating from the other plants and blossoms. His march was now slower, as he was watching for large animals. There was a lonely bull elk grazing in a ridge down below. Farther up, he was startled by the splash of a muskrat jumping on a pond.

It took him two hours till he reached the summit. All along he was wondering what he would find behind it. It would be a big lake or perhaps a freeway going to Denver. If that were the case, he might even hitchhike there to look for his dad. He would admonish him but would leave him alone. He wouldn't ask him to come back, Peter was thinking. Perhaps they could select another town and live together. He knew his father loved him. On the eve of the night that he left town, his father confided in some friends that he could not stand another death right in front of his own eyes.

The disappearance of his father was even more excruciating to Peter than the loss of his mother. His mother's death had been foreseen, but his father's departure was the last stroke. His presence was the last thread connecting Peter with the early untroubled years of his childhood. His father was fond of him. Peter recalled his father, as he flipped through his memory file, his mind floating in to recapture the sweet portrait of his father kissing and hugging him since he was four years old. His father was the kind of man who would not reveal his emotions. Peter never remembered his father kissing or hugging him at all until that spring day.

It was an afternoon day when the last spring snow had melted in the warmth of the rising sun. His mother had gone to the store to buy groceries. Peter, who was six then, was sleeping, as his mother made him sleep several hours during the day. Suddenly he woke up when his father was kissing him affectionately on his forehead and singing him a song. Peter opened his eyes and stared at his father, and the father immediately stopped as though ashamed to be caught kissing his son. Peter found out later that his father always kissed and hugged him when he was sleeping but never when he was awake.

One day in early summer while Peter was napping, and when he roused to notice that his father was kissing him and singing to him, he remained in bed with closed eyes. Peter continued feigning sleep just so that his father would continue to kiss him and sing for him, but his father had discovered the game later when Peter could not resist laughing as his father uttered some funny words. Harry, his father, was disconcerted and left the room at once, and since that day he would only kiss Peter in public sporadically, whenever he was leaving town or Peter was real sick.

When Peter was twelve, he was going to visit his aunt in Michigan. His father had driven him to the airport and when Peter was about to board the plane, he leaned toward his father to kiss him. But his father had said, "You're a young man now, Peter, and men don't kiss. They shake hands."

Now that he reached the top of the summit, the scenery brought him back to reality. There was nothing different except a black high hill higher than the summit where he was standing. There were also more and more mountain ranges and peaks. Down in the valley were rows of aspen and elm trees. He was there alone as far away from people as he ever got. He was told that no one lived around there for one hundred miles. The wilderness here pressed in from all directions and closed altogether the world as he knew it.

Peter examined the other side of the mountain. Waves upon waves of metamorphic rocks had been heaved and tossed on the hills, forming a natural fortification unparalleled by any man-made fort that Peter had seen in the Western movies. There was a deep solitude unbroken except for the sound of the swinging trees and the rushing water in a nearby spring.

Peter did not think about getting lost. Perhaps the idea had occurred to him earlier, but he had discarded it, feeling indifferent to it. Perhaps his inner mind was saying, *So what?* All he was thinking of was, what was there behind the big black hill. How about if there was a secret palace, one that he read about in some of his adventure books. Peter was fond of reading. In fact this was the only activity his mother allowed him to practice. He had several young adult novels, but he would throw them away one after the other. They didn't relate to him. Most of them were about teenage romance, something he was deprived of.

Cynthia did not share his feelings. "Why would she go out with a sick boy, especially one who was going to die soon?" Peter overheard. So he turned his attention to other areas where no other person was needed to fulfill his happiness. He turned to reading. He read many adventure stories. He admired people who were brave and able to get out of a difficult situation. He even read the *Arabian Nights* and was fascinated by their countless fables, stories that augmented his imagination and opened new and strange worlds for him.

The black hill seemed farther and farther as he climbed. At first he started to go circuitously toward it to advance as much as he could before he headed directly for the hill. The area had become very rugged. As he was heading up, he saw a drop off. He began climbing. There were many large boulders on his way. He also saw what appeared to him to be entrances to caves. The broken logs piled up here and there, some of them assuming strange forms. The trees were scarce now, but the thorny shrubs and other small plants were becoming abundant. Before reaching the top, he was forced to turn, going around the hill to avoid a dangerous slope and kept walking around the ridge.

Above him it had become cloudy, with dark heavy clouds replacing the light ones. He was almost near the top when a drizzle started, but he did not give up. When he reached the peak, all he could see were more peaks embracing the clouds, which had descended, obstructing part of the peaks. He lay under a rock to collect his breath. He was short of breath to the point that he was gasping for air. He got up and looked around him. There was a rainbow of colors in trees and rocks despite the increasing rain. The trees in the valley below resembled huge cauliflower heads.

As he examined the clouds, he felt a snap in the air. The wind suddenly intensified. He decided that he had seen enough and hurried to his bike before it was too late. He proceeded to race down the mountain, leaping over the bushes and broken tree trunks. At one point lightning almost struck him. He ducked into a hollow of steep wall and waited, hoping for the rain to stop, but he realized that it could rain for hours. It was becoming darker by the minute.

Peter left his hiding place, and the rain immediately struck him in the face. Up to this minute, his clothes had been relatively dry. There was another flash, followed by a thunderous clap. He was knocked down over the hill. He got up and started running erratically in successive directions. He was panic-stricken for the first time. Then he could only crouch, hanging onto the rocks. He did not have the slightest idea where he was.

A scary idea occurred to him. He was dismayed at the frightening prospect that he might have to spend the night in the wilderness. As the idea penetrated his mind, waves of shivering thoughts went through his body. He might have to look for one of the caves or grottos that he had seen earlier. He decided to find his bike first, and then he would know what to do. It was turning dark already. If he did not find his bike soon, he would definitely have to spend the night in the wilderness. Even with the bike, it would be several hours before he would reach the first house, that is, if he found the path leading to the gravel road.

When he reached the top of the first summit, it had become dark. He had lost all sense of direction. He kept looking in the area beneath the summit to recognize the bushes, but everything seemed strange to him. But where would he spend the night?

Suddenly a great fear took hold of Peter. Would he survive the horrible night? Or would he become food for the wolves and the crows? He asked himself whether it mattered if he died there. "I guess it does not," he whispered to himself. "I was going to die in town sooner or later." But the promises of a better future made him want to live. He wandered for an hour, looking for any sign of civilization, hoping to find a house or even some lights from a distance.

Suddenly he was in front of a big hollow that looked like a rock tent. He had seen similar caves that evening, but this one had a big opening. The inside of the cave was dark, and he could not figure out the depth of it. He stood by the entrance and strained his ears for sounds emanating from the cave. Nothing broke the silence except the monotonous singing of the insects. *Is there a beast sleeping there?* he wondered. *I better find that out now*. He picked up a rock, threw it inside the cave, and waited. There was nothing. He then repeated the process, but this time he threw it more vigorously. If there is an animal inside, he thought, he would know, but nothing followed the sound of the rock. Slowly he staggered inside the bumpy ground, his eyes wide open staring at darkness.

Peter was now starving and wet. If he could be home now inside four walls, he would empty the refrigerator. Aunt Pauline would no longer accuse him of eating less than birds. The wet clothes bothered him and increased his feeling of chilliness. His coughing intensified and he was becoming feverish. An idea occurred to him. He would sleep in that cave, and it was not a bad idea if he never woke up. He remembered the song: "The best he could hope for was to die in his sleep!"

4

Peter woke up during the night startled by the sound of bears calling. "Not again," he whispered. He had just survived the mountain lion ordeal, and now he had to worry about the bears. He reminded himself to be sensible, but he could not help but shake. The cave's entrance was large enough for any animal to enter. Peter thought that he could penetrate deeper in the cave and hide. He strained his ears and figured that the bears were sweeping everything encountered in their way. Peter could hear the stems and trunks shattering and breaking under their feet. The grunts were getting louder, echoing in the wilderness, magnified to hair-raising noise.

As fear and darkness pressed down on him, his thoughts rushed to Mr. Jones, like a sick person who immediately thinks of his medicine when pain strikes. Mr. Jones had told him a great deal about bears. "They have a tremendous sense of smell and can smell animals miles away," he had said. "They can tell between man's scent and that of a deer, and how many of them there are. The only advantage you have against them is vision." Mr. Jones had added that bears have very poor vision and are incapable of distinguishing things at night.

"The bears must have gotten the scent then," Peter whispered to himself. "I'm doomed. But why would the bear attack me?"

He recalled Mr. Jones again. He had said that there were several kinds of bears. The least harmful were the black bears. They rarely harm a person. In fact, they run away when they happen to meet a man. The brown bears, the grizzlies, were the most dangerous. If they charged, Mr. Jones had advised, climb at least ten feet high in a tree. Peter imagined the height of the rock and estimated it to be more than ten feet. He also recalled others advising him to play dead if a grizzly attacked, for the bear stayed away from dead animals. But could he really do that? Peter asked himself. Was he capable of pretending that he was dead in front of a beast without coming up with a movement?

He had heard the story of a hiker who had surprised a grizzly on the crest of a pass amid a rough, narrow set of rocks. The hiker had fallen on the ground and played dead, assuming a cannonball position. The brown bear had come to him, sniffed his body for seconds, then moved ahead.

Peter had also been advised to make his existence known to the bears because they avoid people. Even the grizzlies rarely charge unless they sense danger or were hungry. Since he constituted no danger to the bears and since food was plentiful, he was not in real danger, he thought. *But if bears are full, why then are they walking in the forest at this time of the night? Did they wake up feeling hungry? But how can I make sure when I encounter a beast that he is full? Do I have to wait if he is going to attack me first?* The grunting was now loud, like a drum being played by some African tribesman.

The drizzle outside continued unabated. He could hear it falling on the dying leaves. He could smell its effect on the wildflowers and shrubs. *Perhaps the rain will cover my scent*, he thought.

For a few seconds, he could not hear the grunting. He stood up and slowly staggered to the cave's entrance. But no sooner had he done that than his heart sank. The grunting had become so loud that Peter figured they were less than a hundred feet away. *They must have sniffed the scent and returned*, he thought. He ran inside, not paying attention to the rugged ground of the cave until he bumped his head on a wall. There was such severe pain for a minute that he thought he would faint, but his thoughts were concentrated on the danger. If he had his bike with him, he would get his knife from it, but a knife would not do him much good with these gigantic animals. Mr. Jones, he remembered, always took his pistol and rifle with him whenever he went to the wilderness. If he had either of them, he would shoot in the air and the bears would run away. Or if he had matches, he would build a campfire and he would not have to worry about the bears.

As Peter kept feeling the walls of his shelter, he came across a tunnel leading inside. He immediately went inside, feeling every inch to avoid bumping his head one more time. The fear and excitement consumed whatever strength he had left. He started to cough again. *Why now?* he cried inwardly, flashing into a sudden fury. He climbed a rock that he had made out in the midst of darkness. He exerted great effort, utilizing every muscle and every nerve until he was able to cling to the rock and turn around in it. He squatted, clinging to the ceiling, and waited for the bear to bolt into the cave. He was straining his ears and trying to curb a spree of coughing.

Peter did not know how long he remained clinging to the ceiling, which oozed with water. All he knew was that the heavy footsteps passed by and their sound became fainter and fainter. It took him an hour before he calmed down. That was when he decided to go back to his original place.

It was still dark when he got back, but by now he had grown accustomed to the darkness. Yet he wanted the night to pass quickly. He kept wondering whether he would ever see the first rays of the dawn. Oh, how happy he would be in the morning, if it ever came. The word "happy" stopped him. *Will I really be happy?* he wondered. The first thing he would do next morning was to build a campfire to dry his clothes before heading home.

The grief never left him, however. *The morning will eventually arrive and I will find my bike and head home. But do I have a home? Pauline is the only one left. She is kind but she is also overprotective. It will be back to the same prison: "Stay home. Don't play. Don't swim. It's not good for your health. Don't . . . don't." I guess she wants me to stay home until I join my mother. That might be several years. But as one doctor said to my father, I was going to live until I turned twenty or perhaps twenty-five.*

His thoughts were turned to his mother, Sally. She was a fighter and lived thirty-five years. *But she passed the deadly disease to me. Despite that I will always love her*, he thought. *I know if it was up to her she would have died to save my life.*

His imagination took hold of him, and his mind began to wander. He was seeing himself flying very lightly as he was carried on the layers of air. He was greeted by angels dressed in white. A band of them surrounded him and led him to a courtyard lit by white suns. There were sounds reminiscent of the rustling of the leaves and the sounds of girls' gowns.

The poor woman had found out about the disease ten years prior to her death. At first its symptoms were no more than repeated fevers. After the initial diagnosis, the disease seemed to have left her. The fevers and coughing had stopped completely, but it came back to her to accompany her to her death. The return of the disease signaled a gradual loss of weight. That was followed by her first miscarriage. Peter heard later that she had obtained an abortion. It was enough that she had him. She couldn't put up with another sick child. *But that's not true*, he thought. *She did not want to bring another child into this world to suffer and die early.* It was the hardest thing for a mother to see her child die prematurely.

Peter recalled the long cold winter nights when his father worked at the night shift and his mother would read him stories. He recalled the favorites, such as "Beauty and the Beast" and "Red Riding Hood." As he grew older, she kept encouraging him to read more advanced stories. When he reached twelve, he read his first novel. He went on trying to recollect the details. It had been about a brother and a sister in their teens who spent a summer vacation over at their uncle's house by a lake. The boy saw two suspicious-looking men sailing to a nearby island several times a week. They turned out to be counterfeiters. He took his uncle's boat without his knowledge and sailed there one day. The evil men, however, were waiting for him, and if he hadn't been lucky, he and his sister would have been killed.

Why was the boy curious? Peter wondered. He couldn't come up with an answer that minute. Most people are curious, although they know that curiosity usually led to trouble. Was curiosity something good or bad? "It has to be good," he said to himself. By being curious man invented machines. Then how come man cannot invent medicines to cure all diseases? Why couldn't science save his mother? Doctors had said it was a rare disease that she had contracted from coming into contact with cows.

As the disease had progressed, his father had grown more frustrated. He'd quit his job as a miner and soon turned to alcohol. The company had tried to help him, not for his sake, but because of Sally, his wife, who years earlier had saved a number of miners trapped underground following an explosion. Peter had almost forgotten that incident, but the whole town still recalled her heroism.

Peter was seven years old when it happened, but he recalled all the details, for it had been repeated many times. It had all happened on a cold December night. All of a sudden cries rang out throughout the town. The news was that an explosion had trapped over twenty miners inside deep tunnels of the mine. The company's officials panicked. Nothing like that had occurred before. They were not equipped to handle an emergency of that magnitude. Any assistance from out of town would not have arrived for many days due to the heavy snow. Even then it normally took days to clean the debris and broken rocks to get to trapped miners. Now the wives of the miners were screaming as they stood, helpless, outside the mine.

Sally had awakened, startled by the loud voices. When she learned what the story was, she ran to the mine. She'd told some men to get axes and follow her. She knew a secret way that might lead to the trapped men. The company president, however, assured

Sally that there was no secret tunnel leading to the mine or he would have known about it from the blueprints. About ten men carried all types of available axes and followed her. She walked past the mine and came down a hill about two hundred yards from the mine entrance. Sally, to the great surprise of everyone, took them to a deep well and stood there.

"Why did you stop?" the company president asked. "Where is your secret tunnel?"

Sally pointed to the well.

"This is it," she replied.

"The well?"

"Yes. Notice the well is dry now. It has been dry for the last twenty years since the state provided clean water, but I remember a few years before that. I was a little girl then. We used to play by the well. When the machines were inside the tunnel, we could hear their thundering noise."

She halted for a few seconds and then yelled at the men, who stood motionless, stunned by her story, to get in the well. "What are you waiting for, guys? Come on, move it. Let me see some brave men in the well."

Four men went down the well. They lowered their legs and placed their feet on the stones protruding from the wall of the well and continued going down. When they reached the bottom, a lantern was lowered to them on long ropes.

"Do you hear anything?" the company president screamed at the men.

"No, nothing," their faint voices came.

"Knock your hammers hard on the walls in the direction of the mine."

They knocked three times on those rocks vigorously. The men and women above and behind them, rows of spectators, men, women, and children, waited in silence. Everyone strained his ears and listened for a response. The knock of the men inside was heard as a repeated intermittent beating amid the cheers of everyone. In

less than an hour, several stones were removed from inside the wall. The wall between the well and the mine was only several feet thick. Minutes later, the trapped miners were on their way to freedom. His mother had become a hero of the town overnight. Peter was very proud of her and for all that time of remembering he forgot that he was alone in a spooky cave beset by countless kinds of dangers.

Before he went back to sleep, Peter had this thought. *If my mother ended her pregnancy because she thought a sick child was a useless child, then she was mistaken. She herself proved it wrong when she saved over twenty men. I guess a person is not really dead until he is dead.*

5

When Peter opened his eyes in the morning, his back ached from the many rocks and pebbles that had thrust into his body as he slept. His legs hurt both from the pedaling and also as a result of hiking and climbing the day before. But the mere fact that it was morning shifted his attention from his ailing body to his surroundings.

The lobby of the cave was lighted. Rays of sun shone through the entrance and from cracks in the ceiling. The light and the warmth made him feel safe. The cave consisted of a grand room by the entrance narrowing to a tunnel whose depths Peter could not figure out due to darkness. The walls of the great room were made of vertical stones while the ceiling consisted of mainly hanging rock formations. Some of them were thin on top and round at the bottom, almost like chandeliers. Others dangled like swords, ready to inflict fatal wounds if someone made the mistake of getting near them.

Peter got up, walked to one of the rock formations, and tried to cut loose one of them to use as a weapon for his defense. He was unable to do so due to their large size and solidity. He abandoned the idea after several futile attempts and headed outside.

The wilderness outside the cave was now more hospitable, for the sun shone in the blue sky. It no longer invoked suggestions of hostility, but rather Peter felt so safe that he decided to take his time rather than return home immediately. His coughing had stopped, and he felt rejuvenated. He was not even hungry, although he did not have anything to eat the night before.

Peter picked up his plastic bag and walked away from the cave. Suddenly he remembered the lion. Peter was stunned and started to shiver again. The beast was still sleeping. He went behind a rock and examined the dreadful creature. *It has to be a lion,* he thought. *Only lions have that oval face with white chin and thick mustaches. It may be true that lions do not attack their victims when they are not hungry. But I cannot rely on statistics,* he thought to himself.

His first task was to get his clothes dry even before locating his bike. He started descending the mountain and kept forcing his way around black boulders covered with green and gray algae until he reached a hill on the mountain with a panoramic view to help him figure out where he was. He tried to recognize some of the mountain ranges that he had seen the day before, but he could not. Before him stood a long mountain range with pinnacles of various altitudes. In one spot the mountain rose like a gargantuan loaf from the plateau beneath it. Its walls dropped precipitously to the valley, which was dotted with little lakes. He took off the still-wet clothes, spread them on a boulder under the sun, and waited for them to dry.

Peter felt hungry, but what could he eat? He would like to have some danish or doughnut or anything sweet. If he'd only taken more cookies with him, he thought, sighing. He recalled how fussy he was when his mother and later Aunt Pauline served him food on the table. "I won't eat that." But now he would even eat the leftovers if any were available. He examined the trees, and after a brief search, he concluded that there were no large fruit trees; there were only berries and fruitless trees. He tried to dig some roots and seeds with a stick, but his rudimentary tool did not get him far.

He went back to the boulder and put on his clothes. He looked at the sun through the thick branches and figured it was still morning. He decided to look for his bike and head home even if it took him the entire day.

After wandering for over an hour, he was able to spot the black hill that he'd reached yesterday, but the bike was another story. He tried to remember what kind of bushes he'd put it under and near what kind of boulders. The problem was that there were too many bushes and boulders. He was now puzzled and upset. Should he keep looking for the bike or should he head home on foot? That would be very hard, if not impossible, he thought. The thought of the long trip made him undergo a surge of coughing, which continued for several minutes. Soon he felt the fever taking hold of him. He rested for a few minutes and started surveying the high mountains. *Where is home and what is the shortest way to get to it?* he wondered. He would go in any direction until he reached the first house, and from there he would find a way to contact Aunt Pauline. That is, if she has not already died of grief over him.

Peter followed a grassy path along a mountain range, away from that black hill. He was unsure if he was going in the right direction. He passed meadow after meadow rich in all types of bushes and flowers. The fragrance coming from these flowers practically overwhelmed him. The lily petals with yellow bases were dotted with dark red and violet spots. Wild clover and rose hips were everywhere in the low areas. Berry bushes and small cactus plants with flat thorny leaves covered much of the slopes and gullies. The mist that settled down over the various vegetation gave many familiar kinds of vegetation a strange appearance, as though he were seeing them for the first time. The spruce pines stood in a straight line, as though they were soldiers greeting a dignitary.

At the end of the meadow was a steep rock. Peter went around it and worked his way down. This brought him in front of a small cave. It was much smaller than the one he'd spent the night in. But he continued walking, rejecting a whim to explore. The hiking in the middle of the forest was not as easy as yesterday. The ground was soaked and spongy from yesterday's rain. His sneakers were bothering him. He had not changed his socks for thirty hours now.

The footprints of the various animals were apparent everywhere, but he could not find any footstep of a man, so he concluded that the human beast was not in the vicinity.

As soon as he reached the first pond, he took off his shoes and stood by the water, his mind prey to confusing thoughts. He wondered whether he would have to spend another night in the wilderness or whether he would be lost until some hunters found him; but the question that hounded him, sending waves of chills through his body, was whether he would find food to survive until then.

The calm and clear water drew his attention outward and started examining the little waves rushing to the bank. Soon he saw his image in the still water. He had not changed much in the last two days except that his hair was in a miserable state of havoc and disorder, with wisps of light brown hair stuck to his forehead. His long face was pale and dull looking, denoting fatigue and exhaustion. His dark blue eyes still revealed great determination.

Soon a wave erased his image and replaced it by a different image, blurry and shaking. This brought him back to reality. He took off his socks and started washing his feet. He wished there were fish in the pond so he could catch a few trout and satisfy his hunger, but the pond was too small to have fish. Besides, he had no hook or bait.

His head started giving him signs that a headache was in the making. He would have to eat soon or he would have a harrowing headache.

Peter spent the rest of the day trying to locate the road leading back to town. He rested several times, but he would soon get up and continue the march. He thought of trying some of Mr. Jones's methods of trapping birds, but there was no way to cook them. He did find at one point a deer half eaten by a predator, but he would not eat raw meat. Finally, he started to look for shelter. He went back to the small cave he had passed by and spent the night there.

For the next two days, he remained close to the cave. It was the safest place for him to be. If he had enough food, he could tolerate it. Yes, there were times he was scared, but the first night was the worst. During the third day, he had a terrible headache and went to the dead deer. The hind was still untouched. He cut pieces from it with a sharp rock and ate some, but he spit it out and returned to the cave, his hands trembling due to hunger.

When he slept that night, he did not think he would wake up. All he had had to eat were berries, which were making him sick with diarrhea.

When he woke up the next morning, his headache was gone, but he was very weak. He decided to abandon the cave. He had to leave it if he had any chance of getting back. He went to a pond to drink water. The water was almost freezing. As he was ready to leave, Peter realized that he was not the only intruder in that pond. A porcupine had dropped in to bathe. Peter examined the thorny animal at close range. "But it is not a porcupine," Peter whispered to himself. "That is a hedgehog." Peter started talking to him.

"You little hedgy, you look very small in this widespread wilderness, but you don't seem to be concerned. No doubt you get plenty of food because you know where to look for it and where to find it. And although you're tiny, you know how to save your skin from the larger animals and birds. You can go back to your shelter whenever you want, safe and secure. And most importantly, with full stomach. I wish you'd understand what I'm saying to you, then I'd ask you to be my friend. I need a friend now, whoever it might be. I should be like you if I want to survive. I ought to be quick like you. I should build my shelter and obtain my food. This way you and I would become native to this area."

The animal was frightened and rolled up into a spiky ball. As Peter kept examining the hedgehog, Peter wondered whether the thorny animal was happy and he was immediately stuck on the definition of happiness. Animals have short instances of feeling satisfaction but never happiness, Mr. Jones had told him. Happiness requires a general feeling of euphoria and well-being. Animals act by instinct, driven by factors such as the seasons of the year and climate. They have no hopes or aspirations. There has got to be a difference between man's feeling of happiness and an animal's feeling of satisfaction. But what makes the animal satisfied? It had to be food, Peter thought.

He put his shoes on, letting his socks dry. He stared at the hedgehog for a second and started kicking it as if it were a soccer ball. He was talking again to the spiky ball, posing questions that Peter wondered about himself.

At the end, Peter was bored as the bundle of nails failed to react. He struck the animal strongly, and the hedgehog rolled fast and fell over the cliff. All of a sudden, Peter heard a loud flap in the bushes. This was followed by a wolf, dashing off like the wind. He could tell it was a wolf by the narrow, long gills and the mean brown eyes. *Mr. Jones was right. The wolf is running like a scared chicken*, Peter was thinking. *The wolf must have been devouring his prey when the hedgehog surprised him*, Peter thought. *I'll go and see what it is.*

Yards from where the wolf had run was a brown pheasant bleeding from her neck. Peter picked up the injured bird gently and started examining it. The fangs of the wolf were apparent in the poor bird's neck. Peter's first thoughts were of how to save the poor bird. He needed a sheet of cloth to wrap it around the injured neck. By the time he reached the pond, however, the bird had died.

An idea occurred to him suddenly. Since he was hungry, why not barbecue the bird and eat it? But he was facing two problems. The first was skinning the pheasant and cutting it, and the second was building a campfire. His stay at the cave reminded him of the volcanic-type spikes dangling from the ceiling. If he could find a small spike, an obsidian, then he could use it to skin the bird. That's what Indians did before the white man came, Mr. Jones had told him. He remembered the cave that he'd spent two nights in. He ran there and went inside with the bird in his hands. He went into the narrow entrance and found a thin spike dangling from the low ceiling. With a blow of a stone, he broke the spike. Now he had an obsidian knife.

It was still before noon. He could eat his lunch and then continue to look for home. The next task was to make a campfire. He collected some dry tiny branches along with dry needles and gathered two stones. He set to strike the stones at each other. He got a few sparks, but none long enough to burn the sticks. He tried another method that he had seen in a Tarzan movie. He brought a thick stick and started spinning it against the dry sticks and the dry needles. The area beneath the big stick became hot, but the fire was still a dream. A flint stone would do the trick, but he did not know what it looked like.

Peter tried to eat some of the pheasant meat raw. He could not at first. Then he forced himself to have some. *If the animals can do it, so can I*, he thought. When he put the first piece of the raw meat in his mouth, he wanted to throw up, but eventually he succeeded in convincing himself to accept it and ate some more.

He carried the bird and proceeded north. He was strolling, stopping at numerous spots to examine strange-looking mushrooms or watch a flock of sea gulls heading south. The smart birds, Peter thought, undoubtedly sensed the coming of the ruthless winter and its chilly winds. They were now on their way to the south where the sun would continue to provide them with warmth. They formed a two-sided triangle, as they glided gracefully in the turquoise sky. They were like airplanes doing an air show.

The word "airplane" reminded him of an incident that had been the talk of the town for months many years ago. A pilot and his eight-year-old daughter had disappeared on their way to Idaho. The incident would not have attracted Peter's attention if it hadn't been for the fact that the pilot was his teacher's friend. The search was suspended after one month of futile searching. It was concluded that the plane must have crashed in one of the many lakes in the area. Peter decided to examine all the lakes he passed by to see if he could locate the missing plane.

By now he had reached the top of a hill. As he crossed one rugged terrain after the other and one hill after the other, he expected to hit a road or a trail soon, but there was no road and no sign of any human.

Every step was taking him deeper and deeper into the woods. He climbed a hill to get a better look at the area around him. His hands bled from holding onto so many branches and boulders. His mouth was dry and his lips stuck to each other. Leaves and fir cones clung to his clothes.

As he tried to remove the sticking cones from his clothes, he was startled by a loud wild scream behind a row of pine trees. A fierce fight had ensued between a black crow and a coyote over a rabbit. The powerful jaws of the coyote were almost closing on the crow's neck, but the latter avoided the fatal blow, swerving at the last second. The crow now took off a few feet in the air and landed quickly on the coyote, pecking fiercely at its eyes. The crow would land and take off like a small chopper.

Peter grabbed a broken limb and retreated to avoid the animals, but the lifting of the limb frightened the warring rivals and both fled away from the prey. Peter examined the carcass of the rabbit. It was torn to pieces and its bowels were out, but he was able to salvage the two fat legs, which were untouched.

He climbed the rest of the hill and looked at the valley below. There was a thin blue white line down under. It was a small river flowing in the easterly direction at the foot of the mountain. Suddenly the disconsolate look that had dominated his face earlier disappeared. He felt optimistic for the first time since he'd left the pond. The solution was easy now. All he had to do was follow the river. Rivers originate in high terrain, he reasoned, and flow into low land and eventually to the plains where people live. The only question was how far he had to go before he hit a town?

6

After discovering the river, Peter decided to rest before starting the downriver trip. Although he was in the middle of nowhere, he felt he was already home, but he was not excited about it. Home meant a pathetically confirmed way of life and obeying orders that had become a ritual. A spree of coughing reminded him of his ailment. The headache was tormenting him, but he had to eat before heading to civilization along the river. Now the word "civilization" acquired a special meaning for him. It meant convenience in the fact that supplies of food and other basic services were readily available twenty-four hours per day.

An idea occurred to him for the first time. He would abandon his little town and settle in a big city. His hometown had just become a ghost town. He could no longer walk in its narrow streets, knowing that his mother was not around, that his father was breathing somewhere else, that Mr. Jones was enjoying the Arizona sun. *Cynthia is there but she would shun me*, he told himself. If he were cured of the disease, she might change her mind.

Their relationship had started almost a year ago on a cold morning on his way to school. A boy a year older than he was harassing her. He did not know her then, but he had seen her. Peter had watched as the young man was trying to pull Cynthia's hair. Suddenly, Peter went over to him and pulled his arm. A fight had ensued, but a police vehicle had passed and the boy ran. After that Peter and Cynthia became friends. They went to movies together, but one day, several months later, she suddenly started avoiding him.

He heard later that a boy had told her that if she kissed Peter, she would get the deadly disease, but he did not know who that boy was. *I will try my luck in another town, perhaps Casper or Denver. I will finish high school there. The students in these places do not know me. For them I will be just another boy. By the time I reach eighteen, science might find a cure for my disease.*

As he stood there holding on to the pheasant and the legs of the rabbit, he heard a clamorous flap of wings. This was followed by a movement in Peter's hand. Before he knew it, he saw a crow snatching one of the legs from his hand and flying like a speed chopper. Peter was astonished, for he was sure it was the same crow that he'd seen fighting the coyote. He decided to try to make a fire soon and eat the leg before it was too late.

Turning his glance, he noticed a column of smoke ascending from the east. He got up on his feet at once and climbed a high cliff to get a better view. When he mounted a large boulder, he could see clouds of smoke embracing the mountain ranges. There had to be fire somewhere, he thought. That word *fire*, reminded him of food. The idea intensified his feeling of hunger. He marched fast in the direction of the smoke, heedless of his fatigue and exhaustion.

Peter crossed the meadow beneath the hill until he reached the valley. The river was at this point a narrow, fast-flowing stream. It steeply cut the V-shaped valley. The bed of the river, which was about thirty feet across, was littered with boulders, rocks, and broken tree trunks. The rocks, which stood on both sides of the river, grew pine and other trees. He walked along the rocky twisting bank for about a half a mile and then climbed part of the mountain where the fire was blazing.

He had to stop, as the heat was becoming unbearable. The best thing would be to get a burning log, and take it far away from the fire, and barbecue the pheasant there and the rabbit meat. He had to stay far from the real fire, otherwise he would be overcome by smoke.

Finally, he ran to a burning log, snatched it by one end, and started pulling it. He was short of breath. Severe coughing took hold of him. He hurled the log, ran far away from the fire, and lay down, gasping for air, trying to take deep breaths. As soon as he felt better, he returned and dragged the log until he was safe over a little hill. The wind was blowing in the other direction, so he sat by the brazier. He crushed the log to pieces by means of his knife. It looked like real charcoal. He placed three stones around the fire and used dry sticks as skewers. He cut the bird into four pieces and started barbecuing it along with the rabbit leg.

As the campfire was cooking his food, Peter stood up and watched the wildfire consuming the forest. The fire scorched in series of rapid and consistent waves, sweeping the green branches and releasing layers of black clouds. The smell of the fire was mixed with the meat cooking. Animals were running in all directions, looking for shelters away from the blazing death. There were deer, elk, bobcat, and cougars. Even the chipmunk and the muskrat were in a state of disarray, rushing to their holes.

As the day progressed, the winds gained strength. Peter wondered, as he watched the relentless flames consuming the forest, what would happen to him if the winds changed their course. He would have to abandon his place. The fire might just continue until the entire forest was consumed. He wondered if anyone else knew of this disaster in the forest. If the authorities found out, they should be sending a crew to extinguish it. But how would anyone know of the fire to report it to the proper channels? He wondered whether there were rangers in that part of the state. If so, then fire fighters would be on their way to battle the raging flames.

By now he could smell the delicious odors emanating from the cooking meat, which had turned brown, but the campfire had lost its glow. Peter was starved and could not wait any longer. He looked toward the forest fire and noticed dry sticks on the floor of the forest. He ran toward them to revive the dying campfire.

As he took the sticks and headed back, a chilling surprise was awaiting him. A fox by the campfire was ready to snatch the pheasant. He threw the sticks and ran after the fox. The fox disappeared behind some bushes. Peter returned and turned the meat upside down on the campfire, but no sooner had he headed toward the sticks than the sly mammal resurfaced near the campfire, looking stealthily at Peter. Peter again chased him away. The fox this time did not go far. He stood on a rock close by and started gazing at Peter with brown stubborn eyes as though challenging him and questioning his right to claim a monopoly over the meat. The fox's long bushy tail was up in the air and his upright ears were erect like horns. Peter held his knife, waving it in his hands and advancing slowly toward the fox who fled head over heels.

Peter came back and turned the meat again. "Yes, it's ready," he murmured. He selected one piece and started devouring pieces from it, almost burning his lips. The meat felt strange as it contained no salt or seasoning, but he was in no position to be fastidious. Before he finished that piece, the persistent fox was there, but this time showing signs of submission as though begging Peter to give him some meat. Peter felt sorry for the fox and started talking to him. "You're right, foxy. This is your territory and I am the intruder, but I did not take it from you or even from this area. I stole one piece of it from a wolf and the other from two fighting animals. So as you see it belongs to me."

Peter was uttering these words, slowly looking at the fox straight in his brown-reddish eyes. The slick creature now lowered his ears and allowed his long tail to dangle, sweeping the forest floor. He advanced only one cautious step and stayed there. Peter finally took a thigh and threw it high. The fox jumped, snatching it in the air and disappeared. Now Peter focused on the cooking meat, and in a few minutes, he had finished all the meat. His headache had gradually disappeared.

The fire was almost out by now. Peter rushed to feed the brazier with dry branches. The view of the campfire provided unexplained solace for his loneliness. When the flames mounted, he brought more logs and placed them an almost vertical shape on the fire. Afterward, he brought four logs, dragging them from the valley below. He placed the four logs like a cross so that the fire was positioned at the center of the cross-shaped logs. He would need the blaze if he had to spend another night in the wilderness.

It was becoming harder and harder for him to leave, for the reason that following the river might put him in the way of the advancing flames. Now that he had eaten and was full, he did not mind staying another night there. He would keep the blaze going all night. This would keep all the animals away from him. Hopefully by the morning, fire fighters would be there.

Peter had chosen his temporary shelter near a boulder that was partly protruding from the hill. If it rained, Peter could move under it in a matter of seconds. In addition, the boulder would reflect the fire on him, keeping him warm. He gathered the fallen leaves and kept stacking them near the brazier. *Tonight, I'll sleep over a bed of leaves for the first time in so many days*, he thought to himself. *The brazier will keep me warm. I will not worry about the lion or even the human beast. This raging fire is liable to keep all the predators away for a while.*

Darkness was pressing down on him. The fire in the mountain across from him was blazing with more vigor. The flames lit the sky, reflecting their light on the thin banded masses of thin, high clouds, turning them pink and scarlet. As the night progressed, more dark clouds were moving in. They were high milky clouds, mostly shapeless. The emergence of these clouds cast some doubt as to whether the fire fighters would show up. These clouds were of the kind that produced rain within hours. He knew these clouds in his little town. Whenever they showed up at night, he would wake up in the morning to a drizzle. Peter was worried that if it rained, the authorities would refrain from extinguishing the fire, leaving that dangerous task to nature. After all, the latter works fast and free.

As the sun disappeared, the moon took over as much as the

clouds allowed it. The clouds reached out and grappled with the moon for possession of the night. The quick moving clouds were gliding over the column of black smoke flying in the sky. Peter examined the moon and noticed a shape of a man in it. It was the first time Peter was noticing the man figure in it. *Perhaps he is there to keep a watch over me*, he thought. Before he slept, Peter watched the moon hurrying from one dark cloud to another. In a way the moon was like Peter; they were both on the run.

7

Peter was awakened in the morning by the sound of rain beating like a drum on the large boulder next to him. The fire was still raging in the forest, but his campfire had died down. Most of the wood in the center had been transferred into gray pieces, preserving their shape. He hurried to the huge rock, which stood erect several feet high, and lay on the ground beneath it.

The first rays of daylight were just emerging now. The armies of light were sweeping the forces of darkness. He rested his back and started examining the clouds. They were white, shapeless, and foggy. The high, fluffy cauliflower clouds of yesterday had been replaced by a solid mass of low puffs, promising unceasing drizzle for many hours.

Peter needed a good campfire to keep him warm. Part of the wildfire was not far from him by the river. He ran under the drizzle to the first fire. As he got there, he saw a deer lying on the ground moaning. He examined the injured animal and found no trace of burn. He must have suffered from smoke inhalation. Peter got his granite knife and decided to stab the deer in the neck, but he found it difficult. He had never killed even a bird in his life, but he needed the deer for both its meat and its skin. As a matter of fact, he needed the skin more than he needed the meat. It was getting cold, especially at night, and he badly needed the deer's skin to use as a cover at night and a coat during the day. He had heard that the deer skin keeps the animal warm even when it gets forty degrees below zero and also keeps it cool when the temperature rises to a hundred.

Peter advanced toward the dying animal and started talking to him. "Poor deer, I wish I could do something for you. Besides, I'm not sure if I can save your life." He bent and started examining the deer at close range. It was a buck, a dotted red male deer with two crooked horns. Its tail was thick and short. "What a nice summer coat," he said. He then looked at the deer and whispered, "I'm really sorry, friend, but I have to kill you." He held his stalactite knife and attempted to stab the deer vigorously, but the knife only scratched the beautiful dotted neck. He then closed his eyes and pounced upon the neck, submerging the knife in the neck. The deer shuddered for a minute and then died.

Peter attempted to pull the deer with both hands, but the carcass would not budge. An idea occurred to him. *Why not leave it here for a while? It is safer here as no predator will venture near the fire as long as it is raging. I'll come later and skin it right here. Besides, Mr. Jones advised me to allow a carcass to cool to ensure palatability.*

For several long minutes, he attempted to cut the animal. Finally, he was able to open the carcass. He removed as many internal organs as he could and left them there. He made sure all the blood had drained out of the animal. "Do not eat the animal if a drop of blood remains," Mr. Jones had advised. "Blood is the first thing to become contaminated." He then dragged a burning log and took it to his camp. He broke the log into pieces and made a campfire for himself.

Gradually the red flames were emitting beams of warmth, which made him sleepy again. He moved under the rock and took the burning logs with him. *What should I do now?* he wondered. *Should I leave as soon as the sun shines? Or should I wait here until someone comes by? I think I will go. I'm sure I'll hit a town by tomorrow.* Soon the heat from the brazier started transmitting waves of warmth that penetrated his shivering body. In no time, a pleasant numbness overpowered his weak body and he fell asleep.

When he woke up, the drizzle had escalated to a heavy rain.

The big drops would land on the ground and bounce up to form tiny streams leading downward to the river. He went on watching the rain for a few minutes. Thoughts of town and his mother flashed in his head. He was now seeing the rain from the window of his room. His mother was sitting next to him. He was a few years younger. It had been his first real confrontation with her. He'd wanted to go on a trip to Yellowstone National Park with his classmates and view the geysers and the hot springs, but his mother would not allow him. He did not talk to her for the entire day.

Peter wondered whether children stay too long with their mothers. He observed that all the animals he saw were on their own. Most of the time, the mother leaves the cub within a short time, as he saw on a television program on nature, and the cub is on his own after that. The animal who stays the longest with her young is the wolf, but even the wolf mother stays with the babies for only a year or two. *Maybe that's why they are animals and we are humans. I think a boy or a girl needs a mother.* The love that a good mother gives to her baby, he had heard, is like a fertilizer. Without it the child will grow wild and savage like an animal. Or he may wither physically and mentally before reaching adulthood. In fact he recalled a police officer once saying that prisons are filled with criminals who were deprived of motherly love.

Peter suddenly recalled the deer. By now the heavy rain was light. Peter placed wood on the fire and ran to where the deer was. The forest floor was like a battlefield, with the burning logs falling on already black trunks. He pulled the carcass beneath a huge tree to protect himself from the rain and started skinning it. He recalled Mr. Jones's words: "Start by placing the animal on its back and pull the head upward. Blow as hard as you can in the gullet until the skin is inflated and becomes easy to separate from the meat. Then start coring with your knife around the anus, then make a slit through the skin from the breast bone to the crotch."

As Peter started the delicate surgery, he tried to remember all the instructions. He was careful not to slice into the stomach or the intestine to prevent making a big mess. He was surprised that he was doing a good job. Watching Mr. Jones had paid off. As soon as he removed the skin from the thigh, he cut a piece weighing about one pound. He carried it running to his brazier and started barbecuing it. After he ate he went back to finish skinning the deer.

The most difficult and messy part was the cavity of the deer. He had to make so many cuts, and in so doing, he committed numerous mistakes, rendering his messy task even messier, but finally he removed the innards and did some more cutting. Then he removed the heart, the lungs, and other organs unknown to him. Afterward, he worked on finishing the skinning, making sure that the skin was not damaged.

Several hours later his first assignment was successfully completed. Now he had a complete deerskin. He lifted it and spread it in front of him smiling with cruel confidence. At that second he wished Mr. Jones were there; he would be proud of Peter. He carried the skin along with another chunk of meat and headed for the brazier. There was a surprise waiting for him. For a split second, his heart sank. It was a black bear. He was not supposed to be afraid of black bears, but seeing that humongous creature frightened him nevertheless. The bear had a big smoldering stem in its mouth, and he seemed to be smoking. Columns of thin smoke came out of the burning stem. As soon as the bear saw Peter, it took off, casting away the stem, and disappeared. Peter grabbed the burning stem and was amazed. It looked like a huge cigar. *I can't believe it. A smoking bear*? Peter then gathered some long dry stems and spread the skin over them above the fire. He wanted the skin to dry.

Over the next couple of days, he forgot about his plan to leave. He was busy with the skin. He dried it more until he was sure it was usable. He spread it on the floor beneath the rock and sat on it, enjoying a modest mattress for the first time in several days.

The wildfire in the forest raged off and on, according to the strength of the rain. As the rain died down, the fire intensified. Peter had decided to spend another night there. He would not walk for miles and miles under the rain until he reached a town. He would walk the next day if the weather improved. But how about if the rain continued for several days? Then he would stay there. There were plenty of coniferous trees, firs and spruce, to keep the fire raging for as long as he wanted. Moreover, he had plenty of food to last him for long.

The rain continued for several days, which was sufficient for the wildfire to die out. The smoke from the scorching trees was raging, filling the sky with thick layers of smoke before they died out altogether.

At one point, Peter felt sick and short of breath. When he woke up the next day, he had fever and was coughing. The fever rarely left him for several days. The coughing was severe and continuing. He spent the next few days sleeping, using the deer skin as both mattress and a cover. At times he was short of breath to the degree of strangulation. When his condition improved, he would get up and get water from the river. He wanted badly to make a bowl of hot soup, but he had no utensils.

When Peter felt better, he had no idea how many days had elapsed. He had lost count of the days. There were days that he spent sleeping or half awake. A week later his condition improved. The sky cleared and he was able to see the sun peeking from behind the mountains. Peter could not see the forest, however. The thick fog had swallowed the valley. When the fog finally caved in to the sun, the forest looked completely different in the fire areas. The leaves and the upper branches of the trees had all been consumed by fire. The trunks were blackened. Many trunks were broken.

Peter took his belongings, now the water bottle, the deerskin, and several pounds of cooked meat. He came down to the foot of the mountain in the direction of the river. He was forcing his way through the burned forest. The branches and the trunks had fallen, most turning into charcoal or ashes, some trees discharging black smoke. The river was not any better. Huge deposits of ashes and charcoal fell in the river and onto the rocks guarding it, transforming those gigantic rocks into black giants, striking terror in Peter's heart despite his improved condition.

The waves of water moved from one place of the river to another like the wakes of tiny speed boats. The river at this point had many rapids. After Peter had walked for over a mile, the river was joined by a stream. Now the river was a little larger. Its width ranged from thirty feet to fifty. At some places there were sandy beaches, almost tempting Peter to swim, but it was too cold to do that. He hiked a little farther. He had the deerskin rolled around him so that he looked like a standing buck deer from afar. Soon the river developed basins or ponds filled with fish.

Some distance downstream, the river was joined by a smaller one. The two rivers now formed a fast-flowing channel. The view of the two rivers meeting gave Peter an added feeling of confidence. There was no doubt now that a town would appear in a few miles. He immediately felt better. The severe coughing had stopped. There were now sporadic dry coughs unlike last night when Peter thought he was going to die. He was walking as though he was on a pleasure trip. Perhaps the disease was yielding to a strong determination, which had started to crystalize without his defining it by words. This new determination affirmed his persistence and stubbornness for survival.

The sounds of the animals running behind the elm trees no longer scared him. He figured if an animal attacked him he would just throw him pieces of meat. At one point, he heard a splash in the water. It was a large trout. He wished he had a hook; then he would fish. There was nothing like barbecued fish. As he examined the trout, something caught his eyes, sending waves of terror in his heart. There were human footprints in the sandy beach by the riverbank.

The image of the beast flashed in his mind. He looked around

himself to see if the hulk was still there. He could not resist going over to the footprints to examine them. As he got closer to them, he looked right and left stealthily, straining his ears for any unusual sounds. When he was over the footprints, his body started to shiver. They were those of a barefooted man. They originated from the water and disappeared on the rocks. They were huge and Peter figured they were more than fifteen inches in length. The footsteps were deep, denoting a heavy built body.

His first idea was to get away. But how would he reach civilization without following the river? He looked at the footprints again. They were not fresh, so the hulk could not have been there recently. An idea occurred to him. If he had a boat, then he could sail until he reached the first town. He remembered Mr. Jones. He had once built a raft by tying several logs together, one adjacent to the other. But how would he get the ropes to tie them together? He went to the riverbank and when he saw what he was looking for, he cut some long roots with the help of his knife, but he soon discovered that he could not tie them together. He then found long slender branches by the riverbed and after some tests decided that they would work.

Now he had to find two tree trunks that were several feet in length, had similar diameters, and were light enough for him to drag. It was not very hard, thanks to the fire. He dragged one log after another. Then an idea occurred to him. If he used another log, then he would have almost a V-shaped boat. He found a log that was a little larger than the other two. With the help of the branches, he tied the inner and outer logs together so that the middle log was tied to the two exterior logs. He then carried a stick to use as an oar and to push his three-log boat.

Peter mounted the boat, his eyes glancing in all directions, and sat on the middle log. Soon the boat was drifting in silence. At one point he almost fell as the boat hit a hidden rock. He used his stick several times to prevent the boat from bumping into the fir- and pine-covered rocks that protruded from the bank or from the water. All of a sudden, a side current pouring from behind a partially submerged boulder caught the boat and moved it to full speed. Peter used the stick to slow it. Any misfortune and he was gone, he thought. The perils were numerous. There was the danger from the hidden rocks and the whirlpools. Besides, the existence of the huge rocks in the riverbed created many rapids.

The foamy water rendered any effort by him to spot fish near impossible, but some of them jumped above the water like tiny dolphins. Peter felt proud of himself and his achievement. For a few seconds he forgot about the dreadful footsteps. He wished the world could see him, and especially Mr. Jones. He then thought of Cynthia. If she saw him now, she might laugh at him. She would probably think that he was crazy, but had he really been crazy when he undertook that adventure? Had he really needed it? He did not find an answer. Perhaps, then, he was crazy; otherwise, the answer would rest on the result of this adventure. Besides, would Cynthia admire him if he returned and told her of his adventure or would she consider this a kind of stupidity and irresponsible?

Peter asked himself whether he still cared for her even after she'd rejected him. He was unnerved by the answer. His heart told him that he still cared for her and wished to be cured of his disease and go back to her. Perhaps if he were cured, she would see a different person in him. He wondered if he would change if he was cured. His response was that he would not, but he would definitely be a happier person, especially if he were with Cynthia, holding her hands and taking her out to the park or to the movies. He wished she were with him now to enjoy that breathtaking scenic view. He was smiling to himself. Very soon he would hit a town.

The makeshift boat was now drifting in a narrow funnel that led to a steep rapids. On both sides of the river were more and more hills with high mountains in the background. Peter noticed the barren jagged peaks through the thick vegetation, which the sun turned into reddish brown. A huge vulture soared in the sky above the river. When the giant bird prepared to land, it spread its wings. Peter could not believe his eyes. The wings, according to Peter's estimation, were no less than ten feet.

The vulture and Peter's preoccupation with Cynthia prevented him from seeing the white water ahead of him. The foamy white water was followed by a steep rapids. Before he knew it, the boat capsized. It was overturned so that its front submerged perpendicular to the slope that caused the waterfall, and the three logs broke apart. Peter was thrown out of the boat, flying several feet in the air, and was hurled onto the rocks that surrounded the bank. He felt a severe pain in his head.

Touching his head, his hand came away covered with blood. He tried to stand up but fell. He tried again and again. Finally he managed to stagger for a few steps beneath a big aspen tree when his vision became blurred. He could no longer see anything. His legs could no longer support his body. He collapsed, his knee hitting the ground first; then the rest of his body followed. As he was losing consciousness, a thought crossed his mind. He had been worried all along about the human beast, but now his death could draw near as a result of a stupid fall. His biggest scare was that if he lost consciousness, he might never regain it.

8

When Peter regained consciousness, he did not know how much time had elapsed since the river accident. He had fallen over the grass and the pebbles that blanketed the ground. The first attack was launched by the cold whirling winds striking him in the face. The distant sun shining high in the blue sky provided little warmth. Despite his injuries, he felt an astonishing clearness in his vision and mind. On the other hand, his entire body ached. Pain oozed from every pore of his body, especially in his thigh and hip.

The slightest effort to move was painful. It felt as if needles were pricking his body. He checked his legs to ascertain that he was not paralyzed. For a few scary moments, he could not budge a muscle, but as he applied pressure, signs of life returned to his numbed body. He rested his head on fallen leaves and started taking inventory of his injuries. The pains guided him to those areas. His most severe wound was in the head above the right ear. His right arm had also suffered a deep cut, and blood had dried on both places so that when Peter touched the affected areas the dried blood felt like sandpaper. He had also minor cuts and lacerations in several areas, including the palm of his hand and the middle finger, which was swollen and sprained.

Peter again attempted to get up, but he fell. The best thing to do was to keep warm, he thought. He straightened the deerskin around his body and closed his eyes, feeling sleepy. *I wish I had some hot soup ready this minute*, he thought. He wanted to get up and fetch his venison or some other food, but he could not. As he lay thinking of what had happened, he fell into a shallow doze and drifted into a placid if drug-softened sleep.

He did not know how long he slept this time, but when he got up, the night swooped over the wilderness, but the moonlight provided much needed light. The rushing currents in the river produced a thunderous, monotonous murmur echoing in the valley. He was shivering and there was nothing more to keep him warm. His body continued to ache in the affected areas. His headache was gone, but he was still feverish and the coughs visited him anew. To make things worse, waves of cold, whistling arctic air swept through his joints ruthlessly. He covered his head with the deerskin, but the wind was the kind that roared in his ears after he had taken cover. His clothes and the skin did not help much. He curled around himself and lay like a ball.

The sky was clear and he could see the stars and the full moon staring at him. Peter saw as if for the first time the full sky at night. He was amazed at the hemispherical black dome embellished with thousands of various-sized stars. Brightness varied from a faint almost invisible dot, to a brilliant ball of flashing light dancing in the black hole. He wanted to savor the captivating nature above him, but the pains returned him to his miserable reality, and deprived him of relishing that mesmerizing beauty. The beauty was no consolation for his sorrowful spirit and his agonized heart. The sky seemed to him bleak and dreadful, crammed with invisible monsters ready to pounce on him. Who cares for beauty when one is shivering, hungry, and most of all nearly fatally wounded?

Peter noticed several large stars and started to count them. As he did that, a bright star suddenly fell with astonishing speed toward the horizon. He did not know what to make of it. He recalled Mr. Jones describing that phenomenon to him. Mr. Jones had said that every time a star falls, someone known to the person witnessing the phenomenon has just died. If that was the case,

Peter wondered who the dead person was. Could it be Aunt Pauline dying over his absence? Or was it his father dying of excessive drinking?

He recalled Aunt Pauline saying that if two stars met in the skies, anyone witnessing the encounter could ask for any wish and get it. He went on watching the sky in the hope that this phenomenon would take place. But what was his wish at that time? Was it to get home safely or to be free of his disease? Peter noticed that there were numerous things that he did not grasp.

Peter wondered if he could figure out his exact location. He had heard that one could tell directions with the help of the stars. He recalled his science teacher telling him how to locate the North Star by means of the Pointers. He had said to look for the Big Dipper, which consisted of four stars forming a square, with three additional stars on the tail of one side of the square. The North Star would be a brighter star beneath the Big Dipper, forming a straight line with the two lower stars of the square. Viewing the bright North Star, he was able to recognize where the north was.

But what is the use? I lie here wounded, weak from hunger, he thought. *Add to that, the cold winds are penetrating deep into the core of my bones. Even if the location of the star helps me determine which way home is, that will be of little help, for home could be miles and miles behind these mountain ranges. Besides, there is no guarantee that I won't collapse within a quarter of a mile from here.*

The pains from the injuries were now aggravated by a severe stomach ache and other painful sensations caused by the prolonged lack of food. Peter felt exceptionally hungry for the first time since the river accident. He was so hungry he thought he would even eat a rock, but there was nothing to eat. He recalled how fussy he had been when he got home hungry and food was not ready. He would complain that he was starved to death, but then he was making a mockery of himself. What he called starving to death then was nothing in comparison to the agonizing torment that he was experiencing now. The chunk of venison that he had had with him was nowhere to be found. Besides, he would need fire to cook it.

Peter had to fetch food very soon; otherwise his body would be unable to survive the wounds until the first rays of dawn brought a relief. But what would he eat at this time of the night? He looked around him through the light reflected from the moon. He could only see the dancing shadows of the trees swaying gracefully, increasing their movement as the winds intensified. His ears were strained and tuned to catch the whispers on the wind, but it was generally quiet. There was a sporadic croaking of frogs and the steady singing of insects. When the winds calmed down, he would hear movement in the bushes. But that was the least of his worries now. The forest was alive. Not all the animals were sleeping. *But none of them is hungry*, he thought. He was the only hungry animal.

The monotonous ripple of the water in the river reminded him to get a drink. He got up but he fell. He tried again and as he was dragging his feet, he felt agony and loneliness walking with him in the dark. He almost fell on the way as he staggered and struck a boulder protruding from the water. When he finally drank some water, he got even more hungry. He came back to his place under the elm tree. He expected death all along his adventure but not by means of starvation. Salvation now was getting through the long vicious night, but his mind bulged with rebuke and was revolting and shouting at him to resist everything. He breathed an exasperated sigh and the wild footsteps caused him to stay strong in determination.

Peter remembered his science teacher during one of the lectures. "The human body and that of animals are physically the same," he had said. *Why can't I eat the same food they do? Let's see. What do animals eat?* he asked himself. Experience and TV viewing told him that they ate anything and everything, from the thorny bushes to the despicable insects. *But I can't eat insects, for instance.* Man was prejudiced when it came to food. Many of his classmates would make fun of the Japanese when they found out that they ate raw fish or of the French for eating frogs.

What difference does it make for my body if the food entering it is a beef steak or a snake? Peter wondered. For the body, it was probably the same, but for the human taste, there was a world of difference. As he kept thinking, he felt more hungry. He was shaking and his stomach was growling and screaming for food. His vision was becoming blurred. He got up again and went to some berry bushes nearby. He could not see the fruits at first, but he had seen similar bushes earlier and they were jampacked with little red berries. He cut some and started eating one after the other. He decided to eat a small quantity in the event they were poisonous. Besides, he did not want to have diarrhea like the first few days after eating the berries for the first time. They tasted sour. When the juices from the berries were mixed with his saliva, a painful sensation followed for a few seconds. After he ate a few, he stopped. If he did not get diarrhea by tomorrow and he was still alive by then, he would eat more of the wild berries.

Now he needed a piece of meat or a bread roll with butter. He needed some fat to satisfy his raging hunger. If he had the fire, his problem would be half solved. He would get a frog from the river or capture an animal, any animal, even a chipmunk or porcupine, and if he was lucky, even a wild turkey. He decided to return to the river to get rose hips and raspberries. As he did that, a sparrow flew beneath his legs. He looked at the area where the bird took off. Peter knelt and started feeling the ground, hoping to find the bird's nest. But there was nothing. *If I can just find the nest, I'm bound to find some eggs in it, which will keep me alive until tomorrow.*

At this point he realized that he would never find any eggs. He just remembered his biology studies that almost all birds lay eggs in the spring and summer only and mostly in tree nests.

Peter stood up, grabbed a pine tree next to him and remained in that position for a minute, thinking what the next step should be. As he pulled his hands from the trunk of the pine, he noticed that a piece of bark came with it. He brought the crispy thin layer of wood close to his nose and started to smell it. It had a pleasant smell. The pine tree was a little different from the other trees that he had seen in the last several days. The trunk was thin and long, and it was full of green bark. Peter decided that he should eat some of the bark no matter how horrible it tasted. If it killed him, Peter thought, so be it. He remembered poisonous mushrooms and noxious berries, but he had never heard of poisonous bark. As he started to chew on the bark, he was surprised to find out that it did not taste that terrible. It tasted like bitter celery, but all he could eat was two small pieces.

Peter felt like fainting. He had been standing for several minutes now and his legs would no longer support him. He sat down. Soon, he became feverish and his coughs intensified. A creeping uneasiness surfaced at the bottom of his heart and he felt dizzy, wanting to vomit. *I need some salty foods or I'll always be dizzy*, he thought. *But since I have nothing, I should be strong.* All efforts by him to take control of himself failed. He could not get over the obsessive sense of everything going wrong.

His current condition and the necessity to find a way out of his dilemma made him forget to blame himself. All his effort was going in one direction, to find the light of the tunnel. That would not happen unless he developed self-confidence and convinced himself that there was a goal behind his adventure, and that the difficulties were a must.

His mind slowly started going back, picking up the strings of time. Gradually, he submerged himself into memory. The floodgates had opened, and the torrent was finding its way out. His mind drifted into fuzzy haze.

Suddenly he was home with his parents. He must have been a few years younger, for his mother was sitting next to him at the family dining room. In the room was his father, in addition to Mr. Jones, Aunt Pauline, and the family doctor. They were celebrating a big event, and the table was filled with all types of delicious food. There were grilled geese and ducks, brown and crispy. There were a lot of potatoes and hot rolls. There was even smoked ham and sausage, in addition to numerous kinds of desserts.

But Peter did not touch his plate, although he was hungry. The abstention from food puzzled him a great deal. He wanted just to taste it, but something mysterious in the looks of the doctor prevented him from budging. He noticed that his mother suddenly got up with her suitcase in her hand and headed outside.

As she got to the threshold, she turned to Peter with a tinge of sadness in her blue eyes. "I have to leave, my son," she said as she hugged him. "My train is outside waiting for me." With a wounded look in her eye, she uttered the words "Good-bye, Peter," and started to board the train, whose sirens were now piercing the silence of the little town.

Peter clung to her and asked her to take him with her, but she refused. "You must stay here, Peter, You must," she said with grief lurking in her eyes.

"Now that you're cured, you're leaving me just when I need you most?"

"I have to go, son. I have no choice, but I'll wait for you and you will join me when it is your time."

Peter turned to his father for support, but everyone had disappeared. He was alone and he felt he had to fight his battle by himself. He decided to climb the stairs leading to the train car, but a strong wind blew suddenly, preventing him from coming near it. The bawling winds were so severe that Peter had to cling to the station column and block his ears.

Suddenly he observed his mother in the train. He ran fuming with rage to the window. The wind slashed and shoved him, but he managed to grab the handle by the stair rails. As he tried to mount the train, she pushed him away harshly. He started to scream at her. He was telling her that she had no right to go and leave him there alone, that if she was planning to leave from the beginning, she shouldn't have raised him and brought him to that sick world of hers, that she should have abandoned him when he was a little boy so he wouldn't remember how she looked, just like the animals do.

The train started moving. Other passengers in the train, all dressed in white just like nurses, were staring at him. He gazed at her with mirror brilliant eyes to discover the reason for her sudden departure.

But as the train disappeared, he was calm again. Suddenly, in a breathless instant of release, he was freed.

As the last car of the train disappeared, he was startled when he looked in the direction the train was going. There were conical hills of pure crystal in different colors, silver, blue, and white in addition to transparent clear glass. The hills were in perfect triangle shape, as though drawn by a computer. As the train approached the crystal mountains, Peter wondered how it would pass them since there was no tunnel through the glass mountains. That question became unimportant as he started reading the destination the train was going to. The sign on the back of the last car read "ETERNITY."

9

The sound of an airplane brought Peter back to the world. It was sometime the next morning, for the scarlet disk of the sun was being delivered from the jaws of a jagged mountain range in the form of a blurred and red-blood ball. Peter got up sluggishly and waved his hands in the air in a desperate attempt to draw the plane's attention to his miserable existence. "Hello . . . hello . . . I'm here . . . I'm here," he was repeating incoherently with a raucous voice smothered by his unceasing coughs.

Soon he stopped screaming, realizing that there was no way anyone in the plane would hear him. The plane did not seem to recognize him. It continued soaring in the high altitude, heading north toward the north star, which by now had disappeared. "Why don't they send a plane to look for me? Is everyone happy that I just disappeared? The plane is probably going from Denver to one of the cities in the Canadian Rockies. Perhaps they are the early skiers. Very soon I will be skiing, too . . . forever." His voice cracked with a sardonic weariness. He collapsed on the frosty ground, clearing his throat of a rumbling phlegm.

Peter recalled last year when he'd flown with his father to San Francisco. He had insisted on sitting by the window to see America as he had seen it in the atlas, but that was all he'd seen except it was somewhat larger than the atlas. Patches of green and brown colors filled the place. There were also square and rectangular-shaped fields as though drawn on a piece of paper. The small roads were invisible and only the two-lane freeways would show up as two thin parallel lines. If someone was stranded on the ground just like he was, there was no way the pilot could have seen him. It would never occur to anyone in the plane that in the midst of the cauliflower patches of trees there was a human heart beating with hopes and desires, a human being like them whose name was . . . Peter. For a second he did not know who he was. Perhaps he was not the same Peter any more. It was like the beginning of a new identity for him.

As soon as the plane disappeared, he shifted his attention to himself. As he tried to wet his lips with the tip of his tongue, he discovered that his lips were badly chapped. The deepening cold of mid-October was slowly forcing him to get moving. His fingers and toes were numb. He started rubbing his hands together to prevent any frostbite. Pain did not matter any more. He was now beyond pain. He was simply hanging onto survival, and he had to fulfill a few crucial needs immediately if he was to survive another moon.

Peter needed to make fire and eat. He had to replace the blood he had lost as a result of the head and hand injuries sustained in the makeshift boat incident days earlier. Afterward he would have to look for a shelter, as it would take his injuries several days to heal. The best thing would be to find a small cave, he thought.

As he got up to leave, the nightmare that he'd experienced in the last two days and the scary dream that had followed seemed to him a sight conjured from hell. Death, disguised in various forms, had visited him but for some esoteric reason had missed him, he thought. He had another contract on life, and he decided to take full advantage of it. He decided to get moving immediately in the direction of downriver.

His feet refused to move at first. He stayed at the foot of the cliff and started watching for a suitable place to start his fire. At the bank of the river were many broken branches and boulders. Aspen and Russian olive trees filled the riverbed. There were also some cottonwoods with their leaves starting to fall. The gray bones of the trees were beginning to show. Up in the mountain, the evergreen pine trees embellished the slopes just beneath the snowcapped ranges. The distant foothills were cloaked with velvet composed of a rainbow of colors. The faint rays of the sun filled the hills with purple mist.

Peter continued walking, surveying the area for any sign of human settlement. About a mile downstream, he noticed what appeared to be a hut. His heart thumped against his rib cage. "That is probably the hut of the animal man," Peter whispered to himself. *But why should I be afraid of him?* he thought. *Maybe I should go and pay him a visit. I want to know what he is and why he is there. But I should be careful.*

Peter veered toward the higher elevation to approach behind the hut. The hike was more difficult because of the many gullies he had to cross. Besides, the climbing was making him faint, but he had to see what the hut revealed before making any decision that could mean the difference between life and death. Although he told himself not to worry, his heart was pounding.

As he advanced toward the hut, the fear disappeared and he started to enjoy the danger-excitement feeling that was gradually building in his mind. *Perhaps the animal man is not a bad fellow after all. He may even become my friend*, Peter thought. *I won't be surprised to find him just like me, lonely and without a family or someone to love and care for.* Peter was tired now, so he sat on the trunk of a fallen tree to rest and to watch nature waking up.

The sun had risen, now playing hide-and-seek with a handful of thin, swanlike fluffy clouds scattered across the blue sky. There were more geese and sea gulls making their trip down south. "I'm the only animal lost," he whispered, feeling sorry for himself. *I'm a worthless person*, he thought. *I can't even feed myself.*

Peter tried to compare himself with the birds. *I can notice things*, he thought to himself. *Can the flock of the birds see me as a separate entity creeping on the face of the forest? I can notice the sunshine and the sunset and can observe the rows of trees standing erect in the face of the winds and rains. All these mountains and valleys and clouds, I feel them all and perceive them. I wonder what other thing in these surroundings feel, any other thing here except me.*

Peter got up, feeling he could continue the hike and headed toward the hut. He made his way through a ground filled with wild clover and sagebrush. As he went around a curve near a hill, the hut disappeared. He turned upward and forced his way through a small ravine, taking him to the top of a round hill, and he continued advancing toward the mysterious structure, his eyes never leaving the direction of the hut. At this point he stood and gazed toward the distant horizon above where the hut was supposed to be. He still could not see it. All he could see was the same barren picture of rocks and patches of pines everywhere.

From his location on the hill, he happened to look near the horizon and he noticed an object hidden under the trees glittering under the sun. He kept examining the object that appeared as though it were glass, but the gleam vanished when the sun disappeared behind the clouds. *Perhaps it is just a smooth boulder*, Peter thought. He came down the hill and when he reached a clearing he figured he was about a quarter of a mile from the hut. He walked a little more and then climbed over a broken trunk to take a good look at the hut. At this point he became disappointed. There was no hut.

The broken branches by the river had formed a square wall similar to that of a hut. *At least I don't have to worry about the animal man for the time being*, he thought with relief. *But I sure can use the broken trunks to build a temporary shelter.*

As he got close to the bundle of logs, he noticed an indentation by the riverbank. Despite his miserable condition, he could not stop there and ponder the group of rocks forming a semi-cave. The indentation, however, had an opening from its ceiling so that only half of the aperture was covered by a rock, forming a natural bridge over the rock tent. *This is ideal for me*, Peter thought. *I can use the indentation as my shelter for now. The opening on top will serve a dual purpose of a ventilation and a chimney. All I need is to block the entrance with a few logs to keep the winds and the dangerous animals away from me.*

Having secured a shelter, he still needed the two basic necessities to survive, food and fire. *Let me make fire first and if I succeed, I'll hunt a rabbit or a deer. If not then maybe I should just sleep until I die.*

The bank of the river and its bed next to it were covered with all kinds of stones. *But which one of these stones is flint*, Peter wondered. *The only thing that I know about flint is that it is a hard stone. But aren't all rocks hard?* He grabbed several rocks and started striking them at each other. Some broke easily, forming sharp knives and little spears. Others sprang high in the air in one piece. Peter selected two of the hard stones that did not break and took them to his new shelter, the natural bridge. He then collected dry grass and dead evergreen needles for his tinder and started striking the stones at each other. The sparks produced were tiny and worthless. Besides, one of the stones broke to pieces. He went out and got several more stones and repeated the painful process, but to no avail. The sparks would just fly in the air aimlessly and die down.

Peter gave up when he remembered a western movie. He could not remember its name or who starred in it, but he recalled the four men stranded in the snow mountains between Nevada and California during a bone-numbing night. They had made a fire by means of bow and arrow. Peter sat down and closed his eyes, trying to recapture the dimly remembered details of the motion picture. Suddenly memories of the fire in the movie opened before him as if a curtain had been ripped aside. He remembered the men using a bow, an arrow, a stick, a socket, and a wood board. All the items were readily obtainable except the socket and the arrow.

He got out of his shelter and after a brief search found a smooth stone with a hollow depression in it. "I'll use this as a socket," he whispered with jubilation.

Now he needed a bow and arrow. He cut a branch with the help of a broken stone that he had turned into a sharp knife. He also got a stick and sharpened one end with the rock knife. Now came the most difficult part, for he needed a rope or a string. The roots that filled the river could not be used because they were thick and bumpy and the rope had to be smooth and thin to help rotate the drill. Suddenly a look of relief was drawn on his pale face. He thought of his sneakers with their long strings. In no time he pulled one of the strings from his shoe. It was about four feet long. Placing a board from a broken trunk on the dry grass and dead pine needles, he grabbed the stick, looping the shoe string over it. He then held the stone socket in his left hand and the arrow in his right hand, the sharp end of the stick against the board at the bottom.

As he applied pressure on the socket and pulled the arrow horizontally, the stick started spinning, engraving the board making a hole in it. He continued rotating the stick briskly by sawing back and forth with the bow. The stick was now deepening the hole in the board, but there was no fire and no sparks. Peter did not give up. Without fire, he thought, he would not survive another night. He applied more strength. He began pulling the bow back and forth with his utmost strength. His muscles ached and he was about to faint, but he continued. After a few minutes, Peter became excited as he started to smell the smoldering odor of the burning hole in the board. Soon the hole was widening.

When Peter looked at it a minute later, it had begun to smoke. He became more excited, regaining his shattered confidence and increased the speed of his hands. As he continued the pulling, black powder started to fall and settle on the tinder below.

Peter was now working like a machine. He had started to sweat and the palm of his hand where he was holding the socket got bruised. Even Mr. Jones would have envied his remarkable perseverance and speed. The more he persisted with the movement, the more black burning powder fell on the dry grass and the dead needles. Peter did not stop until he saw a glow in the tinder below. With a blow from his mouth, the flames escalated several inches in the air. He removed his tools and ran to get dry leaves that filled the ground, but he needed something more lasting. He peeled some bark off the trees and collected small branches and sticks that littered the riverbed and placed them over the fire. The fire raged, rising more than two feet in the air. Peter dragged two logs and surrounded the fire with them and then placed three thick broken branches on the fire vertically.

He sat by the campfire, warming his hands for the first time in several days. When the warmth reached them, it was a real revival for his numbing body. He was like a fragile plant that was dying when water reached its roots at the last moment.

His task now was to find food. He needed a fat animal, any animal. He liked both the pheasant and the deer, but how would he catch either of them now? *I would like to catch a few trout, but I don't have a hook or a bait*, he sighed painfully to himself. *A bird will also do, but I need first to make the box that Mr. Jones taught me to make.* He recalled passing by a herd of deer that morning. *But the deer ran before I had a chance to take a good look at them. Besides, I am terribly tired in addition to being injured. Maybe I'll hide behind some trees at the edge of the forest. Perhaps a lost calf or a small animal will offer itself to me. I had heard from Mr. Jones that if one conceals himself at the edge of the forest, deer are bound to pass by, especially if there is a water source nearby.*

Peter strolled for about a hundred yards until he reached a point where the elm and aspen trees ended and the rows of pine trees began. On the other side of the mountains facing him were high bluffs intersected by beautifully wooded ravines. Above them, the few scattered clouds had disappeared. What remained was a turquoise sky filled with gold radiance. But Peter was looking for something to silence his screaming stomach, not some nice scenery to cheer his sorrowful spirit.

Ten minutes passed without any real animal passing. Every now and then, he would observe a squirrel dragging its tail, as large as its body, behind him gliding over a branch. At one point, he observed a chipmunk standing erect, staring straight at him as though questioning his right to be there. Peter stepped forward to examine the little rodent, but the latter withdrew, whistling his disapproval at the intruder, and disappeared in his burrow. He decided to climb the rest of the hill to take a better look at his surroundings.

The winds were becoming stronger, inflicting excruciating pains at the areas of his injuries. Peter realized that he should cover those areas as soon as possible. A hat would be very useful now. The fur of a raccoon would make a great one, he thought. That morning he had seen a raccoon at the river, searching for frogs underwater. He was fascinated by its grayish brown fur and its face with black and brown markings. He decided to hunt one as soon as he was done with satisfying his hunger.

Peter stepped over many cactus plants and wild iris as he climbed the low elevation. Here and there lilies and rose hips decorated the slope. The hardest part was the last fifty yards when he was dragging his feet, holding at times the branches of the scattered pine trees until he reached the top of the hill. When he reached the summit, he scanned the horizon for prospective prey, but there was nothing that he could rely on. He peeked through the branches and noticed a herd of deer grazing at the meadow on the other side of the mountain. He advanced a few steps and stood there, wondering if it was worth descending into the meadow to get a chance at a deer.

No sooner had he made a few steps than all the deer in the herd turned toward him at the same moment as though following military orders, staring straight at him. *Not only do they know about me, but they are also watching me*, he thought to himself with desperation. *If I were strong like before, I might have a chance. As much as I dislike wolves, they would do me a great service if they showed up right now.*

Peter imagined wolves converging on the flock of deer and

one of the deer coming right to Peter injured, ready to be slaughtered. *I'd better stop daydreaming and hurry to my fire for now. In the meantime, I will eat some purslane by the river or catch some trout if I can make a hook.*

Descending the hill, he noticed the object that he had seen in the morning glittering under the sun. It was probably about two miles in the westerly direction. *I'm sure it is a glass door or something made up of glass*, he thought. He moved right and left to take a better look at it, but he could not see anything different. *It has to be a piece of glass or metal*, Peter thought. He decided to investigate the foreign object once he ate, and decided to go to the river.

As he headed down, he was startled by the footsteps of two animals running on the slope beneath him. The first animal was a large sheep. It was so huge that Peter thought it was almost the size of a domestic cow. "This is a bighorn sheep," Peter whispered to himself, examining its huge spiral horn as the sheep dashed in front of him like the wind. No sooner had the sheep vanished behind the trees than Peter learned the reason for the sheep's flight. It was the mountain lion that he had seen at the cave's entrance during his first night in the wilderness. "This is him!" Peter almost yelled. *I know it's him. I can't forget that face of an old man with white mustaches and the small horizontal eyes.*

Peter remained on the high boulder, hoping the two animals would get far away. He was not terribly frightened, perhaps a little afraid. A minute passed during which, though not seeing the animals, Peter was visualizing the struggle aided by his ears. The roar of the lion and the baaing of the bighorn sheep were intermingled with the noise of trees and boulders that the sheep bumped into in its effort to escape the jaws of the lion. Suddenly, Peter became frightened. The lion was cornering the sheep near the boulder that Peter had climbed. Peter got his obsidian knife in one hand and the big sharp stone in the other and waved them unconsciously as high as he could.

The lion stopped and looked at Peter with its watery eyes. Peter stood firm behind the sheep, his heart sinking by the second, but with a blue flame of defiance in his eyes. The sheep froze, not daring to budge. The lion stood there motionless, rotating his glance between Peter and the sheep. He was, it appeared to Peter, trying to choose between Peter and the sheep. On the one hand, he had a boy whose slim pale body did not weigh more than a hundred pounds with very little meat versus the fat two-hundred-pound sheep. The choice was clear and easy to make, and the lion wasted no time with that.

With a quick stroke, he attacked the frightened sheep, sinking his teeth in its throat. The sheep seemed drugged for a second and came up with no movement of defense, its eyes lurking with submission.

Peter was breathless. He watched with horror the slaughter from his boulder. The sheep seemed already dead and the lion ceased being aggressive. The lion turned from the neck to the hind, trying to cut a big piece for himself. It continued biting in the hind area until the sheep suddenly jumped to its feet, charged the lion, and raced down the hill. Peter was frightened as he saw blood flowing from the lion's neck but was relieved as he watched the sheep waddle clumsily toward the river. The lion gave chase as the sheep, blinded by the fatal wound, was bumping at numerous trees until it finally fell over the cliff abutting the river and collapsed only a few yards from Peter's shelter.

The lion, fearful of another surprise from the sheep, pounced on its neck, but before it did that, the sheep charged again, inflicting another wound in the lion's neck and face. Peter could observe more blood flowing from the neck of the lion who, although badly injured, attacked the sheep instantly at its neck and almost severed it. The sheep was now motionless, and the king of the forest again grabbed the hind legs and started devouring the fat hind, but the beast could not continue as the injury was taking its toll on it.

Peter watched with a mixture of fear and joy the king of the forest leaving its prey and heading toward the river. Blood was flowing from its neck, forming a line on the forest floor. The lion seemed blinded by the injury, for he stumbled into the river and soon a current carried it and the lion disappeared. Peter watched with awe the demise of his nemesis, letting out a long sigh of relief. He waited for a few minutes until he was sure that the lion had drowned. He came to the sheep carcass, turning his glance stealthily to make sure that other animals did not precede him. The lion was one less animal to worry about.

The carcass was intact, except for the hind legs. He would eat soon and satiate his hunger, but hunger was not sufficient to divert his attention from his campfire. If the bighorn was a success for him that day, starting the fire was a real life saver, for it meant the difference between life and death. Peter was surprised and somewhat thrilled by his own behavior. He never imagined he could survive such an incident before. He was now proud of himself. Just hours earlier, he was blaming himself for being a trifling useless boy.

The campfire still kindled although the flames were reduced to a mere glow. Peter fed the log brazier with small branches, and the fire raged with a high blaze. He then returned to his prey. He had now a real battle to wage with the carcass, for it weighed no less than two hundred pounds even after the lion's share was gone. As he stood there, figuring out what to do with the sheep, his growling stomach urged him to get food.

10

Peter's task with the bighorn's carcass was far more difficult than that of the mule buck, but the rewards were equally generous. The sheep had a thick layer of light brown wool, promising a cozy blanket for him. The growing pangs of hunger were paralyzing him, but the promise of delicious hot food kept him going.

Peter began by making a long cut at the center of the animal's stomach, commencing at the end as he had done with the deer. He was careful to save the precious skin and its valuable wool. He figured that the art of skinning the deer was not much different from that of skinning a sheep. The only difference was that the sheep wool was thicker and longer than the deer's hair. The sheepskin along with that of the mule buck deer would protect him from now on, no matter how inhospitable the weather was, he thought. He made a similar cut in the thigh and then slashed a piece of meat from it no less than three pounds, making sure there was plenty of fat with it.

The blood flew to the ground in several thin lines, heading in the direction of the river. The smell of the fresh warm blood filled the place, transmitting its scent across the wilderness. With the help of his obsidian knife and the sharp stones, he divided the tender meat into three steaks. He made sure all the blood was drained. After he cooled it for a while in the cold water of the river, he used green sticks as skewers and placed the meat on the brazier.

As the meat was cooking, Peter went and obtained wild berries, which were abundant on the riverbed. He also brought green weed by the river for salad. Peter had tried that kind of weed earlier and it tasted delightful. It would have been perfect with the salad, he thought. He kept going back and forth between the shelter and the slaughtered carcass, to prevent any predator from usurping his rightful property.

Peter continued turning the steaks around and could not help grabbing one of the steaks for a quick bite and then quickly hurling it back on the fire after suffering a minor burn on his lips. Finally when the meat looked brown, he put it on woven sticks that he had arranged like a basket and carried his meal outside, taking with him the berries and the purslane weeds. Unfortunately he had lost his water bottle with the venison when his boat capsized, and he had to drink water directly from the river. Nevertheless it was the first real meal in several days.

Just before finishing the second piece, he realized that he could devour more meat. He returned to the sheep, cut another pound or so, and placed it on the raging fire. He watched his meal with a great exultation, his lips smiling with cruel confidence. Nature was an endless surprise. Wilderness was a natural reference point. It was a mother to whoever sought its offering, and Peter was one.

When he finished eating the other piece, he started thinking of a way to preserve the meat. If he could bring snow from the high elevations, he would bury the rest of the meat. It would last him for a full month, but then he needed to pull the carcass to those snow-capped peaks. The distant peaks were not accessible to him now, but at least he could preserve the meat for several days since the temperature was cold, especially at night. The rest of the meat would go to the other animals.

An idea occurred to him. The animals would come at night to steal the meat. If he could make a cage, he could store several pounds of meat in it and hang it in the shelter. But a large plate would do for now. He got out and found a round flat stone, resembling a big plate, and washed it at the river. He ran outside and as he reached the carcass, several wild animals ran away, startled by his presence. There were three coyotes and two foxes. Peter stood ready to retreat to his shelter, but the animals were faster than him in retreating. He was frightened for a few seconds as he could not trust the coyotes, but went nevertheless, cut several pounds of the meat, and took it to the shelter.

When he returned, he could not see the animals this time, but he could tell that they were not far, probably hidden behind the trees, watching his every movement. His experience with the fox when he was cooking the pheasant was sufficient to tell him that foxes would not give up easily. He stood up, and looking in the direction of the forest, he started addressing the invisible animals: "Just be patient, guys. I'm not going to eat the whole two-hundred-pound sheep. So let me ask for your indulgence and give me just a few minutes, then I can throw a lot of meat to you."

Peter was uttering the words slowly, stopping at every phrase. Although he received no answer, he was, however, convinced that the animals understood him.

He hurried and started skinning the sheep. He worked swiftly, not paying much attention to the quality of the skinning process. The skin was going to be his mattress only. As he finished one area, he cut the meat, climbed a boulder in the middle of the river, and threw the chunk of meat on the other side of the river. Peter figured that a fierce fight would soon ensue between the rival animals, and he did not want any breach of the peace in his territory. Besides, the meat was liable to attract other more dangerous predators, such as the mountain lions and wolves.

No sooner was the meat on the other side of the river than the five animals appeared and jumped across the water, clinging to the rocks protruding from the water. Peter threw more and more meat, repeating the process several times until he had gotten rid of most of it and the sheep's internal parts. As to bones, Peter threw away most of them, keeping a couple to use as tools and weapons. He also kept several small ones to use for soup if he could have utensils. He then carried the skin to the river and washed it, to get rid of drops of blood clinging to it. When the skin was clean, he took it inside his shelter and spread it vertically by the fire. He could afford to wait another day for it.

Having achieved his two pressing goals, there was something additional needed, a real bed. An idea flashed in his mind.

Peter got out of the shelter, brought several long logs, and made a rectangular enclosure about six feet long by four feet wide. He secured the corners with rocks and branches. He then removed the stones from the enclosure and flattened the bulges in the ground. Then he filled the enclosure with leaves and evergreen boughs of fir and spruce, stepping on the boughs and filling the gaps with orange and yellow leaves. On the top, he placed dry grass, moss and ferns. When he had finished, he stood there, his hands interlocked, and gazed at his artifact, letting out a long exhalation of relief. When he patted the homey bed, a blush of pleasure rose to his cheeks, which were regaining their original healthy color. Peter could not contain his smile. It was a wide sweet smile, showing a perfect keyboard of white teeth. It was the closest he had ever gotten to a real bed in the last several weeks. He placed some more wood on the campfire and jumped into his cozy cushiony bed, covering himself with the mule buck deer's skin.

As his fatigued body slid into a thin, long-due sleep, the events of last week rushed swiftly into his restless mind, like a spouting waterfall. His mind started to flip through a mental atlas of all the places that he had passed by in the last two weeks, commencing with the jagged mountains and ending with the river.

Suddenly a dim ripple ran across his anxious mind as he recalled the nightmare that he had experienced the night before when the ghost of death paid him a visit and the dream that followed. Something in the dream was sticking out. It was probably the train. *Why is it going to eternity?* Peter wondered. *Was it the train of death? If so, why aren't I in it?* He could have easily clung to it, but some mysterious power prevented him from joining the train. *If so, what does that mean? Does it mean that I died the night before, but I returned to life when the train refused to take me?* His mind was swamped with a flood of questions that Peter did not even attempt to answer. *Somehow I have to sort out my thoughts, arrange them, and impose some sort of order on them*, he thought. *Otherwise I may lose my mind.*

If death is going to spare me, what should I do with my life? Should I go back to civilization or should I stay in this shelter for a while? I know now I can manage almost any situation. Peter was astonished at his resistance and perseverance. If someone had told him before what he would go through as he did last week, he would never have believed that he would have survived the river accident and the onslaught of nature during those weeks. He rechecked his injuries and they were dry. Finally sleep came rolling, its wheels sweeping away the unanswered questions.

When he woke up, it was still light. He felt so relaxed that he remained in bed for several minutes. The first thing that drew his attention was the campfire, which had died completely. Peter figured that he had slept no less than four or five hours, for that was the time he estimated it would take for the fire to die out. He ran outside and brought dry needles and small sticks, and started blowing in the fire. Luckily for him there was some glow, and soon the needles started to burn and so did the sticks. In no time the fire was flaring. He would need it because the winds were turning cold as the day passed by.

Peter felt like drinking some tea or coffee, but all he had was water. If he could have some hot water, then he would boil some plants, perhaps the dandelions or the chicory plants that he saw by the river. *But what can I use for a container?* He had heard from Mr. Jones that Indians used birch bark to heat water by folding the moist, cup-shaped bark inward.

Peter went out, obtained birch bark from a tree, and made a large cylinder-shape container. He submersed it in water for a minute and filled it with water from the river. He brought it and placed it on two skewers, making sure the flames did not reach the container. It took a long time, but finally the water got warm. Peter thought of another idea. He heated some clean pebbles and dropped them in the container. He then went outside and cut dandelions and other plants and put them in the container. A few minutes later, he had what looked like Chinese tea. Peter developed the container and made a more sturdy one. He would try to make soup from now on, he thought.

Peter spent the next several days resting. His wounds were healing, and his body was getting stronger. His coughing was becoming less severe, and in fact, he felt he was already cured of his disease. Days passed slowly, processionlike. All Peter did during those autumn days was gather firewood, eat and sleep. Each day was better than the day before. Peter was adjusting to the food provided by nature.

His hunting skills were improving. Three days after his arrival at the new shelter, he had caught a wild turkey. It was in the late afternoon when he heard a flap by the river. At first he thought it was a coyote messing with his food. Then he heard the rooster turkey crowing. Peter took his knife and approached the big bird step by step. If he caught the turkey, he could even celebrate Thanksgiving, which was getting near, Peter estimated, but he had lost count of the days. He had to figure out a way to keep up with time, otherwise he wouldn't know what day or even what month it was.

Peter crept through the aspen tree cloaked with multi-colored leaves, as most of the leaves had fallen by now. Suddenly he picked up the motion of the turkey and froze. Peter was moving now inch by inch, and an inch by an inch, he raised his knife as the turkey approached. Peter's heart sank as he watched with admiration its purple bold head and brown red neck with a big red beard under the long clothlike beak. The feathers were like shingles of an old roof.

On the fifth day, there was the first snow of the season. Luckily for him, the sheepskin had dried up completely. It had become frosty in the past, especially in the mornings, but on that day, there was at least an inch of snow on the ground. The weather had started to cool the night before. The relatively warm breeze had, toward dusk, turned into gusty winds that knifed lungs and tingled bare skin. By dawn the fierce winds were shrilling toward the river. Peter was awakened by the deep cold. He fed the brazier with more wood, placing the logs like a small tent. No matter how cold it got, he was protected by the two animal skins, he thought. He closed the opening with another log, but the snow-chilled wind was still sneaking from the openings. The wind was now rushing out with snow in its breath. Any remaining leaves would now fall, Peter thought. By the morning he expected to see all the trees naked.

When Peter woke up in the morning, snow covered the valley, turning the brown ground into an ocean of snow, submersing all the small plants. The bushes and tall grass, however, rose swaying in the air, staggering under the blows of the fierce winds.

Standing by the entrance of his shelter, Peter wondered what would happen to all the birds and animals and doubted if they would survive the bone-numbing winter. The river seemed particularly fascinating as the water glided through white fluffy banks covered with snow. The trees, as he guessed, were mostly naked and chunks of snow clung to their branches.

Peter was lucky, though, as he still had much of the turkey and purslane, in addition to green plants that he had found by the river. He had tried them two days ago and they tasted delightful. Peter also tried another type of what he called "Chinese" tea, using a different kind of flower.

The next day, as he finished his breakfast, he was surprised to find out that the sun was shining through the openings in the shelter's entrance. The snow was already melting. The water from the melting snow was dripping all over, and some of it came inside the shelter from the natural bridge covering it. By noon the snow had melted except on the grassy areas, and by afternoon, there was no trace of snow.

On the next day, he woke up with increased energy. He felt that all his wounds were healed. The cut on the arm had now closed altogether. He even felt that his disease was gone altogether. He had to make the decision whether to remain there in his shelter or continue downriver until he hit a town.

Suddenly, something flashed in his mind. It was the gleaming object that he had seen two times during the first day in this region. He had forgotten about it in the midst of his effort to survive. As the image of the glistening object flashed in his mind, he savored the idea that the gleaming object was a house. Only glass gleamed that way, Peter thought. It had to be a glass object then. *If this is true, then I'll find people there or find evidence that people were there. Either way I'll get some directions as what to do.*

His fire was still raging. He cooked some turkey and soup. He would decide after eating if he was going to remain or move out of there. Peter watched the turkey drumsticks cooking, then turned his glance to other remaining turkey parts. He had saved the features, although he did not know what to do with them right away.

The turkey reminded him of an incident he had forgotten. It was in a way similar to the circumstances that he was experiencing now. It had happened when he was nine or ten. He and his friend Johnny were playing on a turkey farm near town. On the same farm, there were many buildings and several silos to store wheat and fodder to feed the turkeys. Johnny had suggested playing hide-and-seek since it was a Sunday and there was no one there. Johnny's turn was first and so he hid in one of the buildings housing turkeys. But Peter had found him in no time. When it was Peter's turn, he climbed the silo. It was a tall, cylindrical structure with three locked windows, one on top of the other. Peter had climbed the thin ladder, and in no time he was inside the silo, which was almost empty.

As he got inside, he realized that he was trapped. If Johnny did not discover his place, he could be there for days or even weeks. He started screaming and yelling, but his voice would not travel beyond the thick walls of the silo. He was hoping that Johnny would at least go and tell his parents that Peter had disappeared.

Peter realized that he had to depend on himself. He searched the area for any doors, but there weren't any. There were the three windows, but they were high. He would need several boxes to stack on each other to get to the window, but there weren't any. Peter sat there on the grains, almost suffocated by the stuffy smell of the grains. He had to get out and soon, but all he could do was sit and stare at the smooth walls. There were no tools whatsoever. Any attempt to reach the first window was impossible. He started carrying the grains in his hands and throwing them around. He was doing that unconsciously as his mind was searching for a way out.

The grains were several feet thick, but he did not know exactly how thick they were. There had to be a door on the ground level, otherwise how was the grain extracted from the silo? He started removing the grain, and suddenly his eyebrows rose in obvious pleasure. His hands had grabbed the handle of the door. As he pulled the handle, the door sprung open and the remaining grain poured to the ground along with Peter.

The memories of the silo came crowding back like a hidden current, forcing Peter to compare his situations at the silo and in the wilderness. He was astonished to find out that they were similar. In both situations he had to rely on himself and had to make a decision whether to find a way out of the predicament or wait for help from outside, but if he had waited for help in the silo, he might have starved to death or died from dust inhalation. Similarly, if he stayed in his new shelter, he might never be discovered. Therefore he should continue downriver until he reached civilization, but he had to discover the gleaming object first.

An hour later he was on his way to the hill where he had observed the gleaming object before. This time he was able to reach it with relative ease as he had become familiar with the area and he had grown more robust. When he reached it, he started looking for the object, scanning the rocky horizon, and when he did not find it, he climbed a cliff and looked in all directions. The meadow on the other side of the mountain stretched in an easterly direction, merging with another range of mountains. On the other side, the rows of pines on the high elevations were intersected by ravines.

It was a while until he saw the small object glistening under the sun in the easterly direction, lying by some fir trees in a rocky area far away from the river. Peter's heart pounded as he realized that the object could be a human settlement. He started the march of what he estimated to be two miles, his gaze glued to the foreign object. On his way there, he lost the object several times but would find it eventually. Peter was so preoccupied with the object that he overlooked the birds and seagulls that took to the air to enjoy one of the last warm days of autumn.

At one point he was mounting a small peak, which allowed him to take a better look at the object, which was by then about a mile far. Peter's heart sank as he realized for the first time that the object was a small cabin surrounded by glass doors. Peter was amused but frightened. Very soon he would either discover people or find a way to get him in contact with them again.

But what is the object? he wondered, after an agony of suspense. It looked round with several glass doors. *Could it be a small house? If so, who would build the house here? It can't be that of the beast man, as this structure required modern techniques.*

As he got closer to the object, his heartbeat increased. He kept rubbing his tongue against the back of his teeth. When he passed the trees, he reached a clearance and the object was in front of him. For a second, his confidence abandoned him. The object was a small airplane. It was hidden by several rocks and boulders from one side and pine trees from the other.

11

Peter hid behind a boulder and examined the plane. *There are probably people trapped inside it*, he thought and imagined he could smell decomposed bodies.

Following several minutes of dreadful waiting, his agitated nerves caused him to hear strange voices and menacing laughter, but when he concentrated, he could hear no sounds.

When he got ten feet away from the plane, he halted and strained his ears, tuning them to pick up the slightest whisper in the air. Lately, he had discovered that his senses were becoming more acute, especially his hearing and his smell. Now he could hear the faintest moan of an animal and the slightest movement in the woods.

Nothing, however, disturbed the agonizing silence. Peter looked around stealthily, examining every boulder and every tree, his eyes trying to penetrate through them to make sure there were no people or animals lying in wait. He also examined the ground for footprints, but there were none.

Before coming closer, he clapped his hands loudly. He then advanced step by step, walking on the tips of his toes.

The plane was small in comparison to the one that had taken him to San Francisco last year. The cabin was no larger than that of a sedan car. The little plane had some numbers on its side, some of which were erased, but there was no company name. Time had taken a toll on the plane, for rust was mixed with mold and dirt. *It has to be a private plane*, Peter reasoned. *It's got to be the missing plane that went down several years ago. No wonder it was not*

found. The trees and rocks completely obstruct its view from air.

Peter clambered through the front door and gazed inside, his heart pounding. *The pilot and his daughter must be skeletons by now*, he thought. He looked inside and the interior of the plane gradually became visible to him. The cabin was empty. He scrutinized the interior for a sign of blood, but there was none. The plane was clean, except for some spider webs. *The pilot and his daughter must have survived*, Peter thought. *But where are they?*

He jumped to the ground and went around the plane. The right wing was broken so that it dangled down to the ground. The left wing was intact, but it tilted downward, leaving it erect at a forty-five degree angle. The front end was sound, except for a broken glass by the pilot's cabin. The tail was badly damaged, rampant with cracks. Peter figured that the plane had crashed on its tail tilting toward the right wing.

Peter mounted a boulder, wondering what to do. The chilly wind continued to linger, although it was getting warmer. The treetops swayed with the whisper of the warming breeze, gradually replacing the cold morning winds. The purple lavender at the end of the meadow still frilled themselves in the shining sun, defying the chilling winds. Herds of Canadian geese and sea gulls filled the skies rushing south. Peter watched them glide gracefully indifferent to Peter and his world.

He went back in memory and tried to recapture the dimly recalled events that had taken place several years ago when this plane had disappeared. The search had continued unabated for over a month, but there had been no trace of the plane or of its pilot and his daughter. The wilderness had swallowed them, and as a matter of fact, one of the members of the search team speculated that a geyser must have swallowed the plane. The question that hounded Peter now was what had happened to the two people? It was evident that they'd gotten out and gone somewhere. But where did they go?

The answer was not easy amid the maze of natural paths in

the mountain ranges and hills. The widespread wilderness pressed in all directions. If Peter had not seen civilization, he would have thought the world to be one endless wilderness. If someone told him there was a different world beyond with buildings, streets, cars, and people, he would have laughed at that person.

Peter took a glance at the valley. *If I were stranded here like the pilot and his daughter, where would I have most likely have gone?* he asked himself. *Would I have headed toward the valley or the mountains? Someone who just survived a plane crash would be weak and incapable of climbing. Besides, the valley looks greener and more hospitable. I'll head toward the river and hopefully I'll find a trace of them there.*

Before heading toward the valley, it occurred to him to go inside the plane. He would use its communication system to call for help, but he dismissed the idea as silly since if the system was operable, the pilot would have used it himself.

Peter climbed the cabin, nevertheless, and reached for the door handle and pulled. The rusty door refused to open. He left it and went to the other door, which was damaged. He was able to open it easily.

Opening the door, he was surprised by a big bird dashing out. It was a falcon, which soared to the sky. Peter went inside and closed the door. The cabin consisted of the pilot's dashboard, crammed with various types of instrumentation. Behind the pilot's seat were eight chairs, four on each side. Above him the sticky spider webs covered the place as though the plane had been sitting there for a hundred years.

In the back was a wash room, drawers and compartments. Peter opened all of them but found nothing. Peter was about to leave when he saw a small briefcase and a newspaper under one of the seats. He opened the briefcase and found men's clothes inside, a pair of socks, underwear, two shirts and a sweater. There were also a brush, toothpaste, and soap.

Peter turned his attention to the newspaper. It was the sports section of the *Denver Post*. Peter read the headlines, which put him in touch with the world again. The Detroit Tigers had scored a decisive victory over the Boston Red Sox. There was news of local and high school football games. There was also a big sale, items of food that Peter badly needed. He took the briefcase and the paper.

Strolling down the plateau, his thoughts were storming his mind with dreadful possibilities. He feared that the man and his daughter had run into the hands of the beast. As he rushed through the evergreen pines, he could hear the splash of the river, roaring in a monotonous song, never changing its tone for a million years. Peter figured that he was about two miles downstream from his shelter.

He mounted a branch abutting the river and sent his glance across the river, surveying the downstream. There were more broken trees and bushes, but nothing else. He wondered if the survivors found the river, and if they did, whether they headed downstream or upstream. *They couldn't have gone upstream as I would have found a trace of them during my journey*, he thought. *They must have gone downstream, reasoning just like I did that they would eventually find a town.*

Peter grabbed the newspaper and started flipping the pages. On the second page, the story of an athlete stopped him. It was about the baseball star Oliver Sands, who had made five home runs in the last game. The amazing thing about the story was that Oliver had just one hand. The story included an interview with his mother, who indicated that Oliver had been born with the left hand only. During high school, not only was he an excellent player but also a good student, with straight A's. But his heart was always in baseball. He would hold the heavy bat in one arm and strike the ball. Next thing, the ball would be soaring high, landing at the first rows of the spectators who hurried to grab the ball, everyone trying to get a piece of the action.

If this young man could perform miracles with just one arm, then I shouldn't give up no matter what, Peter thought. *If Oliver could become a baseball star despite his handicap, I should be able to get out of this wilderness. The only difference is that I don't know what nature has in store for me.*

Peter put the paper away and walked downstream. He could not resist the urge to try to track down the missing pilot and his daughter. After several hundred feet, the river curved to the south. He marched a few hundred feet more, but he could not see anything unusual. The lonely wilderness stretched all the way to infinity, unbroken by any sign of civilization. The distant mountains loomed up from both sides of the river, like impregnable prison walls. The river continued its journey in the southeasterly direction, winding its way like a long giant serpent in retreat, its scales glistening under the sun.

Peter was turning to go back to the shelter when something on the riverbank startled him. There was a piece of napkin crumpled on the ground, clinging to the underbrush. He knelt and examined it. It was still in good condition, which meant that it had been discarded recently. He examined the area around it thoroughly, placing more emphasis on the eroded and arid soil. His heart pounded as he found what he was looking for. There were footprints on the sandy areas of the riverbed. They were light prints barely visible to the naked eye.

The prints were nothing like the huge prints he had seen on the riverbank several weeks ago. These were small prints of a normal human being. He knew they were not his, since he had not reached that spot yet.

Peter followed the steps until he found an area where the prints were deeper and more conspicuous. He knelt on the ground and examined them at a close range. They were prints of human shoes, more exactly those of a woman. The prints formed a pair of little holes in the ground. *The prints are recent; perhaps the pilot and his daughter are alive*, he thought. *But where are they?*

An idea occurred to him. *The two might still be around here;*

otherwise, they would have made contact with the outside world. But why have they stayed here all these years and why haven't they attempted to leave? The only logical explanation is that they are unable to do that. If this was the case, they were either living in isolation or... here Peter's heart sank as the more plausible possibility was that they had been captured by the beast. But soon he rejected this idea, too. If they were captives, what were their footprints doing here?

Peter found no answers to his questions. *Could it be that the beast allows them to move around freely?* But it did not make sense. *If the beast allows them to move freely, then they are not captives, and so the beast is not evil after all. But if they are not held against their will, why are they still with the beast?*

Peter stood there baffled and perplexed. He closed his eyes trying to piece things together, hoping for a flash of revelation to solve the riddle that was hounding him.

He felt hungry and remembered his campfire again. *I'll go back and rest. Afterwards, I'll think of what to do, but I'll first have a drink in the river.*

Heading upstream, he stopped by a spot where the water was easily reached without getting down. He mounted a rock abutting the river and knelt to get a drink. Just when his lips touched the water, he noticed an object under a rock hidden under a rotten trunk. It seemed like a brush covered with mud. Peter pulled it slowly, but his eyes opened wide as he learned that the object was a doll. He picked it up and cleaned it. The beautiful slim blond was about a foot long. This doll had to have belonged to the girl, he thought. She must have dropped it when she and her father were by the river.

Peter laid the doll on a boulder, and his mind went back in history to when the plane disappeared. The doll must have meant a great deal to the girl since she took it with her when she and her father were most likely running for their lives.

12

Carrying his new discovery, Peter proceeded upstream, his mind prey to conflicting thoughts. No sooner had he made a few steps than he heard a flutter in the trees by a slope above him. *It has to be a large animal running. Perhaps it's another sheep being chased by a lion*, he thought. He came out to an area with thick broken trees and hid behind the dense vegetation, but he could not see anything. He climbed a trunk several feet high so that after he did that the whole valley became visible to him.

More than a minute passed during which he heard intermittent bustling sounds. Then there was complete silence. All of a sudden, his eyes snapped with horror as he saw a black bear running upstream by the slope abutting the river. The bear passed Peter and then stopped about one hundred feet from him with a horrified look in its eyes. He recalled Mr. Jones saying the black bears bolt away when they see a human being, but the bear had not seen him yet, unless there was another person there that the bear saw or sensed. Then, out of nowhere, a creature materialized, immediately striking terror in Peter's heart. It was a huge hulk, closer to being a giant gorilla than a man. The giant creature had emerged from the riverbank and stormed the bear with a long machete in his hands. Peter recognized the dreadful creature as the infamous human beast, although he had not seen him before, but all the descriptions that he had heard before suited him perfectly. The semi-naked hulk was taller and larger than the bear itself, his face coated with a natural grotesque mask unmatched in any Halloween party. The bear, realizing that he had no chance of flee-

ing, started to fight back and charged the beast man, snapping his jaw on his arms.

Peter froze in his hiding place. Every nerve leaped and shuddered. His breath was coming heavy and despite the cool breeze, he felt beads of perspiration forming on his forehead. He had finally seen the human beast. He seemed to Peter a wicked beast assaulting a harmless fellow animal, charging him like a vicious monster. By now the struggle was almost over. The bear had released his jaws from the huge arms of the animal man under the latter's relentless blows and also by virtue of the bleeding in its neck. The bear fought again, and Peter could see him charging the animal man, lifting his front limbs to reach the face of the human beast. The latter, instinctively on guard, like a pit bull in a ring, grabbed onto the limbs of the bear and started thrusting his machete in consecutive rapid blows almost effortlessly to the neck and head of the bear. The blood flew abundantly from various places in the bear's neck like faucets opened abruptly and simultaneously. The beast man muttered a few unclear words as he set to finish his victim. Soon the bear ceased struggling and collapsed. The animal man moved with a snap and approached the dying bear cautiously. His laughter rattled and roared in the wilderness as he finished the bear with his machete. He lifted the bear's head, but the animal was motionless.

Peter's heart had gone into sudden shock. He had never witnessed such brutality in his life, especially with the use of a machete. Peter observed him now, kneeling on his prey, trying to carry the carcass away. He watched with horror as the man-beast lifted the four-hundred-pound bear as if he were picking up a pillow and deposited it on his shoulders. As he passed by Peter, he noticed that the beast was limping. Peter was startled by the big hole on the forehead, which resembled a golf hole. Peter almost coughed, but he curbed the cough in the last second. Lucky for him the coughing had stopped because one single cough could have cost him his life.

As the animal man was only a few yards from him, heading downstream, Peter watched him through the dense vegetation, wishing he had a gun, then he would empty its bullets in his head without any hesitation. This was the nemesis that he had to vanquish if he was ever going to return in one piece to civilization, but he reasoned that the task could require an army of heavily armed men.

The animal man weighed no less than three hundred pounds. He was seven feet tall, taller than any basketball star in the National Association that Peter even knew. The hulk was fashioned like a beer wagon with two huge hands. His muscles bulged and slid under the red-bronze tan. His squalid long hair grew upward and outward in great filthy masses of curls, falling almost to the dark eyebrows covering his forehead. The forehead had a hole in it, almost the size of a big walnut. The eyebrows consisted of an inch of thick long hair above the deep eyes almost uninterrupted, even above the small round nose. The smoldering fox-colored brown eyes almost disappeared in his rigid, bony cheeks. His dark, hawkish face was covered with a thick mustache and beard that never knew a comb.

His clothes consisted of a torn shirt and other rags covering his middle parts, tatters that did not resemble any form of clothing known to Peter. He was barefoot and each foot was as huge as that of a real Bigfoot.

The beast man had finally disappeared behind the trees with his prey on his shoulders. Peter thought of following him to find his shelter. If he did that, he would know where he stayed so that he could avoid that area. *If his shelter is by the river, all I have to do is climb the mountain and hike for several miles until I have passed him.*

Peter leaped to the ground and started strolling cautiously, trying to give chase to the beast without being seen. It was not a difficult task, for the beast was laughing like a lion's roar. At times, however, Peter was finding it difficult to keep pace with the beast due to the thick vegetation and the fallen trees that projected like hurdles in a racing field. Peter would opt for the easy way and sneak beneath them and continue the pursuit. At one point Peter had to mount one of the fallen trees, and as he attempted to come down, he fell off the trunk of a fallen tree. He clung to a branch, but the branch gave way and broke, emitting a loud cracking sound. The beast halted for a second, looked at the area of the noise as Peter crouched breathless, then he continued.

The river roared incessantly as the beast continued his journey home. It was still windy and was getting colder. The high ridges surrounding the river from almost all directions provided much needed protection from those winds. Peter was now going around a granite bowl akin to his indentation shelter but without the natural bridge over it. In the distance, the jagged mountains preceded by craggy elevations loomed up, embracing the blue sky that was turning gray. The sides of the granite indentation were dappled with white bark pine, smeared with crust-like lichen where moisture constantly inundated the algae green rocks, flooding them at times with foamy waters.

But his undivided attention to the beast deprived him of seeing all that beauty. Everything had become invisible and inconsequential except the awkward giant some hundred yards ahead of him. All the sounds of nature had died down except for the sounds of the footsteps of the beast breaking small plants or shattering broken trees. Peter had decided to trail the beast, even if he had to spend the entire day following him at the risk of losing his campfire.

Nearly a mile downstream, the beast veered to the north, leaving the river. There, on the top of a cliff, Peter could see a real cabin the size of a farm barn about one hundred yards away from the river. Peter climbed a tree to enable him to see the cabin clearly. The hulk placed the carcass in front of his house and started cutting it without skinning it. The giant was chopping the carcass indiscriminately. Peter examined the area around him, scrutinizing every point in the rugged wilderness to see if there were other houses or huts, but there were none. The wilderness stretched without any sign of man, and the valley was getting wider and wider as the river continued its unending journey.

The earlier harrowing line of questioning was still tormenting him. Where was the girl who left the footprints that he had seen earlier that morning? *If she is not with the giant, does she live by herself?* he wondered. *Could she be his wife or daughter? But that's impossible*, he thought. *If he walks barefoot, then his wife or daughter would be uncivilized like him.*

Several minutes passed and the beast was busy chopping the bear. When he was done, he stood up, turned to the direction of the cabin, and uttered a sound that Peter could not distinguish. He strained his ears and opened his eyes to their fullest. It appeared to Peter than the giant was calling someone from inside the cabin. And his calculations were right. Seconds later a girl emerged from the door of the barn. Peter was dumbfounded as he looked at her. She was an attractive young woman of about fifteen or sixteen years of age. She was wearing a one-piece track suit in gray cotton melton, with a red sweater on top. Her light brown hair framed an oval pale face and elongated neck. The beast seemed to be asking her to take some of the bear's meat to cook it. Peter stared at the enchanting girl and then examined the clumsy giant. The scene was truly that of the beauty and the beast. He remembered that the girl had been nine or ten at the time of the crash. *She's been here in this wilderness with the beast for six years*, he thought. *But where is her father?*

The view of the meat and the fire reminded Peter that he was starved. He came down from the tree slowly and headed back to his shelter without even taking a look behind him. His mind was like a whirlpool with all kinds of ideas racing through it. He would decide what to do after he had eaten something and received adequate rest, but before he left, he wanted to see her father. He waited for another hour. The girl and the beast were exchanging some words, but there was no trace of her father. They were alone.

The trip back to Peter's shelter took two hours, although the distance could not have been more than three miles. Peter was exhausted and stopped to rest several times on the way. Just before he arrived at the shelter, he almost fainted. He started coughing again. His disease seemed to be returning to him, but he finally made it home without any serious incident.

Lucky for him the campfire was still burning, thanks to the big logs that he had placed vertically on the fire. These logs had insured the life of the fire. As the fire consumed part of the log, the log would recede and replace the burned parts. Peter fed the fire and ate the remaining turkey. He was then ready for a long sleep.

13

When Peter woke up, it was dark. The trees outside could still be seen as shadows, soon to be swallowed by the prince of darkness. The first onslaught he noticed was waged by the cold winds rushing briskly through the wide openings of the shelter. The bawling winds moaned and wailed, like a mad witch in a haunted Halloween house. These winds would normally strike horror in Peter's heart, but by now he had grown accustomed to them.

He got up sluggishly and crawled near the blazing campfire. He watched the embracing wood snapping as the fire rose around them, its golden flames cuddling the exterior parts of the logs in preparation of consuming them.

Peter tried to get up to feed the fire with more wood, but his legs would not support him. He was so drained from that day's long hike that he could not carry the light logs. He felt like a marathon runner after completing the twenty-six mile race. He sat on the edge of his rustic bed and closed his eyes. Although he was physically exhausted, his mind was clear.

Peter started replaying the incidents of the day. It was the busiest day so far since he left town. He had started that tempestuous day by discovering the crashed plane, then the small footprints followed by the hideous beast man, and finally the beautiful girl. Here, Peter stopped his train of thought. *Is this girl the same one whose plane crashed years ago? Could she be someone else? No, it can't be. This girl is about fifteen and her age fits with the pilot's daughter. But what would she be doing here? And where is her father? Could he have been sleeping or hunting when I was there? No, I don't think so. They would be hunting together. Then did he escape and leave her here alone at the mercy of the beast? But if this is the case, why didn't he contact the authorities?*

Peter turned his attention to the girl again. *Why doesn't she escape? She does not seem to be his captive; she appears to be free. She was alone today while the beast was hunting. Besides, she can get rid of him when he sleeps. What is the secret behind it?* The question was hounding him. "I've got to know," he whispered to himself with determination. There was another question scaring him. What if the beast came to his shelter? He had to find a solution.

By now it had become totally dark outside. The winds were intensifying, and the temperature was plummeting. Peter sat close to the fire, fiddling with the burning logs, using a long stick to arrange and rearrange the logs over the fire. Soon his interest was exhausted. He turned to the briefcase and got the newspaper, but he could not see much under the dancing dim light of the blaze. He threw the newspaper away and turned to the doll. *I'll surprise the girl with it when I see her.*

Soon he was hungry. He checked his inventory of food and found a turkey drumstick left. He grabbed it and hung it over the fire by two sticks. He had to get some more food tomorrow, he thought. That would be his priority the next day. He also needed more firewood, as he had only several logs left, but food was more important for the time being. He tried to think of what to get. He wished he could catch some trout. They would taste delicious when he barbecued them. Birds, too, would be great if he could find a way to catch them.

When the drumstick was ready, he started biting on it quickly, indifferent to his burning lips. When he was ready to go to sleep, he felt the winds rushing through the cracks with snow on its breath. He looked outside and he saw the snow flurries clinging on the rocks outside his shelter.

Peter was awakened in the morning by the sound of a robin singing. He had heard it singing since he took refuge in that shelter but had never seen it. Nature outside was clothed with a thin layer of white snow. He crept to the shelter's entrance and looked outside. The eternally evergreen pine trees were now white, and the aspen had become naked overnight. They were coated with a transparent crystal layer of ice. He looked for the robin, and he was able to spot it standing on an aspen branch. It was larger than a sparrow and had an orange breast and a brown neck with a small sharp beak.

Peter then turned his attention to the fire. He had to keep feeding it every couple of hours. It was like a small baby that required constant attention, and he was happy to do that. Soon the scene of the girl and the beast flashed in his mind again. He would very much like to meet with her as soon as possible, but he had to wait for the right day.

Yesterday's events were still like a long dream, but they were real and they could be the key to his new life as a new man. Yes, the beast was real and he had the evidence, but now the girl lived with him. He had made up his mind to meet with the girl on the next day and give her the doll. She might be the key to the entire mystery and eventually to his getting out of the quagmire alive. Somehow the mere thought of her titillated him. She was another human being like him, and that allayed his feelings of solitude and seclusion.

Peter thought that her stay with the beast was suspicious and would remain a puzzle until he met her. *But what should I tell her? I think I'll first try to find out what happened to her father and then ask her to leave the giant and come with me to civilization. She may by now know the way out, but I have to watch the beast and find a way to approach her.* This thought provided him with much-needed relief and solace. It was as though he was already home. The thought of going home tickled him, although he was not sure whether he was totally cured of his disease.

Peter felt hungry, but he had no food and he had to start hunting. He had a taste for some birds, but the snow had driven most of them away. Deer were abundant but he had no way to hunt one. Birds were also plenty, but how could he catch them?

Suddenly his eyes shone as he recalled one of Mr. Jones's methods of catching birds. But he needed a bait. He got out of the shelter and came to the river area. After some searching he found a decomposed fish mostly buried under the snow. He took a sharp piece of wood and sharpened it from both ends. He then buried the sharp stick in the decomposed fish and left it in a conspicuous place near the river.

When he was done, he examined the rushing waters of the river. It had to be loaded with big trout and cutthroats, Peter thought. *If I can figure out a way to catch the fish, I will solve my food problem once and for all.* The river was about one hundred feet wide. As he stood there watching the river, an idea flashed in his mind. He set to carry it out immediately. He hurried back to the shelter and brought his knife along with a large sharp bone that resembled a hatchet. He dug a small canal from the river to an adjacent dry basin. He then widened the canal so that even the big fish, such as those weighing several pounds, would easily pass through. He was hoping that some of the fish would go in the canal, thinking that it was an extension of the river. When they did so, they would be trapped in the basin.

Now that he was hopeful that one of the two methods would be fruitful, he headed to the broken branches and started gathering fire wood. All he had to do was collect the logs from the river bed and break the big ones.

Peter was getting more and more hungry. He checked his decomposed fish, and it was there untouched. It had failed to fool any birds yet. His basin was getting filled with water, but it was free of any fish. He needed some food right away. His heart was shaking, and he was about to faint. He walked to the cliff and started throwing rocks at some of the cardinals that would fly by or nibble in the snow. The snow by now had intensified, covering the ground with a white thick layer, but he was not lucky anyway.

His hands froze from holding on to the stones, and the birds were faster than he was. Finally, he decided that the only abundant animal was the deer and he had to develop a weapon to get them. He needed a bow and an arrow for that purpose. He could use a sharp stick that he could fashion with the help of his knife. At this his eyes shone with a smile. *I can use my knife as an arrow.*

Soon his knife was tied with a string to an arrow that he made from a stick. He then fetched his bow, and soon he had a good bow and arrow. Peter put on his warm clothes in addition to the deerskin and went out. He chose an area at the edge of the forest and stood there. There were herds of deer here and there, but he needed one that would get close to him without being detected. As he stood there motionless, he recalled Mr. Jones's advice: "Stay still. Don't move no matter what. Don't even breathe, if you can."

The deer seemed to know about his plan, for they stayed away for a while. Some of them stared straight at him from a long distance as though they were wondering what kind of creature he was. Soon Peter's thoughts turned to the beast. *What if he discovers my footprints? What if he saw the smoke coming from my shelter?* he thought. *It could be my end. All my plans would evaporate. I wish there was a way to fortify my shelter.* But how and what would stop this human beast who had destroyed the bear as though he was smashing a puppy?

Before he knew it, there was a sole buck coming his way. Peter's heart sank. His breath was coming in heavy as though he was climbing a steep hill. Inch by inch he moved his hand, lifted it up, and released the arrow. Unfortunately, it broke in the air because it was not tied properly. He took the knife and incised it into the stick from the other end, which was not as sharp as the edged one. This created a more robust and reliable arrow.

Peter started the waiting process again, but this time he climbed a tree. He decided to shoot the deer in the neck in order to insure that the deer would collapse right there. From his location above the tree, he noticed a big hole not far from the tree. *This is it*, Peter whispered. *I just thought of a way to keep the human beast and the other animals away. I'll dig a pit at the shelter's entrance and cover it with branches and leaves. This way I can sleep easier without worry.*

It was only a few minutes before a herd of deer passed by. It consisted of one mule buck and three females. Peter wanted to shoot the buck, but one of the females was closer. Peter started lifting his hand a mere fraction of an inch at a time. Then at the right second, he released the arrow, pointing it at the animal's neck. The arrow flew and pierced the neck of the female deer and it fell. The other deer dashed like the wind. The injured deer soon got up and started running as though it was not hit. Peter gave chase but after a hundred yards, he decided that he should not jeopardize his life. His footprints were all over. He turned back and headed toward the shelter.

Sitting by the fire, he noticed that the knife was gone. It had penetrated and lodged in the deer's neck. That meant that the deer would not go far. He was startled when he realized that the wounded deer might fall into the hands of the beast. The beast would then realize that there was an intruder in the wilderness. At this thought, Peter got up and decided to chase the deer.

Soon he was at the point where he had shot the deer. The bloodstains had already frozen. Peter followed the drops of blood and the hoofprints, which headed toward the river, then went upward in the direction of the mountains and then were lost in the thick woods. But there was no trace of the deer. Peter was tired and almost returned when he heard a noise not far away from him. He went in that direction, and he could hear a coyote devouring its prey. As he got closer, he saw the wounded deer. It was now dead, and the coyote was already biting into it.

When Peter got close to the coyote, he was surprised that the dog-sized mammal did not flee. He just continued devouring large pieces of the venison. Peter stood far away and waved a big stick, but the coyote did not budge. At one point, he stopped eating, looked quickly at Peter, then continued his lunch. *I should avoid any confrontation with the animal*, Peter thought. *I'm weak and hungry. Besides, there is plenty of meat out there for both of us.*

Peter waited for a few minutes until the coyote left by itself. He then approached the carcass and soon found his knife. It was still in the deer's neck. He took some of the untouched meat and left. When he was returning, the snow was getting heavier. Peter was no longer worried about footprints. The snow was doing a good job of covering them.

After eating Peter took a shower. It was a creative way that he had invented. He would fill a bark container with water and place it over the fire until the water temperature was fairly warm. He would then get a clean cloth wet and wipe his body with it, then dry it with one of his clean shirts. Since finding the airplane and having an additional inventory of clothes, he had started taking his daily shower.

The snow continued for several days. During that time Peter's supply dwindled to nothing. He could only keep the food for several days. Afterwards he would throw it out. A week later, as he left his shelter looking for food, he remembered the stream that he made. He hurried there.

To his surprise the basin had several trout swimming in it, unable to go back to the river. Peter caught two of them easily with his bare hands. They were each about fourteen inches in length and each weighing more than two pounds. He took the fish to his shelter, feeling invincible. He looked at the fish, which were still alive, as a hungry man looks at his steak. The fresh smell of the fish excited him more. He cleaned the two fish quickly and barbecued them on his fire. It was the most delicious meal he had since he left his home.

During those days, Peter kept thinking of the girl he had seen at the giant's dwelling. He was so anxious to talk to her, but he was waiting for the right time. He wanted to go to the beast's cabin on a sunny warm day, but the weather would not cooperate. Peter spent a few more days waiting for the good weather to come. During that time he had started digging the hole in front of his shelter. It took him two full days to finish. The digging was much harder than he thought. Peter would dig an inch, then stop as his hands would freeze. He even used his clothes as gloves.

When Peter was finished, he had a pit three feet in diameter and four feet deep. The fall of the beast or another animal in the pit might not kill the intruder, Peter thought. It would, however, give him plenty of time to escape. He then started digging more. He had decided to dig another foot deep and widen the diameter another foot. This part was the hardest because the digging was down and the place was too small for him to work. Besides, there were many stones that got in his way. That day he had remained until late in the afternoon.

When he had finished, he was so tired and so hungry that he started to shake. His inventory of trout was finished. He had eaten the last fish in the morning, and the basin was devoid of any fish. It almost looked as though the fish got smart. Peter recalled Mr. Jones telling him that fish are the dumbest creatures among all animals. *I wonder if he was right this time.*

Peter threw his axe and the knife aside and collapsed near the pit. *Would this big hole stop the beast or a bear?* he wondered. *It's now about five feet deep. It may trap a smaller animal, but I'm not worried about the small animals. I want to trap the beast and the bigger animals.* Peter looked around him and saw large rocks. Suddenly an idea occurred to him. *If I place some sharp stones at the bottom, that may cause some cuts and bruises to the assailant and it will give me additional time to escape.*

The next task was to cover the pit with branches and small sticks to look natural. When he was finished, he smiled to himself, looking at his work with admiration. *Now I can sleep without having to worry about a surprise attack from the beast.* Just before he finished, he heard the noise of a bird singing in a rapid and continuous way. It was as though the bird was in some danger. He hurried there and his trap was this time successful. There was a big falcon by the decomposed fish. The sharp stick had pierced his neck and the bird was dying a violent death, but Peter was by now part of nature. He had to kill to survive. It was a game that he had mastered well.

Peter took the bird to his shelter. He was careful not to fall in his own pit and went around it. It looked so natural that he almost fell in it. That evening he had one of the most delicious meals as of late. The half-pound bird was so fresh and delicious that he wanted more of it. In fact he went back and hid the sharp stick again in the decomposed fish that was by now frozen.

The temperature rose quickly in the next day. He was awakened by the robin's singing as usual. The two had become friends in the last two weeks. Peter would sit down often and just watch the bird with admiration, as it stood on the branch unconcerned with the cold winds. Its orange breast was distinguishable in the gray surroundings.

Peter would every now and then talk to it, and the robin seemed to listen.

"Thank you, Robin, for staying here with me," Peter whispered one day. "I know you'd rather leave for the south like the rest of the birds where it is warmer. I appreciate your staying with me and keeping me company."

The robin would always sing in the morning, no matter what the weather was. It seemed always happy to live another day. The bird reminded Peter of his father. He would wake up and no one could even say a word to him before he had his first cup of coffee.

The day was getting warmer. Within hours all the snow had melted. The temperature had risen to the mid-fifties, Peter thought. It almost felt like the beginning of the spring, although it was only mid-November. It was time now to meet the girl. Since the snow was gone, there would be no trace of his footsteps. *I'll have to leave tomorrow at dawn. I'll go at dawn when the beast sleeps and wait for him to leave alone so I can talk to her.*

After spending a few hours away from his shelter, searching for food, he returned. His plan was to get everything ready for tomorrow, especially the fire. He had to put enough logs on it to keep it blazing for hours. When he arrived at the shelter, there was a surprise waiting for him. The branches covering the pit had fallen in the pit and Peter could see drops of blood inside it. Apparently an animal had fallen in but was able to escape.

14

Peter woke up at dawn. It was still dark, but the birds were already announcing the advent of another day. He stocked his fire, making sure the logs were stacked high. He then picked up his knife and the sheepskin and left. The snow had melted, but the ground was still wet. Lucky for him the half moon provided some light that he badly needed.

The marching was effortless, for, by now, he had grown familiar with the area. He proceeded down river, strolling on the edge of the riverbed. The winds were strong and at times blew violently, but the prospect of a meeting with the girl fully occupied him. Besides, Peter used a second sweater to cover his head and face. His feet, however, annoyed him due to the wet ground. At one point he nearly gave up and wanted to return to his shelter, but he persisted. He had determined that meeting the girl was a step necessary to his own survival. By the time he got near the beast's cabin, his shoes were spongy.

It was slightly before daybreak when he arrived at the cabin. Peter swerved around it and started climbing a hill directly behind it. His plan was to climb a high point and watch the place from there without anything obstructing his view. The climbing was difficult, not only due to the chilly winds, but he also had to climb a steep rocky hill before reaching the summit. When he finally accomplished that goal, he saw what appeared to be a natural den molded from gigantic rocks crumpling from the high elevation and settling at the edge of the mountain. The result was something similar to a grotto housing a saint's statue that Peter had once seen in a church. He took shelter there and collapsed inside.

The singing of the birds mixed with the swaying of the trees did not stop. After he had enough rest, Peter got up and looked at the cabin. It was visible now and Peter guessed that the grotto was not discernible from the cabin because he himself had not seen the den when he was on the cliff. The reason was that it was blocked by trees and boulders.

The scarlet ball of the sun was now emerging from behind the rugged horizon. Nature was taking off its dark mourning garments and replacing them with brighter, exhilarating colors. The dead woods were coming to life as though the red disc of the sun had revitalized them. The fresh smell of the trees and the unsullied air, coupled with the singing of the birds, could have provided solace to Peter if it weren't for the monster lying several hundred feet below him. Deer movement was apparent everywhere. They would even walk in front of Peter without fearing him. The squirrels were coming out of their holes. It was the first sunny day in over a week, and all the animals seemed to be taking full advantage of it. The wild berry trees were still blooming, and their evergreen branches were loaded with little berries.

Coldness was now creeping to Peter's feet. His teeth were chattering, and he wished he could make a campfire. He was also becoming hungry. He started moving his limbs to generate warmth. He got up and strolled in front of the den. At this second, he hurried back in a snap. The beast was coming out of the cabin accompanied by the girl. Peter was greatly disappointed and felt devastated. He was hoping the beast would leave her alone to go hunting on that sunny day.

Peter climbed a tree to get a better look at them as they were descending the hill. The beast was dressed in jeans and a heavy jacket. The girl was dressed in long pants and a coat. Seeing the huge dent in his forehead, Peter wondered how such a beautiful girl could withstand such monstrous looks. As soon as they left, Peter came down the hill gradually and hid behind a tree until they disappeared in the slopes. He then walked to the structure step by step, shaking with fright and excitement. He examined it quickly. It was a wood cabin about thirty feet long by twenty feet wide. There was also a small storage area behind it. He then hurried and pushed the wood door. The squeak of the door was so frightening that Peter was paralyzed for a few seconds. *Maybe they're going hunting together*, he thought. *I think it will be some time before they return.*

The inside of the barn consisted of two separate beds at the posterior of the barn and a table and two chairs at the center. Near the entrance was a broken wooden shelf stocked with bread and fruit. On the other end was a small round table with a jug of water. At the very right, Peter saw a stack of firewood and next to it a primitive fireplace not much different from his at the shelter. When he finished his cursory examination of the room, Peter turned to the loaf of bread and the fruit. He was so hungry, and had not seen bread for close to two months.

He stretched his hand to reach for the bread, but stopped when he heard voices outside. Peter was dumbfounded. *They are coming back*, he thought. They would discover him and it would be his end, but he would not give up that soon. His mind raced to discover a course of action. He crept under the bed and hid there. Moments later he heard the door open. It emanated its spooky noise. Although he could not see a thing, Peter could tell that the beast and the girl were piling bags on the table. In fact, Peter heard the door open and close as more items were being brought. Finally Peter was able to hear the girl speaking.

"Is this all, Billy?"

"Yes, Tracy."

This was what Peter heard the beast saying. His voice was a terrible keening groan, springing from somewhere deep in his throat.

"Did you bring the blanket, too?"

"Yeah, here. Now I go hunting."

"Okay, don't be late."

Peter heard the footsteps growing fainter. He waited a few minutes, debating whether he should stay longer or come out at once. He also wanted to know how to start. Once he passed that stage of the first encounter, the rest would be a smooth downhill ride, he thought. He crept out of his hiding spot a little until he could see her feet.

Peter waited until he saw her leave, then he came out. When he saw her coming back, he gathered his strength and stood in her way.

"Hello there," Peter said.

The girl was startled and froze for a few seconds. She looked at Peter from a corner of her eye. Soon the look became threatening and she frowned, knitting her thick brows. In no time, she jumped to the side of the barn, grabbed a stick, and got ready to strike, but she stopped in the last second as Peter stood smiling, spreading his hands to apprise her of the fact that he was not armed.

"Who are you? And what are you doing here?"

"I got lost in the wilderness and could not find my way back to the city. I'm sorry if I scared you."

The girl stepped back and stared at Peter, examining his eyes with confidence, but she said nothing.

"I come as a friend," Peter added as he got closer to her. "And I need your help."

"What brought you here?" the girl responded firmly. By now she seemed to have regained control over herself. Peter examined her for a second. *She's even better looking than Cynthia*, he thought. The first thing that caught his attention was her green eyes. Her hair was long and in a state of disarray, as it had never known a brush or a comb. Although her face was that of a child, her height was that of a woman.

"It's a long story," he said. "Can I sit down first?"

"Go ahead."

The girl said that in a cold and rude manner. She remained standing, holding onto her heavy stick, not moving her glance from him.

Peter sat on a chair by the table, which was filled with the new grocery bags. "Aren't you gonna sit, Miss?"

The girl sat reluctantly. She frowned at Peter and said, "Tell me who you are and where you come from."

"I've been lost for about two months. I don't even know exactly how long. Maybe longer."

The girl gave him a cynical look, but her lips remained sealed. Peter could read skepticism drawn all over her face.

Finally, she opened her mouth. "Do you think I was born yesterday? Why don't you tell the truth?" She said that in a strong voice that struck terror in his heart.

"What do you mean?" Peter asked in a submissive and frustrated voice.

"They sent you to look for us. They sent a small boy so we don't get suspicious."

"What are you talking about? I've been lost in these mountains. I was scared to talk to you when I first saw you with the giant. It is the first time I've seen a human being in weeks. Please try to understand me."

"Then what are you doing here in our house? And why are you hiding here?" she asked.

"Well, actually, I came to give you something you dropped."

"What are you talking about?"

"Didn't you drop your doll?"

The girl's eyes widened, her interest rising. Her eyes stared at the ceiling for a few seconds. "What doll?" she asked.

Peter got out the doll wrapped in the newspaper and showed it to the girl, who stood there motionless, staring at the doll. Peter did not say anything and watched her eyes wander. Peter figured that she was struggling to recall some dim memories, to retrieve an item that the years had deposited all kinds of objects over.

Finally, she grabbed the doll and examined it.

"This is Cookie. Where did you find her?"

"By the river," said Peter.

"You know, it's been many years and I almost forgot about it."

Her voice was softer, and Peter realized that she was beginning to believe him.

"Well, I thought you would like to have it back."

"So then tell me about yourself. And I hope everything you say is truthful," said the girl.

"I told you I have been lost for a couple of months."

The girl still seemed skeptical. "Prove to me that what you're saying is the truth."

"What proof do you need?" he asked and pointed to his clothes. "Just look at my sheepskin and my clothes. Examine my torn shoes. Besides, I can take you to my shelter."

"So you've been lost since the end of summer. How did you survive all this time and how did you get lost?"

"I survived by mere luck, and let me tell you how all this happened. It was at the end of last September when I left my hometown and ventured deep in the wilderness on my bike, but I forgot how to get back."

As he spoke, he examined her green eyes to see if she believed him, but her face revealed no expressions at that point. He told her about the first night he spent in the cave scared to death of the mountain lion and the bears, his incurable disease that seemed to have left him, his third day when he discovered the wildfire, his accident when his makeshift boat capsized and how he almost died, the discovery of the plane, her footprints on the riverbed, and finally the beast.

Peter tried to project ingenuity and honesty. He substantiated the episodes of his story with details that made the girl look at him with admiration.

"I believe you because Billy was there when the forest fire

was blazing. He told me all about it."

"I was hoping the wildfire would bring the fire fighters to save me, but no one came."

"Nobody has been here and that's why they did not discover the plane."

Peter wanted so badly to ask her about her father, but he decided to wait. "So there are no people around here?" Peter asked.

"I haven't seen anyone in the last several years."

"How about these grocery bags?" Peter asked, pointing to the bags the beast and Tracy carried to the barn just then.

"Well, Billy knows of a small town, but it's far away from here."

"Have you ever been with him to this town?"

"No, he doesn't take me," said Tracy.

"How long does it take him to go and come back?"

"A whole day and sometimes he does not return for two days."

"And you stay alone while he's gone?"

"Yes, and you know what, I never thought I could do it."

"I, too, thought I could never live alone for more than a day, but as you can see, I have been alone for about two months. I was so scared that I thought I'd just die without anyone knowing about me."

The girl looked at him with admiration. "Tell me about yourself. I heard the giant calling you 'Tracy.' Is that your name?"

"Oh, I forgot to tell you. Yes, it's Tracy."

"Can I ask you a question? You were in that plane over there," and he pointed to the hills where the crashed plane lay.

"Yes, my father and I were traveling to Idaho Falls when our plane developed a problem, but my father was able to crash-land it without anyone being hurt."

"So where is he, if I may ask you?"

"Oh, my father . . . I almost forgot. I'll tell you in a minute. You must be hungry. What do you want to eat?"

Peter was starved, but he wanted to hear what had happened to her father first. She went to the grocery bags and examined the contents.

"What would you like to eat?" Peter did not believe himself. Before that he would eat anything. Now he got to choose for the first time.

"Can I have eggs and toast? Also tea or coffee, please."

"Sure. It will be just a couple of minutes."

Tracy took several eggs from a basket and a frying pan and put it on the fire. She also boiled water for the tea. Peter examined the grocery bags at close range now that she was busy preparing breakfast. There were bread, fruit, cheese, and soup cans. There was also a new blanket lying on the floor. *He probably raided a town recently*, Peter thought. *That means that there is a town not far from here.* He then remembered that it took the beast more than a day to go and come back. *The town cannot be close, then.*

Peter enjoyed his first breakfast for a very long time. He ate all the eggs and about a half loaf of bread. He drank two cups of tea with milk. Now that his stomach was appeased, his curiosity wanted to be satisfied. He wanted to know about Tracy's father.

Tracy told him that the beast had stopped them several hours after the plane crashed. She then sat and started her story.

"Billy was nice to us. He offered us food and a place to stay. He told us that the closest town was miles and miles away and that he did not know how to get to it, but we felt that he wanted us to stay with him. Every time we wanted to leave, Billy would come up with an excuse so he wouldn't accompany us.

"Finally my father was fed up and left on an early morning when I was still sleeping. I have never heard from him since."

"Did you try to follow him later?" asked Peter.

"Several times, but every time I hiked for several miles, I got scared and came back."

"Could the beast . . . I mean Billy, have hurt him?"

"No way. Billy has never hurt anyone in his life. He's really nice once you get to know him."

Peter had heard terrible things about the beast, but he did not want to bring them up now. He also wanted to say that the beast was the one who had killed her father. Instead he asked, "Why is he so filthy? His long dirty beard, his messy hair, his clothes . . . "

"I don't know. I guess that's how he likes it. He's been in the wilderness since childhood."

"Did he tell how he came here?"

"No, he never told me when or how he came. I asked him once about it, and all that he said was that he was afraid to go back to civilization."

Peter wondered why he would be afraid unless he had done something wrong. He also wanted to know more about her father. He decided to come back to the subject of her father. "If your father made it to civilization, he would have contacted the authorities; but since he did not, then the only possibility is . . . "

Peter did not want to say it, but Tracy completed the sentence. "The only possibility is that he is dead."

"If he is, who would have killed him?"

"How would I know? Perhaps a wild animal."

"You followed the river downstream, didn't you?

"Yes, several times, but like I said, I would come back scared to death," said Tracy.

"Did you see any trace of human settlements?"

"No, I did not."

Peter paused for a second. He was unsure how she would receive his next question, but he had to say it. The beast may be coming soon and it might be too late. "Would you come with me and get out of here?"

"I don't know. I have to think about it. I'll talk to Billy about you and me."

"Please don't. I don't want him to know I'm here."

"It seems to me that you don't like him."

"I don't know him. I have heard so many stories of his vicious crimes."

Peter said that and looked outside at the river through the door. He was making sure the beast was not there.

"What have you heard? I want to know too."

"Well, he has killed many people, including many children at an Indian village in this area."

"Let me tell you there is no Indian village around here. I have toured all these mountains and I have not seen anything, and you yourself have been hiking for several weeks. Have you seen any traces of a village?"

"Not really, but couldn't the village be hidden in a valley or something?" asked Peter.

"I have gone in every direction. Besides, if there is a village somewhere, wouldn't there be a trail or a road to it?"

"You're right. I didn't think of that."

"As you see, all you heard were rumors. There is no truth to it," said Tracy.

"I don't know. I still don't trust him, and I would really like you to come with me to civilization."

"I don't think any one of us should go, at least not at this time of the year. We don't know where the closest town is. We could be marching for a week before we find anything. Very soon the snow will cover everything. What is going to happen to us in that case?"

Peter had to admit to himself that she was right. He then remembered the grocery bags when she mentioned the village. "You said the closest village is too far, but didn't he just raid one recently?"

"Sure, but he won't tell us how to get there."

"How can you then trust him?"

"I have no choice. You see, he feels that he won't be able to live without me."

"So what do you think I should do?" he asked.

"Stay here with us. I'll talk to Billy about you."

"No, no. I can't. Please promise me you won't tell him I'm here."

Peter looked again. He knew the beast would be coming back soon, for he'd been there for several hours now. "Let me go back to my place for now. But how will I get in touch with you in the future?"

"Just come here, like you just did."

"What is the best time to come here without him seeing me?"

"In the morning when he has gone hunting."

Peter stood up and as he opened the door, he saw the beast at the river area. "Thank you for the delicious meal, Tracy. But again, please do not tell him I'm here. I'll contact you within three days."

Before he heard an answer, he sneaked outside. He hid behind the tall pine trees outside, and then went behind the cabin.

15

Peter hid behind a rock. He still could not trust the beast. Even if there was no real evidence against him, the manner in which he butchered the black bear was so vicious that Peter had to believe the stories he had heard. Peter left the cabin and returned to the shelter.

Back in his shelter, his mind was still in the cabin. What he saw there was tempting. It was an easy life, plenty of food and comfort, and most importantly Tracy was there. He and she could be good friends. The beast might be a decent creature. Peter could befriend the beast and then might find a way home. Before he slept that night, Peter had decided to present himself at the cabin and ask Tracy to introduce him to Billy the beast.

When he got there in the morning, he was not as careful as before. The sun shone high, providing a false sense of warmth. Tracy was there alone. She smiled as she opened the door. When he finished eating, he told her he wanted to stay.

"I'll tell him about you today," she said joyfully.

"But are you sure he'll allow me to stay?"

"I don't see why not. There is plenty of food here. Besides, he may ask you to accompany him on his hunting trips."

Peter felt excited for a moment, then a cold chill traveled through his body. *I will stay with Tracy and I will convince her to leave with me for town*, he thought. He then imagined going on hunting trips with the beast. *But will the beast allow me to accompany him on his hunting trips, or will he ask me to stay at the cabin? Even if I stayed, it would not be a bad idea. I will make Tracy trust me.*

"So, Tracy, how do you spend the whole day?"

"Making food and yarn."

"Yarn? Who taught you?" asked Peter.

"My grandmother did. I almost forgot, but after Billy brought some yarns, I remembered how to do it."

"My aunt back in town is one of the best in that. You see this sweater? She made it for me."

Tracy got up and ran to a drawer. Peter watched her as she maneuvered around a box on the floor and could not stop watching her until she came back with a shawl in her hands.

"I can do the same thing," she said proudly.

Peter was impressed. It was of good quality. "This is nice. This is really nice, Tracy."

"I'll make one for you."

Peter got up to take a better look at the shawl when he saw Billy coming. His appearance struck horror in Peter's heart. Without any hesitation, he leaped out of the cabin, whispering to Tracy to keep him secret until he came back.

Over the next week, Peter visited Tracy daily. They spoke a lot about their respective hometowns. Tracy's memory was returning gradually. Her recollections of childhood events were dim, but she remembered a lot. Peter would listen attentively. He would often stop her and ask her to clarify something. They were becoming friends. Peter had started to fall in love with her. As they were cooking a pheasant one day, he wanted to hold her hands, but he hesitated. He was afraid she would not like it.

Peter wanted to face the beast and talk to him, but something told him to be careful. He wanted to find real evidence to either incriminate the beast or vindicate him. Then he would know what course of action to follow.

One morning when Peter arrived at the cabin, Tracy was

screaming. At first, he thought the beast was attacking her. He ran to the cabin and listened carefully. Tracy was calling on Billy to rescue her. Peter pushed the cabin door and opened it. A coyote was inside and Tracy clung to the wall, screaming. Leaving the door open, Peter hurried inside. He wanted to give the animal an opportunity to leave before he confronted it, but the coyote would not budge.

Peter then thought of an idea. He grabbed a piece of meat from the cabin, came to the animal, and started speaking to it. "I know you're hungry, friend, so here you've got plenty of meat, but I want you out now."

Peter started backing away gradually and the coyote followed him. When he was out of the cabin, Peter threw the meat as far as he could. The coyote rushed to the meat, snatched it in its mouth, and disappeared.

Peter went back inside the cabin. Tracy was still shivering, her eyes closed. Peter approached her and held her hand, but Tracy threw herself in his arms. He held her tightly and closed his eyes.

He did not know how long they remained in that position, but when he opened his eyes, she was still in his arms, their faces touching. When he attempted to kiss her, he heard sounds outside. Soon he realized it was the beast. He ran to the door, but it was too late. Peter crept under the bed. Next, he could hear the heavy footsteps of the beast entering the cabin.

"I saw big coyote running this way. What happened?" the beast asked.

"He came inside and I had to throw him the meat."

"He gone now."

The beast came to sit where Peter was hiding. Tracy immediately ran and stood in his way.

"Please go after the coyote, Billy. He is hiding there. I'm scared."

"Oh, don't be afraid. He won't come back."

"Yes, he will."

Tracy pushed the beast gently toward the door. Peter was shivering under the bed, holding his breath.

"All right, all right," said the beast.

Peter heard his steps going toward the door. He wasted no time and came out of his hiding spot. He held Tracy's hands for a quick second and examined her dark green eyes. There was a great deal of meaning in that look, but that was all he had time for.

When he was safe in the grotto, he was overcome with emotions. He closed his eyes to conjure the image of Tracy embracing him. He envisioned her in his arms. It felt so good. There was no feeling to match it. The only question was whether she had the same feelings for him, too.

Peter came early the next day, but the beast was still there. He stayed in the grotto for two hours, but he did not see the beast leaving. He looked behind him and wondered what was there in the back of the mountain range. *I'll climb to the top*, he thought. *When I come back, the beast should be gone.*

He headed there, hiding behind the evergreen pines. With every step he looked behind him stealthily. Suddenly an idea occurred to him. *If I can discover Tracy's father, then I'll know what to do.*

Minutes later he was climbing the steep mountain. His mind was clouded with perplexing concerns. *If I climb the hill, I may discover a town or a settlement that Tracy has not seen. That would save me the trouble of hiking for miles and miles until I reach town.*

The climbing was not difficult. Peter had eaten a nutritious breakfast and had enough rest. The mountain consisted mainly of a linear slope overflowing with rocks and boulders. In other areas, there was a deep gully and a steep slope. Peter took a detour, which put him near the summit. The evergreen pines were becoming scarce and were being replaced with boulders.

When he came close to the top, the mountain had turned into a barren rocky summit. The climb would have been joyful if it weren't for the powerful winds waging one wave of ruthless attack after another. The handful of sea gulls and other birds seemed oblivious to the winds, for they crouched on some of the cliffs next to each other.

When he finally reached the summit, he looked back in the direction of the cabin, but everything had disappeared. He looked in the other direction of the mountain, and there was nothing. He then climbed a tall rock and started examining the other side of the mountain. Suddenly his heart started to pound. There was a village at the foot of the other side of the mountain. Peter looked across the unending wilderness for other signs of civilization, but the wasteland aside from that village stretched for as long as his human eyes could see.

Peter wasted no time in heading toward the village. The descent was effortless. Besides, the slope was not as steep as the other side. As he got closer, the village disappeared behind a cliff, but then reappeared. Peter was happy and excited. Soon he would see people who would give him a ride to his town. Suddenly an idea flashed in his mind. The beast must have known about the village. It was only a couple hours of climbing and descent.

But I didn't see any footprints of him on the way, Peter thought. *Perhaps he does not know about it.*

When he passed the cliff, the village was in front of him. Something struck him instantly, however. He had not seen anyone yet, although it was noon. *Why is it so quiet and where are the farmers*? he wondered. *Where are the barking dogs and the children playing in the open fields*? By now he was passing the first farm with its collapsed wooden house.

On a little hill was a house next to a big cabin and several fenced areas. The adjacent farms seemed neglected for a considerable period of time, for the weeds and dry thorns of various sizes grew all over. He continued the march and passed by more farms and houses. Finally he reached a gravel road leading to the heart of the village. The few shops on the street were closed and empty, their glass mostly broken. The street finally led to an unpaved road going in the northeasterly direction.

Peter stood in the middle of the road, perplexed and frustrated. *Why is this village deserted? Where are all the people? Am I revisiting one of the fairy lands in the One Thousand Nights and One Night?* An idea clicked in his mind. This had to be the Indian village that was abandoned following the raids of the beast. He recalled reading about it in a local newspaper. He also recalled his conversation with Mr. Jones. *Tracy has not been here, as she could not climb the mountain*, he concluded.

"Here is the evidence that I need to show her." Peter was talking aloud to himself. "The village residents must have abandoned it to escape the wrath of the beast. It's all clear to me now, but should I go back and tell her about the village or follow this road away from the village to safety?"

The untrodden narrow road streamed along the lower parts of the slope until it vanished behind the hills. *It's true I don't know how long I have to hike until I reach a real town, but it has to eventually lead somewhere. There has to be a settlement soon*, he thought. Otherwise how did the villagers obtain supplies and other necessities?

Peter rested on a boulder by the road, debating what course of action to follow. He could just follow the gravel road to civilization, or he could go back and warn Tracy of the beast. *But why the sacrifice?* he thought. *I can go to the nearest police station and return with an army of rangers and police to arrest the beast.*

Finally, he decided to go back to see Tracy as soon as he toured the abandoned village. *I think I'll go inside some of these houses*, he thought. *Let's see if I can find something useful for me.*

Peter walked to the nearest house. It was a small ranch whose porch had partially collapsed. The only front window was broken, its glass shattered. Peter had to walk carefully around the glass to avoid being injured. When he pushed the sagging wood door, it opened, emitting a scary sound.

The inside of the house was filled with old furniture and rags. Tattered worn garments were scattered on the floorboards. There were old tools, mostly rusty, such as hammers and nails. The smells of rotten wood and decayed floorboards were overwhelming. Old appliances were there, but nothing worked. Peter turned on the faucet and the water sputtered, then gushed in a thin line. He left the house and went into another. It was similar to the first one. There was nothing to eat, but there was plenty of firewood if he wanted to build a fire. Both houses had fireplaces so they would provide a real shelter for him. There were also plenty of old utensils and silverware here and there.

Leaving the old house, Peter's heart sank. He noticed smoke coming from one of the houses. He examined silvery smoke and wondered what was going on. He hesitated for a few seconds, then walked directly to the house. There was nothing unusual about it. He stood outside and watched for a few minutes to see if someone might come out, but there was no sound. *Could someone be living here?* he wondered.

Peter waited for a few more minutes and then yelled, "Hello . . . anyone here?"

When no one answered, he repeated the call, but again there was nothing. He went to the door and knocked. When he heard no answer, he knocked again and then pushed the door. To his surprise, it opened.

From the first look at the house, he could tell that it was occupied. The place was warm and furnished. Just when he wanted to yell again for people inside, the board underneath him sprung open and he could see a well below. Peter was able to cling to its edge just in time to avoid falling. He finally got up, took a position in a corner, and drew his knife.

There was an unbearable silence. A minute later an old man emerged from the foyer. "Who're you?" he asked. Peter instantly recognized him as an Indian.

"Why don't you tell me who you are? You were gonna almost kill me."

"I'm sorry. I thought you were Billy the beast."

16

Minutes later the two were sitting by the cozy fire, drinking coffee and eating homemade corn bread. Peter could tell that the old man was in poor health. His hands shook and his lips trembled. Peter told him his story, including his encounter with the beast. The old man then started telling his.

The village was evacuated last winter following the killing by Billy the beast of a family of three in their home. The rangers came by after the incident and asked everyone to evacuate the village.

"So then what are you doing here?" Peter asked.

"The family that was killed was mine, my son, his wife, and their daughter. The beast broke into their house one night to steal food. When my son resisted, the beast simply chopped everyone with his machete. I came here to seek revenge. You see, if the beast comes to the village again, he'll notice the smoke, just like you did. And when he steps into the house, he'll fall in the well. He won't be able to survive like you did. He is so heavy that he'll just plunge into the well."

"The well?"

"Yes. The well you almost fell in. The house was built over it. It is over thirty feet deep."

The old man's face turned pale and his eyes gloomy. He seemed too tired to talk. But he went on, "When I do that, I'll watch him starve to death."

"How long are you going to wait for him to come by?"

"I hope he comes soon because I'm running out of time."

"What do you mean, sir?"

"As you see, I don't have too long to live."

"Maybe I can entice the beast here," Peter said.

"So you know where he lives?"

"Yes, he stays in a cabin by the river on the other side of this mountain range with a girl."

"A girl?"

Peter told him the story of the missing plane and how the girl and her father survived. Peter's thoughts turned to Tracy. *I should bring her here to stay with the old man until I get help. I should entice the beast to the village and then to the trap. Then we can leave for civilization. Why not get directions and come back with the police?* He immediately turned to the man. "How far is the main road from here?"

"About five miles."

"How can I get there?"

"Just take this road for about three miles, and then turn left by the crossroad. Keep your eyes open for a tall flat rock by the crossroad, since the road is covered with snow most of the time. You'll find a restaurant and a gas station once you go there."

"That's it? Just five miles?" Peter was excited.

"Yes, my boy."

"Then I have a better idea. I'll go to that gas station and call the police from there."

"That's probably best because I don't want to die before getting him. I know my days are limited."

Peter stayed with the old man for the rest of the day, thinking of his trip to civilization. He wanted the old man to accompany him, but he seemed too weak for the five-mile trip. That same evening Peter told his host that he wanted to leave in the morning.

"Why so soon?" the old man asked.

"I want to get you a doctor."

"Don't worry about me, son. I will be fine."

"Do you need anything else . . . like food?"

"I have enough food for months. There is plenty of corn. Besides, we Indians know which plants and herbs are edible. I'll show you which ones to eat and which ones to avoid."

Peter's attention turned to the upcoming trip and he closed his eyes for a second. The thought of seeing people and contacting Aunt Pauline was not leaving him, but the image of Tracy was competing with that of the idea of going home.

The next morning, Peter got up early. The old man had made breakfast of coffee, cheese, and corn bread. After promising to be back in the afternoon, Peter left. He did not anticipate any resistance especially now that he was armed with more facts.

The trip was easier than before, as he had become familiar with the area. When he got to the grotto, everything was quiet. No sound came from the cabin. Finally, he knocked on the door and hid behind a boulder, but there was no response. He went inside. The cabin was empty.

Peter stood there, examining the naked elm trees and the snowcapped mountains, thinking of his next plan. He wanted to go back to the old man when he thought of his old shelter. He still had some belongings there. He would take them. Besides, he did not want the beast to discover the place and know that someone was staying there.

An hour later he was by the shelter. He felt that something was wrong. A minute later he discovered that his feelings had not betrayed him, for no sooner had the shelter become visible through the branches than he heard the beast screaming. Peter hid behind a boulder in the river area and watched the beast as he tried to get out of the pit. Apparently, the beast had just fallen inside it and was screaming and yelling profanities.

Tracy had rushed to his assistance. Billy's bare feet were bleeding because the sharp pebbles and stones in the pit had inflicted cuts and bruises. The beast struggled and finally was able to get out. He entered the shelter and collapsed on the bed that Peter had made. Tracy rushed to him and surveyed his injuries. The beast pushed her aside angrily.

"Why are you pushing me, Billy?" she yelled at him.

"You do this to me."

"What are you talking about?"

"You and your boyfriend."

"My boyfriend? Why, that's ridiculous, Billy. Who in the world gave you this idea?"

The beast's face became red and blotchy with anger. The opening at his forehead disappeared when he got angry.

"You took me here to kill me. Boy and you do this to me. I kill him. I kill boy."

Peter realized that Tracy had told the beast about him. For the first time since he'd met her, Peter could tell she was frightened of the beast; but she did not seem to be concerned about herself, for Peter heard her say, "The boy was lost and I told you everything about him. He probably dug the pit to protect himself from animals."

The beast did not seem to hear what she said, for he was repeating to himself, "I kill him, I kill him, I kill him."

Tracy got angry. "He can't hurt you; he's just a small boy. He needs someone to help him, not kill him."

The beast did not listen, for he got up and ran outside with his machete drawn. Peter's heart sank. The beast looked in all directions for several minutes before returning.

Tracy looked at him for a few seconds. "Let's get going to the cabin. I'll treat your cuts there."

She held his hand and led him like a small boy. The two passed just above Peter.

He watched them until they disappeared, then decided to follow them. He had forgotten to get the rest of his belongings. He just took a glance at the shelter one more time, wondering whether he would ever see it again.

Peter followed them as the two walked silently until they got to the cabin. He hid outside and waited for the beast to leave so he could talk to Tracy alone. Minutes later, she came out and seemed to be looking for something. Just before she returned, Peter whistled softly. She stopped, looked behind her, and saw him. She opened her mouth and stifled a scream of joy, then gave him a signal to wait for her.

Peter waited outside, impatient and ready to run at the first sign of danger. He still did not trust Tracy fully. Minutes later she came out alone. She walked to where Peter was hiding. He took her hands and squeezed them warmly.

"Listen, Peter, Billy is looking for you to kill you."

"I know. I was at the shelter. I saw everything." Peter examined her face. "You seem worried about me. Do you really care?"

"Don't be silly," she interrupted. "What are you going to do?"

"Listen carefully." He looked at the cabin stealthily. "I'm going home and I want you to come with me."

"Do you know where you're going exactly?"

"Yes, yes," said Peter.

"Do you know where the next town is?"

"Yes, I do. And now what do you say? Will you come with me, Tracy?"

"I'll go with you wherever you go, but tell me about the town."

Peter wanted to tell her about the old man in the village, but he was fearful that she might unintentionally give the beast a hint about the old man. The beast would then go and kill him.

"I'll tell you everything later."

"I don't want to know a great deal now. I know there is no chance for me to escape by myself. Perhaps God sent you to save me, Peter."

"Please trust me, Tracy. I want the best for you."

Tracy smiled, causing him to shiver inside.

She got closer to him and held his hand. "I trust you, Peter. Do what is best for us." She heard the beast calling her. "I wish you good luck, Peter." She turned to the cabin and whispered to Peter, "I'll be waiting for you."

He watched until she disappeared in the cabin, then rushed to the grotto. From there, he watched the cabin for a few minutes, thinking of Tracy. He had started to fall in love with her, but did she also love him? He would come back no matter what. But next time he would not have to hide. He would be with an army of heavily armed policemen.

In two hours, he was back at the village with the old man. He told him about his encounter with the beast.

The old man sighed and shook his head. "This beast man is more vicious than all the wild animals, and nobody can get him except by a trick."

"Don't worry. He will be in police custody in a few days," said Peter.

"I wish to revenge myself before the police get him."

"You might be able to."

Peter and the old man ate turkey and bread. After the meal they sat by the fire. The man wanted to know more about the beast and Tracy. Peter was happy to provide him with the details. Peter then got up and checked the old man's inventory of firewood. It was getting low. Peter went outside and brought enough wood to last several days.

As soon as Peter entered the cabin, he sensed at once that something was wrong. He glanced around quickly. Then he noticed the old man lying on the couch, his head resting on a pillow. Something about the man's face made Peter catch his breath. The old man was pale and still. Was he breathing? Peter strained to hear. A moment later, he knew it was no use. The old man was dead.

Peter did not know what to do. This was the first time someone had died in his presence. His mother had died in a hospital and Aunt Pauline had not allowed him to see her body. Peter could not stay under the same roof with the body of the old man. He left the house and just wandered in the deserted village for hours, not knowing what to do. He then came back just when it was becoming dark. Peter then carried firewood and went to the house next door and built a campfire there.

In the morning Peter came to the house, hoping that by some miracle the dead man would be alive, but he was disappointed. Peter wrapped the body in some clothes, dug a pit in the backyard of the house, and buried him there. Afterward, he sat down, thinking of going back to the cabin, but he was tired and just wanted to get it over with by contacting the authorities.

Peter left the village and headed outside toward the road. He had finally decided to go home. He stood for a second, examining the lofty mountains, while his memories conjured images from his home. Would he find anyone in his town? *Perhaps I will find it deserted just like this village*, he thought. *Aunt Pauline may be dead. Even Cynthia's parents may have moved to another town, but I don't care for her anymore.* His thoughts took him to Tracy. *I would have kissed her if the beast hadn't called her. I will be with Tracy all the time from now on. She has no parents and she will stay in my house with my aunt.*

Peter felt a blush of pleasure. He could not help but smile or even laugh at his own gloomy thoughts seconds ago. Now he was already savoring the wonderful sense of being with real people again.

"I think I'll just hike the five miles non-stop until I reach the restaurant on the road."

A quarter mile down the road, there was another farmhouse. At that point the road narrowed and curved in the easterly direction. There was a little wood bridge that he had to cross. When he passed it, he almost stumbled onto a huge bison crouching by the brook. The colossal animal was startled at Peter's sudden movement and jumped to its feet. Peter leaped from the bridge and ran. The bison was infuriated. It charged Peter, injuring him slightly in the thigh. Peter ran toward the farmhouse. The bison gave chase. It was running so fast that Peter thought his end was near.

As he reached the farm, he realized that the bison was gain-ing on him. His only chance was that if he reached the fenced area, he might be spared. Peter felt the teeth of the bison grabbing his shoulder, inflicting a severe wound to it, and fell to the ground. As he was about to faint, he saw the bison charging again. Peter grabbed the round head of the animal and clung to it.

The bison carried him and started to shake his head to drop Peter, who was holding firmly to the animal's horns. The bison, who could no longer see, ran with Peter still clinging to its head. Peter noticed that the bison was getting close to the fence. He collected his strength and jumped to the ground. He ran the few steps separating him from the four-foot fence and jumped there. Peter was about to lose consciousness when he saw the bison grappling with the fence. Excruciating pains seared through his injured shoulder and thigh. Blood was flowing out of his injuries, and he fainted.

17

When Peter regained consciousness, it was still light. It took him minutes before he realized what had happened. The bleeding from the shoulder had stopped, leaving a small pool of blood on the barren ground. The pain was unbearable. He touched his shoulder. The laceration was the size of the palm of his hand. The cuts in the leg were not serious. He ripped off the sleeves of his shirt and used them to dress the wounds.

Cold penetrated into his bones. He pulled the thick coat over him and looked across the farm where he had taken refuge, but the bison was gone. Inside the pig's den, Peter tried to get up but could not walk. He crawled until he reached the little house adjacent to the farm. He pushed the door, but it was locked. He thought of returning to the old man's house, but he had no strength.

Peter wanted to break the window, but he remembered he needed a sealed shelter if he had to stay there for a while. He crawled around the house and found a side door, which was also locked. Next to the side door were stacks of firewood. Peter grabbed a large log and struck the rotten side door with the little strength he had. A few minutes later, he succeeded in springing the door off its hinges. He made a hasty inspection of the house, then proceeded to the living room. There was a sofa and other furniture.

His first task was to make fire. Now that he felt safe, he needed to stay warm. He brought several logs from outside and arranged them like a pyramid in the fireplace. The problem now was finding some matches. He hoped he didn't have to go through the intricate bow-and-arrow process again. He looked in some trash that was left in one of the corners, and luckily for him, there was a book of matches. He brought dry leaves from outside, and in a few minutes, he had a nice cozy fire.

His next task was to find food. He was too weak and too sick to go to the old man's house. But even there, the old man had died before he told him where he had hid the food.

Peter lay on the ragged sofa by the fire for a few minutes. When he felt he had enough rest, he went outside. He looked carefully for any traces of the bison, but the animal was gone. *It was my fault that the bison attacked me*, he thought. *I surprised him. I should've heeded Mr. Jones's advice always to make noise when hiking in the wilderness.*

Peter went back to the road and started examining the area. There were neglected crisscross corn fields across both sides of the road. The corn fields seemed to occupy the whole valley until it was swallowed by the mountains. Peter figured that some of the plants would be carrying corn and decided to return when he felt better.

Peter returned to the house where the old man had died, and he built a fire. He checked the inventory of food in the house, and there was bread and cheese that would last for several days. He also made coffee. Afterward, he placed coffee on the wounds and bandaged them again. He sat by the fire, wishing that Tracy was there, then she would take care of him just as she cared for the beast. Peter thought that the wounds would heal the moment she touched him. *If I could walk, I would go to her this minute*, he thought.

The food left in the house was gone in two days. *The old man must have a secret place to store the food*, Peter thought. In the last several weeks, Peter had grown lazy in his effort to hunt and find food.

He recalled the corn fields and strolled outside, examining the ground. The pain in his shoulder was pestering him. He wanted to return to where the bison attacked to get the corn, but he hoped to find similar fields closer. He walked to the next farm and could not believe his eyes. There were countless good ears of corn on the ground. Peter gathered several spikes and took them to the house. When he returned, it had started to snow. He cooked some in the campfire, and after he ate several spikes of the corn, he slept.

Thick snow covered the wilderness in the morning. This time, however, he was inside a house with a real fireplace. He stood by a window and watched the white flakes fall sluggishly, landing on the ground that had already been blanketed by a thick layer of the white stuff.

The snow kept Peter a prisoner for several days. His body, however, needed to rest and recuperate. His wounds needed the time to heal. The worst wound was on his right thigh. It was the last one to heal. After removing the first bandage, he just let the wound dry. He had no medicine other than coffee, and he was leaving the healing task to nature.

Peter spent the next several days in bed and left only to get food. At one time he shot a deer with a bow and arrow, but the wounded animal escaped. He had no strength to chase him. Instead, he was able to kill a rabbit. Rabbits seemed to be abundant there. Peter would hide behind a tree or a rock and kill one with a rock cast from his hand. In the latter days, when his wounds were healed, he would run behind a rabbit, and on one occasion, he was able to outrun the swift animal and catch it.

The bleakest hours for Peter were during the night. The image of the beast visiting him was frightening, although he was protected by the trap. He also thought of the old man buried in the backyard.

A week later, Peter took a walk along the gravel road away from the village, but this time he made plenty of noise so that he would not surprise another vicious animal.

After hiking for about a mile, he found out that there was a canyon leading in the direction of the cabin. If this canyon led there, he reasoned, it meant there was a way to the cabin without climbing the lofty mountain. He decided to explore that possibility in the near future when he was fully recovered. His leg was almost healed, but the shoulder still ached.

The days were getting shorter and the nights longer. Peter figured that by now it was December. He wanted to see Tracy before the snow would impede his movement and paralyze him for several months. The snow was already heaping, covering everything except the trees. He was too familiar with winter due to living in the town, as the snow kept him and his family under house arrest for weeks. He recalled his mother stocking up on all types of groceries.

Peter waited for a warm day for his excursion. The snow had to melt also because he did not want his footprints all over. That day came two weeks later. On that sunny day when the temperature rose, he followed the canyon along the creek where he had been attacked by the bison. In less than an hour, he was at the river. Peter figured that it had to be the same river due to its width and proximity, but he could not see the cabin. He wanted to head upstream to discover the cabin, but he would not take any chances now.

Peter returned to the house where the fire was blazing. He had decided that the safest method of seeing Tracy was to go early in the morning when he could watch the beast leaving. He would not return without her. Peter even envisioned plans whereby she would meet him by the grotto before the beast got up, and he would accompany her to the village, then take the gravel road.

The next day he prepared his brazier so that it would last for hours. He also took the book of matches with him. He would need it if he had to build fire away from his home.

Peter left the house armed with a real knife he had found in the house and went back through the village. He preferred the mountain route because it was safer, although it was more treacherous. He had not climbed a mountain since the bison incident, and he had to rest every now and then.

Peter looked behind him and sighed. He felt a great deal of loss. Here was a site that, not long ago, used to flourish with life and explode with activity. If it hadn't been for the beast, Peter would have seen farmers working on their farms and early laborers rushing to work. He would have heard dogs barking and roosters calling, announcing the advent of another day. He would have seen the lights shining, turning the wilderness into a place full of life and action.

When he reached the summit of the mountain, it was light. The easterly mountains loomed in the horizon like a thin dim line, which almost by the minute was getting brighter. The first rays of light assisted him in determining where he was. He was standing just beneath the summit by a big boulder that he recognized from his last trip. The first thing to do was to find the grotto quickly to escape the winds. Peter could withstand their bone-chilling temperature but not their severity and vigor.

A half hour later, he was there. His feet were wet. His toes and fingers were turning grayish from the cold. By now, it had just become light, but there was nothing to see except the naked trees, the leafless shrubbery, and the handful of the evergreen trees swaying under the shrieking winds.

The first assignment was to collect firewood. He started with broken stems and sticks. He then placed his dry woods on the sticks, and soon he had a cozy fire. Now it did not matter much how long it took before the beast left. He had decided to settle it with Tracy once and for all. Old Man Winter with his severe weather was at the door. Spending winter in that endless wilderness made no sense for either him or her.

Peter got out of the grotto and came down to view the cabin. Peter was lucky this time. It was about an hour later when the beast left the cabin. He was dressed up in a huge coat, so Peter gathered that he was going hunting. Peter immediately covered the fire with dirt and went to the cabin.

Minutes later, he was at the cabin's door. His heart was pounding. He did not know how Tracy would receive him.

Tracy was there alone. "I thought you went home. I've been so worried about you."

"I was attacked by a bison and I stayed in bed for several weeks," said Peter.

"And where were you all this time?"

Peter told her about the Indian village and about the old man and the fact that he was there to revenge the murder of his family by the beast. He was no longer worried that she would tell the beast. The man was dead and there was no one else the beast could harm.

When he was finished, she paused and shook her head. "Tell me more about the old man. How did he die?"

"He was very sick. The poor man died before realizing his wish to revenge the death of his family."

"Are you sure of his story?" asked Tracy.

"Yes, and that's why you're coming with me."

"You know I would not hesitate for a second, but I'm afraid we'll get lost and die like my father did."

"Do you still believe your father died in the wilderness after what I told you about the beast? I'm sure he killed him, although I do not have the evidence."

"I find it difficult to believe you."

Peter exploded with anger. "Stay here and rot, then. You probably deserve it."

"Fine. Go and leave me alone."

"You know you're so stubborn that I don't know what to do with you. I think I'll just go by myself."

"Go and get killed in the woods. I'll be fine here."

"You're crazy. Sooner or later the beast will kill you."

Peter turned around and left angrily. When he was about a hundred feet away, Tracy called him, "Come back, Peter. I'm sorry I angered you. I'm just scared."

Peter came back. "Please get ready then."

"I'm still worried that we'll get lost."

"And even if we do, we'll still survive. Just look at me and imagine what I had to go through."

"It's easier for you to survive without me. Besides, I may be a burden on you, but anyway, why don't you have something to eat?" asked Tracy.

"Do you think it's safe to be here? Would he be coming back soon?"

"No, don't worry about him. He'll be gone for several hours. And if he does not find something to hunt, he may be gone all day."

"Good, then I can relax for an hour or so."

Peter examined her as she was leaving to prepare breakfast for him. Then he watched her as she worked. He was alternating his glance between the door and Tracy. It would be nice if he could be with her all the time.

Peter enjoyed his breakfast. It consisted of quails and eggs. The cold and the long walk made him eat a great deal, but before he finished eating, he decided to bring up the important subject again. "If you're worried about us getting lost, you can stay in the old man's house until I come back with the police."

No sooner had he finished than he heard a snap in the trees below. It was the beast returning. In his awkward walk, he resembled a monster. Peter jumped up and sneaked outside.

18

No sooner had Peter left the cabin than he was face to face with Billy the beast. It was too late for Peter to seek shelter from Billy, who was holding a machete in his hands. For several seconds Peter stood motionless, thinking of an appropriate course of action. His mind told him to speak to the beast and try to befriend him, but his heart urged him to bolt. The mere look of the beast scared him. No matter what Tracy said about the beast, he would not trust him.

Peter was seeing the beast for the first time at this close range. They stared at each other, their eyes trading hatred and animosity. That gaze was an abrupt declaration of war between them. Peter was scared of the beast's reddish eyes. His dirty brown beard danced as he yelled profanities. His thick eyebrows formed a straight line beneath the grimy hair.

Peter did not budge from his position at the cabin's door. He was shaking, his glance fixed on the beast, ready to flee if the beast shifted a foot. Tracy stood by the door, urging the beast to drop his machete. The beast gazed at Peter with fury, not paying any attention to Tracy's pleas. The anger hung in the air like an invisible dagger, and any word was liable to release that fatal weapon.

"Billy, I told you to drop the machete," said Tracy. "Don't you hear me?"

The beast continued to stare at Peter.

"What's wrong with you, Billy? Can't you see? He's only a boy. Why do you need the machete? I'm asking you to drop it."

"He smart boy," the beast said, turning to Tracy for the

first time. "I kill him, I tell you. I kill him."

"He hasn't done anything to you."

"He dug the pit. He want to kill me. I kill him, now."

The beast's voice roared like a lion. It echoed in the wilderness, providing an extra source of horror for Peter. The beast's eyes shone with a burning spark, and his forehead had contracted, concealing the hole there.

Peter took advantage of the beast's preoccupation with Tracy and examined the area around him. There was a tree that he could climb in seconds, but the beast could eventually cut its trunk. He could have climbed a boulder, but it was only a few steps from the beast. His best bet was to run behind the cabin to the grotto and eventually to the village, but the beast would find out about his village shelter, and Peter would have no place to stay.

Peter half-closed his eyes in his attempt to discover a deliverance from his dilemma. He was, however, glancing stealthily at the beast out of the corner of his eyes. He was no longer paying much attention to the heated exchange between the beast and Tracy. All her appeals had fallen on deaf ears. Peter was ready to make his bold move.

In no time he swerved backward, mounted a rock, and climbed the cabin's roof. The beast, having recovered from the surprise move, pounced in his direction, waving his machete in the air. Tracy went inside, cursing the beast, who went around the cabin looking for a way to climb it. Peter kept circling the roof, whose top looked like a small tent. Finally the beast brought a chair from the cabin. At this point, Peter was deliberately standing on the back end of the roof. The beast mounted a chair and started climbing. Peter threw a rock at the beast, who, in his attempt to catch it, fell from the chair to the ground.

Peter jumped to the ground and went in the direction of the river. At first, he wanted to go upstream, as he was more familiar with the area there, but the hope of finding people downstream seemed more promising.

Peter followed the riverbed and struggled through broken stems and crashed trunks. At first he did not look behind him, as he was certain the beast was tailing behind him, but after sprinting for some distance, he realized that the beast was not there. He wondered if the beast had broken his leg or if Tracy was able to convince him to leave him alone.

But the fact that the beast was not visible to him provided little consolation for his terror-stricken heart. He continued the hike downstream, defying the countless rocks, bushes, and broken trees impeding his progress. He felt a special power taking hold of him. He could run as long as it took, even if he had to run to the end of the world.

The river roared, its currents generating white waters, which were making clouds of foam and bubbles that would disperse when they struck a hidden rock. Vapor flew in the air and struck him in the face, wetting his dry lips. The water tasted refreshing.

Peter knew he had to move fast. Even if he had a boat, it would not be safe to sail. If he fell, the freezing water would pull him down instantly. He looked toward the horizon in all directions, but there was no trace of humans. He decided to continue running until he was outside the beast's reach.

Finally he stopped and glanced behind him. When he found no trace of the beast, he took refuge behind a curved rock above the riverbed. It was like a triangle wall and provided a temporary cache in addition to some protection from the winds. *I need to rest if I have any chances of defending myself. I will wait here for the beast. If he does not come, I will go back to the village.*

Peter examined his surroundings. The slope from the westerly direction descended sharply. The valley was getting wider. Upon a cursory inspection of the shape of the mountains, he realized that he had been there before. It was weeks ago when he followed the creek and saw the river. Now he knew exactly where he was. *Maybe I should entice the beast to the village and then make him fall in the well, but it is a long distance and the beast can easily gain on me*, he thought.

Peter touched his knife and it was there, but the knife was no match for the hair-raising machete. He would have to shoot the beast with an arrow, but Peter realized that he was not good at that. He had tried it several times with the deer, but he'd missed most of the time.

A mile downstream he was at an area filled with little rocky hills and piles of broken trunks. At that point, the river went down abruptly, forming small waterfalls. Beneath him it was plain and smooth all the way to the hills. Peter could also see a small lake next to the river. He selected a hill and hid behind a rock.

A funny smell filled his nostrils. He was familiar with that smell, as he had been to the hot springs. It was phosphorus. Peter no longer felt cold. As he sat, something caught his attention. It looked to him as though the smoke was coming out from a pond, but when he stood and took a better look, he realized the smoke was actually a cloud of steam from a hot spring. He wished at that point that he had seen it before. He would then have gone there regularly to enjoy the hot water.

But where is the beast, he kept wondering. *Did he change his mind about killing me?* It was now close to an hour since the confrontation.

Peter looked all around him, and he found more hot springs in the flat land beneath him. *I must be close to some real village or settlement. I'll be even happy to find a paved road. I'll just stop a car and it will be the end of my misery. I'll then go home and find Aunt Pauline there waiting for me.*

A flap in the broken trees below brought him back to reality. His heart sank and the blood rushed to his head. He moved cautiously and glanced across the river in that direction. The beast was less than a hundred feet away, trying to cross a trunk with the help of his machete. When he accomplished that, he started examining the barren earth. Peter knew that the beast was looking for some human footprints, his. Peter was paralyzed. He clung to the rock and resisted an urge to cough. He did not even attempt to think what would happen to him if he was killed. It was something that he ruled out. He could not die, at least not then. The beast was to die first, he thought.

Peter watched the beast advancing slowly. He watched the beast strolling and muttering some unclear words. At one point, he stopped and looked in the direction where Peter was standing. Peter crouched, thinking that the beast saw him. He held his breath.

Several long seconds passed before the beast turned away and walked downstream. Peter stood up and let out a long sigh. In the process, he coughed. He tried to curb it, but it was too late. Peter rushed to his position and waited there in the hope the beast had not heard him, but he was disappointed when he heard the footsteps returning.

I'm doomed, Peter thought. *He knows where I am now. I must defend myself.*

The beast proceeded in Peter's direction, holding the machete in his hands. He walked slowly on his toes, his face turned to the left and yet his glance was turned to the right. He did not seem to know where the cough had originated from. He stood there and examined the rocks and trees in the area, paying special attention to the boulders, which could provide a hiding place for a boy like Peter.

Peter took advantage of the beast's confusion and reflected on his course of action. He looked around him and saw a cliff consisting of steep rocks. If he could climb it, then he would be safe for a while. He did not think the beast with his huge size would follow him, but going there would expose him. Besides, the beast could wait for him until he came down. The beast kept examining the rocks, advancing step by step until he finally came and stood in front of the rock where Peter was hiding. Peter's heart sank. He could even hear the heavy breath of the beast. He could not wait any longer. He stood up and dashed like the wind. The beast followed after him, cursing and threatening.

Peter ran from one place to another, jumping at times from a rock to another in his attempt to find a way out. He figured the best way was to attack the beast, to slow him if not to kill him. Otherwise, the beast could be chasing him all day, but he stood no chance of attacking the beast. He had to use something against which the beast could not defend himself. He thought of throwing stones at him and injuring him. He ran and hid behind a boulder, picked up several stones, and waited for the beast. As soon as the giant approached, he cast the first rock and missed, but he was lucky with the second one as it struck the beast in the face. Blood flew from the face immediately, but the beast did not seem to care.

Peter ran in all directions and realized that the beast was not going to give up.

Peter now reached the hot springs. The funny smell of phosphate overwhelmed him. He could see the water boiling in the various-sized and -shaped geysers. *If I can get the beast to fall into one of these, he'll die right away.*

Peter got up at once and ran to the edge of the geysers. He deliberately chose the slippery areas next to the geyser in the form of a bubbling pond about twenty feet in diameter. The water was simmering and at certain points forming minute fountains so that the geyser resembled a giant teapot with its clear water adulterated with red color.

Peter sped around the steaming craters, the beast on his tail, holding firmly to his machete as though it was the key to his power. But the beast did not fall, as the ground was full of holes and cracks, which rendered it rough, and Peter was tired. He climbed a cliff next to one of the geysers and waited. The beast came to the foot of the cliff, waving his machete. He smiled at Peter with confidence, as though he had Peter cornered.

"I kill you, boy." The beast smiled. "I kill you now."

"Just like you killed Tracy's father."

The beast giggled. His loud grotesque laughter echoed in the wilderness. "Yes, boy. I killed him. Now I kill you."

"Try, if you can, ugly baboon," Peter said with a special wide smile, which fury lurked beneath, holding firmly to something in his hand.

As the beast advanced toward him, Peter threw a stone, hitting the beast in the left eye. The beast covered the affected eye and started to curse again. He proceeded again, step by step with such a confidence that it scared Peter, but he continued to cover his eye all the time.

The beast watched Peter standing up, attempting to flee, and as he did, tripped on a tree trunk. The beast leaped like a monkey and grabbed Peter by the shoulder.

"You bad boy. I kill you," the beast said and threw Peter several feet in the air.

Before Peter was able to rise, the beast picked him up again by the collar of his shirt and lifted him up in the air.

Peter screamed to let go of him. The beast threw him on the ground and drew his machete. He pounced on Peter and thrust at him. The machete missed Peter's head, but struck his shoulder. The beast stood on top of Peter and started to giggle. He was celebrating his victory. Peter lay there on the damp ground, shaking. He did not feel the pain immediately, but a minute later, he felt the pang. He knew he had been hit in the shoulder and decided that only a trick would save him.

The beast was about to strike again when Peter, with a quick movement, rolled down and the machete missed. The beast was enraged. He picked up Peter and threw him down the slope. Peter's body rolled down the hill and settled near a hot spring. With great amusement the beast watched Peter rolling down and then disappearing behind a boulder. Something then fell into the geyser. The beast ran to the geyser. The bubbles were rising up and ascending, their commotion caused by the fall of the thing in the already simmering waters. The beast knelt down and touched the water, but he pulled his hands out instantly as the tips of his fingers were burned. "Good, boy's dead now . . . boy's dead."

The beast laughed loudly and was repeating the phrase like a child who had just scored a small victory. He waited for a few minutes as though he was fearful the boy would come out of the boiling waters of the geyser. When he saw the water still boiling, he turned back and headed in the direction of the cabin.

Peter, crouched beneath the cliff, stood up slowly, glancing stealthily in the direction of the beast. When the beast disappeared behind the hill, Peter let out a long sigh of relief. He smiled and sat on the ground for several minutes, breathing heavily in full, satisfying silence. Nevertheless, he was still shaking. As he was leaving, the last minutes when he came near death lurked in his mind. He had jumped to the ground at the same moment when he had thrown a rock in the geyser.

Peter hiked upstream for about half a mile. At this point he noticed an indentation by the river, almost like a cave. He wanted to go in but changed his mind at the last second. The beast or some other creature might be waiting for him there. He had just survived his first bloody encounter with the beast. In addition he was injured, and he did not even know the extent of his injuries.

Peter followed the creek on his way home. It was a shortcut that saved him much-needed energy. The hike seemed longer than the last time. The winds were getting stronger and blustery, but the hope and the wonderful sense of going to his new home and starting a campfire made the hike more effortless.

In about an hour, he was at his home by the Indian village.

19

Peter's first chore was to build a cozy fire in the fireplace. Luckily, the book of matches was still in his pocket. At first the icy logs resisted igniting, but ultimately the campfire was set and blazing. He then dressed his wound with coffee and a clean cloth. Now Peter was ready to doze off for many hours. He stacked the fireplace with dry logs, arranging them diagonally to facilitate their kindling and to minimize the smoke.

For the first few minutes, he was shivering, but after the logs turned red, warmth radiated to his body. When his eyelids became heavy, two images flashed in his mind. The first was that of the beast in the form of a monster who was going to hound him forever. The second was brighter and restored confidence and optimism in himself. It was that of Tracy embracing him.

The two images competed for attention. His first round of the duel with the beast had already started that day. The other rounds would follow soon. It was going to be a bloody match that had to end in the demise of one of them. As his bed was becoming warmer, sleep came nudging in among his thoughts.

It was still light when Peter got up. He proceeded to the fireplace to feed it with more wood. But before he reached it, he stopped, horrified. He heard noises outside. His heart sank and the blood rushed to his head. He strained his ears and listened. The noise was that of footsteps coming from outside. *The stupid beast. It has to be him*, Peter thought. *He must have found out that I did not fall in the crater and then knew about the village. But how did he find out about this particular house? Could he have seen the smoke? Or could Tracy have told him? No, no way.*

Peter again turned his ears to pick up any sounds outside. The footsteps were definitely coming his way. They were not animal footsteps. He could tell that from the monotonous tumble of the steps. He immediately ran to where he could lower the board to throw the beast in the pit. *Maybe I'll make the task easier for the police.*

In a few seconds, he had devised a plan to destroy the beast if he survived the fall. He would lie in ambush by the entrance, concealed by the edge of the wall. If the beast survived the fall, he would then surprise him with a quick thrust in his chest. At this thought, his body shivered due to the image of blood flowing out of the beast. *I have to regain my self-control if my plan is to succeed.* His steadfastness supplied him with courage and hope. He felt more relaxed and started to control his anxiety.

Peter walked to the window and peeped through the window, taking extra care not to show his face. No longer had he looked than he smiled and threw the knife aside. The comer was Tracy, carrying a bag in her hand. She was alone.

Peter was suspicious about her visit. He thought the beast might be following her, but nevertheless he ran to the door and opened it. A wave of arctic air rushed inside, but Peter did not even feel it as he was busy looking at Tracy, not believing he was seeing her. Her cheeks, tinged red by the cold, made her look most beautiful. Tracy hurried to him and hugged him.

"How did you know I was here?" Peter asked, closing the door.

"It was easy. I looked for the chimney with smoke, and yours was the only one."

Peter helped her remove her boots, which were covered with snow. "Come and warm your feet by the fire. But tell me, doesn't the beast think I'm dead?"

"Yes, but I knew you were too smart and resourceful to die

that quickly. I was terribly worried nevertheless. But thank God you're alive."

"Did you speak to the beast after he came back?"

"Yes, he returned about two hours later. He was so joyful that he offered to prepare food for me. I refused to eat and asked what had happened to you. He said you'd fled, but I could tell from the funny way he acted that he'd killed you or at least that's what he thought." She rubbed her hands by the cozy fire. "Tell me, Peter. How were you able to dodge him?"

"At one point in the struggle, he lifted me and threw me from a cliff. I fell near a hot spring and then threw a stone in it to make him believe it was me who fell. He still thinks that the crater swallowed me."

"So now you can relax without having to worry about the beast," said Tracy.

"I won't relax until I see him in a cage."

"How are you going to do that?"

"I'll go to town and get the police."

"Don't go, please."

"Why not? We could be in town in a couple of hours. In fact, we should leave right now."

"Let's eat first. I brought some food."

Tracy opened a plastic bag and put its contents on the table. There was bread, two apples, a piece of red meat, and cheese.

"How did you leave without him knowing about you?"

"I was so mad at him. I left his food untouched and I accused him of killing you, so I asked him to leave me alone. He left to go hunting and I came here," said Tracy.

"How about if he returned and found out that you were gone?"

"He'll think I went to bring water from the river or something. He thinks that I'm too scared to try to look for towns and people."

Peter cooked the meat. When it was done, they ate together. They were both starved. When they were finished eating, he looked at her to determine if it was the right time to bring the subject of leaving for town.

"It seems to me you're still hesitant to come with me."

"We should ensure our safety, Peter, before everything else."

"The old man told me the place is only five miles away."

"In that case, I'll stay here and wait for you."

Peter realized that there was no reason to push her to come with him since he was going to return in just a few hours with the police.

It was the afternoon, otherwise, Peter would have left then.

"Since you're staying, I'll leave in the morning."

"That soon?" asked Tracy.

"Don't you want to be settled once and for all?

"Yes, but . . . you gonna leave me here by myself?"

"You're safe here, Tracy. Besides, it's you who does not want to come with me."

"Why don't you stay here?"

"What do you mean? Don't you want me to come back with the help?"

"Not really."

Peter was dumbfounded. He thought he knew Tracy a little, but now she had turned into a mystery.

"Why don't you want me to come back with the police?"

"Because I want you to stay with me."

"I will stay with you, sweetheart. I'll never leave you."

"I mean stay with me here," said Tracy.

"Stay here for good?"

"Yes, Peter, and forget about going back to town."

"How about the beast?"

"We'll get rid of him somehow."

"And then?" asked Peter.

"And then you and I will be together here."

Peter noticed that she was examining him at each word she was saying.

"Just you and me, Peter?"

"Why can't we live happily in town?"

"Well, I have never lived with people since I was a little girl. I don't know how to act. I'm scared of civilization. I can't even read."

"You'll learn and adjust. I'll help you. I won't leave you for a second."

Peter came close to her. He held her hands and examined her eyes. He knew he could trust her completely. Almost inadvertently, his hands went around her hair, caressing the honey-brown locks. He wanted to kiss her, but he was not sure how she would react. Suddenly, he heard a terrible noise outside. It sounded like something falling.

Peter got up and rushed to the door. He could not see anything suspicious outside. Peter and Tracy strained their ears and listened. They could hear heavy footsteps outside.

"What could that be, Peter?" Tracy asked fearfully.

"It's probably a bear."

They listened again. The footsteps were getting closer and closer. They would stop at times as though the one causing them was lost or looking for something.

Peter wanted to tell her that it was probably the beast, but he did not want to scare her. There was no question that the footsteps were those of a man.

"It's the beast. Isn't it, Peter?"

"I think so. Let's put out the fire. This way he'll never see the smoke from the chimney."

"It's too late. He's already seen it by now."

Peter then thought that the opportunity might not present itself again. "But on second thought, why not finish him up once and for all?"

"How?" asked Tracy.

"The well. I have not told you about it yet. We'll trap him there. But let's make sure it's him first."

They went to the door, and although he had a plan to trap the beast and kill him, Peter was horrified. He immediately grabbed Tracy and led her gently into one of the rooms. He then took a position by the door, holding a knife in his hand. Before he could take his position, there was a knock on the door.

"Tracy . . . Tracy," the beast roared.

Peter realized that the beast was only looking for Tracy. He could allow her to go with the beast while he went to get the police, but the beast might get suspicious and find out that Peter was there too. He had to decide what to do as the voice of the beast continued roaring again and again, "Tracy, are you here? Open the door."

Peter collected his strength. "Yes, she is. Come in, stupid beast."

Peter figured that by infuriating him, the beast would recklessly burst into the house, something Peter hoped for, so he could push the button that opened the mouth of the well.

As soon as Peter uttered those words, the beast pushed the door vigorously and it opened. The beast froze as he saw Peter, but he was able to recover from the surprise and advanced slowly. Peter waited for the beast to step on the right spot to trap him, but when he saw the frightening creature, he could not wait any longer and pushed the button. The beast, who almost grabbed Peter, staggered and fell down. His hands, however, clung to the edge, but Peter kept stabbing the hands until the beast fell in the well.

For the next few seconds, there were no sounds whatsoever coming from the well. Tracy had now joined Peter in trying to observe the beast in the dark well. His body lay there motionless.

"Is he dead?" Tracy asked.

"Looks like it."

"What are we going to do with him?"

Peter leaned forward, watching for every movement in the dim well. "I don't think he's dead. Look, Tracy, he's moving."

The beast had started to move his arms. The two watched him with awe as he sat on the wet ground of the well. Soon he seemed to have realized what had happened, for he looked up, and when he saw Peter, he stared at him, using profanities. Peter's thought focused on the possibility of the beast getting out of the well, for he did not seem to be badly injured. There were cuts on his legs and on the palms of his hands due to stabs inflicted by Peter.

Peter examined the walls of the well. They were made of smooth rocks. The little cleavages between the rocks were too small for the huge hands of the beast to use them to climb. This made Peter feel safer. He placed his arms around Tracy and went on watching the beast nervously.

"I'll kill you, boy! I'll kill you!" cried the beast.

Peter pushed Tracy aside gently and signaled to her to stay away and listen. This was his best opportunity to secure incriminating evidence from the beast.

"How are you gonna kill me, Billy?"

"I kill you. I kill you."

"You seem to enjoy killing innocent people."

"Shut up, boy."

"Tell me about the three Indians you killed in the village."

The beast looked at Peter with interest.

"The old man told me about it. He just died a few days ago, but not before he told me everything."

"Yes, I killed them and I kill you, too."

"No. I think I'm the one who will kill you this time. But before I do that, I want to ask you a question. Where did you hide the body of Tracy's father?"

"I won't tell you."

"Why did you kill him?"

"Shut up, boy, and let me out."

"If you tell me where you hid the body, I'll let you out."

"First let me go."

"No way," said Peter.

"If you don't, I come out and kill you."

The beast struggled to climb up the well, as he was threatening to get out and kill Peter. When he realized that he was trapped, the beast called on Tracy to help him out.

"No one is gonna help, stupid ape. We'll go and get the police."

"You can't go. It's far. You get lost. There are evil animals on the way. I'm the only one who can kill them."

"How far?" Peter wanted to examine his veracity.

"Two days on foot if you don't get lost."

"The old man said there is a restaurant and a gas station five miles from here. I'm sure you robbed them several times."

The beast did not answer. He continued to strike the wall with his machete. Peter left him and went to Tracy, who was crying silently.

"So now you know he is the one who killed your father."

"And I've been with him all these years."

"Now you must come with me."

Tracy did not answer. Peter thought that he could make the five miles in a couple of hours. If he left in the morning, he could be back in the afternoon with the police, but how could he trust that the beast could not get out of the well? He went again and examined the well. It was about twenty feet deep. Peter looked at the thick board covering the well. He went to it, flipped it, and covered the well with it. He then dragged a heavy sofa over it and kept piling furniture on it until he was sure that even if the beast climbed up, there was no way he could lift the bulky plank.

That night, Peter slept with one eye open just in the event the beast attempted to get out, but he did not hear any movement from the side of the well. In the morning, he and Tracy ate breakfast and he told her he was leaving at once. He could have convinced her to accompany him, but he thought that she might delay him.

Outside, the sun peeked through the light clouds. There were still a few inches of snow on the ground. It had snowed heavily in the last week, but there was no snow in the last several days. It was cool and Peter estimated the temperature to be around thirty when he checked the board covering the well and left, his thoughts shifting between the beast and Tracy on one hand and the real people that he was about to meet in a few hours.

20

Peter started the march an hour after sunrise. He made a great deal of noise as he hiked to avoid another encounter with another vicious animal. The winds were cold, but Peter was wearing warm clothes, plus the sheepskin. He turned to glance at the mostly cloudy skies every now and then, fearful the heavy clouds would invade the friendly skies in a split second.

Peter passed by the little bridge where he had been attacked by the bison. The gravel road stretched for as long as he could see, passing by a plateau amid gray rolling hills, but he could not see the flat rock as the ground was covered with snow. He was able to tell where the road was by the boulders and bushes around it. Also the road was lower than the rest of the ground.

Peter could not resist thinking of the "new" world with which he would be soon in touch. The first thing he would do was contact Aunt Pauline. He was already thinking of his first words to her. He wondered whether she would like Tracy.

Meanwhile, he kept looking for the flat rock and the other trail on the left, but the trail kept going in a straight line for a quarter of a mile. It then descended toward the valley, curving alongside another creek. The trail was about twenty feet to the east of the creek. The broken trees littering the creek bed extended to the trail. Peter figured that no vehicle had used that trail for a long long time. The high mountains looming in the horizon were getting farther away. He gazed out over the sunlit white peaks.

An hour later more clouds moved in from the northwest. They were mid-level banded masses, breaking up periodically to provide brief sunny periods. The scudding froth of clouds against the blue sky reminded Peter that a storm was brewing. He nevertheless continued to hike on the gravel road, not paying much attention to the unsettled weather. He expected to see the crossroad any minute now. He could continue despite the storm. He was no longer the frail sick boy terrified of the storms. He would conquer the weather, if he had to. The temperature was rising, and he was expecting to see the cars on the paved road soon.

On his left was a mountain range that was winding upward. Peter figured that a paved road had to be located at the edge of the peak, so if he did not find the crossroad or the flat rock, he should be able to see the restaurant anyway. Even if he got to the road far from the restaurant, he would hitchhike to the nearest town and call the police from there.

On both sides of the road, snow patches spread over the top of the hills. There were still sparrows circling the evergreen pines in great abundance, apparently challenging the Wyoming winter, but they were all on the move. He wondered why suddenly the birds were agitated. He wasn't able to spot any animal, but at one point he saw a porcupine running as Peter advanced. Deer could also be seen but in smaller number than before. They, too, seemed to be on the move and seeking shelter. At one point, he stopped and listened carefully to the sounds of nature. The heavy stuffy breeze whistled, but he was unable to interpret its meaning.

By now he could hear the slightest noises in the wilderness. There was nothing to alarm him. He heard clearly the rustling of the leaves being shoved by the winds. He could hear the small animals moving, although he could not see them, but he could not tell why the animals were running.

As he strained his ears, the faint clamor of the animals was vanishing rapidly. A deep silence was replacing everything, stealing all the sounds of nature except the whistling of the winds and the gurgling of the stream that intensified at times when it pummeled a rock in the water. He then smelled the air. There was something special about it. It was becoming stuffed and heavy, but that did not stop him and he continued hiking.

Peter had hiked for several miles when he realized that he might have passed the crossroads and looked back. Still the flat rock would not show up. *What happened to it? There is no way I could have missed it*, he thought. The only possibility was that the rock had collapsed by the force of the winds. He blamed himself for not asking for more specific directions from the old man. Also, if Tracy was with him, she could have helped him look for the road.

Peter had now another problem to worry about. The silver clouds were becoming tall and rippling, towering in the high skies, promising a heavy snowfall.

He had hiked for three hours when he felt tired and cold. He was also angry. Why didn't the weather cooperate just for one day? The sky was shrouded by ice crystal clouds. The winds, which so far had been calm, were getting stronger and colder. The temperature began plummeting rather than continuing to rise as Peter expected and hoped. He had seen these clouds before. They were often a sign of a severe weather to come.

He blamed himself for leaving the safety of the Indian village. *At least I had a roof there and a fireplace, along with Tracy. I could have waited until the snow melted. In that case I would never have missed the road.* He wondered what would happen to Tracy if he did not return for several days, or if he did not return at all and the beast somehow managed to get out. He did not even want to think of that possibility.

Peter sensed that it was going to snow soon. It wasn't only the dark low clouds that overshadowed an ominous day but something peculiar in the air. Waves of wind were striking with a new ferocity. His senses told him that a severe storm was brewing.

I should have returned over two hours ago when I first sensed the storm, he thought. *It's probably too late now.*

It was a winter storm that could easily convert into a blizzard. Besides, he did not have to rely on his own predictions. The birds and the other animals were doing the job for him, already getting ready for the worst. In one minute he had to decide whether to continue the march or return. In fact, he did not need the full minute.

Peter immediately turned back and started running in the direction of the village. At least there was a warm place for him there. Besides, Tracy's idea was not bad. He would stay with her in the wilderness until the spring.

His powerful legs were plowing the snowy road. It had taken him more than three hours to get there, but the storm would not afford him the chance to get back, for he had only been running for a few minutes when the snow started to fall accompanied by howling winds. The snow fell slowly. Soon it became heavy and the winds blew the snow in all directions, forming whirlpools of white dust. *Will I make it?* he wondered. He decided to take refuge under some rocks, but the blizzard would soon cover everything.

Another quick glance at the skies revealed the dark clouds floating over the wilderness. The running was not difficult at first, for the snow was still shallow, but now even the trail itself became hard to distinguish if it weren't for the fact that it was slightly lower than the adjacent terrain. *The best thing for me is to locate the hills I passed by earlier this morning,* he thought.

Peter was exhausted and could no longer run. He had been running off and on for over an hour. His heart pounded and his chest heaved convulsively. He had to resort to a shelter, at least temporarily. Fresh snow covered his head. Although the sheepskin was wrapped around his body, he could feel the wind striking him when it blew fiercely. He had to stop. He was covered with sweat, despite the frigid temperature. The melted snow trickled down his neck in icy rivulets, causing pain and discomfort.

If I don't stop immediately, I'll die, he thought. *And if I die, Tracy will die too. But stop where? I can't stop. I have to continue until I reach the village.*

His wishful thinking was far from reality. The snow had sloughed onto the trail in high drifts. Tons of snow and debris from broken trees were gathering momentum. The drifting snow piled up around him in the form of small mountains. The hiking became almost impossible. Peter's feet dipped in the snow. As he pulled one foot out, the other would sink deeper. His shoes were filled with snow and his toes became numb. It was quiet, and nothing was heard except the howling winds and the periodic falling of trees.

Peter figured that he was now probably five miles away from the village. Five miles normally meant a couple hours of fast hiking in ideal weather. But now it would be night before he got there, if he made it at all. Over an hour passed since the snow had started to fall. He looked around and recognized some of the rock formation that he had seen earlier. There was one that looked like the jaws of a whale. *I should've recognized the ominous signs. Maybe I should look for a shelter in those rocks. I should not go down the valley just in case an avalanche covers it altogether.*

A large rock directly across the path promised a temporary haven. Rushing in, Peter struggled through the heavy snow. Finally, he reached the shelter beneath the rock about a hundred feet above the creek. The triangle rock, the size of a passenger car, stood on the slope like a giant teapot challenging the weather. Beneath it was an indentation the size of a dog house. Peter hurried and crouched there, but the wind rushed to him from the big opening, so he went out and pulled several broken trees and covered the opening of the indentation, securing the ends under the heavy snow. The damp logs were heavy, but he had to bring more of them to secure his shelter.

Peter got out again and saw a few broken trunks. He grappled through the deep snow to get them. Just as his frigid fingers grabbed the logs, he heard an explosion at the top of the hill. His heart sank as he saw huge chunks of snow and ice crashing down the slope toward him. He abandoned the logs and hurried to the rock. In his effort to hurry, he fell in the knee-deep snow, but he got up swiftly.

Peter watched with horror as a huge sheet of snow flew on the air in his direction. A large chunk of ice fell past him in a blur, slightly missing him, followed by rock and more chunks of snow. Masses of powdery material struck him. Peter, covered with snow, fell to the ground. He attempted to get up, but his frosty hands would not cooperate with him. He crawled toward the rock like an injured dog. *This is the avalanche that will finish me*, he thought.

After a full minute of crawling, he got inside the new shelter. It was the longest minute in his life. Through the cracks in the logs guarding the entrance, he could see the powdery snow engulfing the universe like a spinning churning whirlpool of heavy fog. *If I survive this avalanche, I'll never die*, he thought. But he was mistaken, for he had not seen the avalanche yet. A second later, he heard a much louder explosion, followed by a shower of churning snow as though it was being pushed by a gigantic snowblower.

The next thing he saw were masses of snow burying the rock and his shelter. He suddenly found himself in complete darkness. He lay back, rubbing his hands against each other, trying to bring life back to his paralyzed legs.

Peter did not know how long he had been huddled inside the hole when life returned to his hands. He took off his shoes and emptied the snow from them. He rubbed his toes, too.

He needed to preserve his strength if he was to have any chance of survival. But how would he get out of that snowy grave? At this thought, Peter felt startled. He was truly in a grave. He was being buried alive! He had heard of people being buried alive, but not like that. He didn't know how thick the snow was above him. *It could be ten feet*, he thought.

The temperature inside the snowy grave was getting warmer. At least he wasn't feeling the bone-chilling winds. Peter touched his pockets, as he could not see anything. The two ears of corn were still there. The place was too dark and too crowded for him to eat. He had to think of a way to get out of the grave.

After minutes of deliberation, he decided to dig through the snow before it froze and turned into hard ice. Luckily for him, his knife was still in his pocket. He pulled one of the logs from the opening and started to dig a hole in the snow ceiling. He had to utilize his hands if he wanted to move at a faster pace. More snow fell over him. But soon, the relentless cold turned his hands into a sheet of ice. He stopped and rubbed his hands again. Soon, his knife was doing more digging. The snow fell on the shelter in small chunks and almost filled it. He kept applying more force until, in a split second, all of the snow covering the shelter collapsed as it fell over him.

Peter was covered to his chest with snow. He climbed the logs clinging to the big rock and sat over it, shaking violently. It was almost dark now, but he could still see the fury of nature around him. In the valley below, the broken trees were visible only as shadows above the mounds of snow, while he was covered with snow. He had to escape the winds and find another shelter, and soon. Nightfall was imminent and the winds were penetrating his clothes as though he was naked.

Peter sank in the fresh snow. He started heading toward some larger rocks by a cliff. As he struggled to reach them, he continued through the knee-deep snow. He fell several times but stood up as soon as he fell. He did not waver when a bleak thought crossed his mind that his situation was hopeless. It was already dark, and he needed to find a shelter or he was as good as dead.

As he fought waves and waves of snow, the thought of a miserable death took hold of him. He was able to escape the wrath of the beast, a fellow human being, but would he be able to escape the fury of nature?

Following the fatiguing bout of falling and getting up, he reached at last the rugged area where he hoped to find a cave. It was honey-combed with chasms and crevasses, but it was his only chance.

All I need is a place to protect myself from the wind so I can make a fire, he thought.

Peter touched his pocket, and the matches were still there wrapped in aluminum foil. *I'm sure I can find some dried firewood inside the cave.*

Focusing his eyes on the darkness, he scanned the rugged area again. In his effort to cross a rock partially covered with snow, he was struck by what felt to him like a flying wave of snow. He felt himself being propelled through the air like a cannonball and fell. Snow clung to his face and especially beneath his nose. *I have to make it no matter what, but where is the cave?* he wondered hopelessly. *I still have to cross these ridges to reach the area I need.*

Peter hurried, dragging his feet, pulling them from the snow. Swallowed by darkness, he fell into a chasm and started to roll over until he settled near the creek. He got up and could not believe his eyes when he saw what appeared as an entrance to a cave. He crawled on his belly in that direction. He was now face to face with a steep wall about twenty feet high. He looked around but could not see anything in the dark. He walked around the wall until he was able to climb to the cavity opening.

Inside, a strong odor of animals filled his nostrils. *What's this smell?* he wondered, *a graveyard for dead animals?* He looked around, focusing his glance at the darkness to explore the cavity.

That's not a cave, but it's more like my first shelter by the river, he thought.

It was an indentation the size and shape of a grotto. He could see animals lying there. He was no longer afraid of them. *I'd rather die here in this grotto than be buried in the snow. I hope they are not bears or bisons.*

Peter came close to them, and he could hear the bleating of sheep. He relaxed. *If there are sheep here, then there can't be wild animals with them.* Peter heard more sounds of sheep. *They have to be many. I'll make a fire, and that should keep me warm until tomorrow.* He pulled some dry twigs from the shelter and got out the matches, but his frozen fingers could not even open the aluminum foil. His hands were turned into a sheet of ice. He could not even tighten the sheepskin around him.

Peter was getting weaker by the minute, shivering violently. He had to get warm immediately or he was dead. He crawled inside the shelter, but he was still cold. The bleating of the sheep was coming to him in the form of slow motion sounds coming from far away, as though he were in a dream. His feet could no longer support him. He wanted to get closer to the sheep, but he could no longer crawl. He fell to the ground and tried to move, but his frigid fingers could no longer grasp the damp and frosty pebbles blanketing the floor of the indentation.

As he was about to faint, the idea of death swept over him. *I'll just die and there will be no one to protect Tracy. The beast may somehow find a way to get out and he will cut her to pieces.* His eyes were heavy, and he fell into unconsciousness.

21

When Peter opened his eyes, it was dark and the storm still raged outside. He felt dizzy, but he was no longer as cold. Although it was dark, he felt his body covered with something. He could smell the heavy scent of sheep. Peter tried to move his head, but an attack of dizziness paralyzed him. *If I make it tonight, I'll survive the blizzard*, he thought. He knew that he was suffering from hypothermia, which afflicted people exposed to severe cold weather. Mr. Jones had warned him against staying too long in the cold.

Peter moved his hands after a while, and they were no longer frigid. He felt the area around him, and he touched the thick wool of the sheep. The warmth of the wool supplied him with hope and restored his confidence. He could hear the sheep's sounds as they moved or mooed.

But how did I get here? I was near the entrance when I fell. I can't concentrate anymore.

Slowly, his clear mind was abandoning him and he was becoming delirious. His body was shivering violently. The howling winds and the intermittent explosions of avalanches were continuing. Peter buried himself under the sheep and soon lost consciousness again.

When he opened his eyes again, it was light outside. Everything was quiet. The sounds of the explosion were gone, and the howling winds had vanished. What remained was the gurgle of the creek.

Inside, the sounds of the sheep mooing were pleasant and relaxing. Peter was still partially buried under the sheep. He tried to look outside. It had stopped snowing, but a mountain of snow blocked the opening of the shelter. He closed his eyes fast. The dizziness increased as he opened them. His body ached. Moreover, he had suffered frostbite in his hands and legs. But he could tolerate all that if he was not hungry. *I'm starved*, he thought to himself. *I'd pay anything for a warm bed and a hot glass of milk.*

For the next several hours, Peter dozed. During the times of wakefulness, he would tighten his cover and close his eyes to relieve his headache. At one point he gazed at the sheep around him, and he was surprised. They looked like a family, two adult sheep and three young ones of varying size. One of the little ones would creep under his mother and grab her breast, sucking on one of the four nipples quietly. The lamb would stare at Peter as though inviting him to share.

As soon as his mind cleared, the image of Tracy and the beast jumped to his mind. He was worried about her for fear the beast would kill her. It had been several days already, and Tracy must be getting worried to death.

A terrible noise interrupted his thoughts. Peter figured that a huge chunk of snow must have fallen, for he saw clouds of snow blowing near the shelter entrance. The sheep did not budge with the sound, and Peter wondered if they knew what was going on. The two adult sheep were smaller than the one killed by the mountain lion. Each had a pair of horns and long woolly coats the color of coffee cream. The little ones had snow-white wool but no horns. The adult sheep ignored Peter. They just lay there, waiting for the weather to improve.

It was light now, and Peter felt well enough to examine the shelter. It was an irregular round room, approximately fifteen feet in diameter. The room had a cathedral ceiling rampant with gaps and crevasses. The floor was damp at the entrance but was dry by the end where there were twigs and dry leaves. *It would make a perfect shelter if I could build a campfire and had food*, Peter thought.

When he opened his eyes again, it was dark. He was hungry, but what would he eat? He was too weak and sick to go out and look for food, and there was nothing in the shelter. Then he remembered the corn. He looked for it in his coat and it was there untouched.

But I can't eat it raw. I have to build a campfire.

Peter studied his surroundings and concluded that it would be impossible. For one thing, the sheep may burn or they may run. He threw the corn to the sheep, which they started eating at once. He then lay down again by the sheep and slept.

When he woke up again, it was still dark. He noticed he was sucking on something. It took him a full minute to realize that he was sucking on the doe's udder. He stopped immediately and looked at the mother sheep. She didn't seem to mind, so he returned to breast-feeding to satisfy his hunger.

Peter woke up the next morning to a severe cold, but the headache and the dizziness were gone. Although he was shivering, he felt more energetic. He looked around him and noticed that the sheep were gone. He sat up and noticed that his feet were hurting him. He took off his shoes and socks. The skin around the toes was snowy white and mushy. He wiped his feet with his hands and decided to clean his feet as soon as possible.

Peter walked to the shelter's entrance. It was the first time that he was seeing the area in daylight. There was a gigantic pile of snow in front of the shelter, at least twenty feet higher than the gorge below. Across from his shelter, the snow mountains loomed on the horizon, shining under the distant sun. The sun was attempting to pierce the entrance through the gleaming glasslike layer of ice, which had formed due to the melting snow.

The temperature rose rapidly. It was the first time in weeks that the temperature had climbed to the fifties, but the snow was everywhere and in great abundance. Mountains of the white crystals littered the valley.

The rising temperature was melting the snow. He could see

it in the water dripping from the smooth bark of the naked aspen trees in round drops, then disappearing in the snowy ground. He could witness it in the increased flow of the creek, which the melting snow had turned into a fast-flowing river.

Peter advanced a few more steps to get a panoramic view of the universe in its new snow-white gown. Everything was fresh and pure. The stillness added serenity and magic to the scene. *Nature is neutral*, he thought. *Its beauty would have manifested itself even if I were buried dead under the snow. Nature has changed one hundred and eighty degrees in the last couple of days.*

Even the wind had stopped, except for a sporadic breeze. The fluffy piles topped with the glazed deposits of snow glistened under the sun. In the flat sections near the creek, the drifting snow had created series of hills akin to white sand dunes. As the gentle breezes fondled them, the snow dunes stirred lightly, like waves in a quiet lake.

Peter noticed the sheep's footprints in the fresh snow. The double deep tracks formed a fresh trail, leading out of the shelter. His eyes followed the tracks until they disappeared behind a chasm. He strained his ears, and he could hear the sheep. They could not be far. He moved in the direction of the sound until he could see one of the adult sheep nibbling on the bark of the pine trees.

Peter returned to the shelter and wondered if he should return to the village immediately or wait another day.

Tracy may get worried because I have been gone for several days. I'm also tired and hungry, and I can use a good campfire. But I won't be able to find my way back. The road will not become visible until the snow melts. If I hit the road now, I'll need some snowshoes and I have none. I'll just sit still here and build a fire.

Peter gathered more twigs from the shelter and then went outside for some real wood. There was plenty, but it was wet and cold. Nevertheless, he carried several logs to the shelter. The hardest part was pulling the heavy wet logs from under the snow.

As he was struggling to pull the logs, he thought of how he had often complained when Aunt Pauline asked him to shovel the snow from their driveway. It was a task lasting for only several minutes, after which a hot meal would be waiting for him on a nicely set table.

At first, the logs refused to burn. Finally, he had a nice fire going. For the next half hour, he stayed by the fire, warming. Even the odor of the wet logs smelled pleasant. He was enjoying every minute.

Peter shifted his attention to food. All he had in the last three days was milk from the sheep. Leaving the shelter, he observed the sheep anew. *I can go ahead and kill one of the baby sheep, but I couldn't do that*, he thought. *They kept me warm.* He looked round, but there was no sign of food. He noticed that one of the baby sheep was coming his way alone. *Why can't I kill it? If I don't, some other animal will.* The little sheep stopped only a few feet from him and looked at him, crying *baa, baa, baa.*

Peter found himself in a dilemma. On the one hand, he was hungry and he was getting hungrier by the minute. On the other hand, he could not raise the knife held in his hand. The sheep in a way was his sister. They had fed from the same udder. The little sheep continued to cry. He could no longer remain there. He left and returned to the shelter.

Peter thought of fishing, but there were no fish here. The creek was too small for any fish. At this point, he noticed that some of the birds were returning to the forest, following the rise in the temperature. He had seen a robin crouching on a branch singing. *But how will I catch the bird*? he wondered.

Peter returned to the shelter, placing two logs on the fire. He then left, allowing the black smoke to fill the shelter. He followed the creek downstream, hoping to find some birds. *They are the easiest to cook and the most delicious*, he thought. Hiking in the wet snow was fatiguing. Soon he was exhausted and decided to return to the shelter. *I'd rather use my energy in carrying more wood to the shelter for the night than in wasting it in the futile search for food.*

Beneath a young spruce were several logs partially submersed under the snow. Removing the snow around them, he started dislodging the logs one after the other. He had managed to pull three when he heard a noise of something moving under one of the logs. It was a faint moan of an animal.

Peter stepped back and drew his knife. *It can't be a snake or another reptile. They must be all hibernating now. I'll remove the logs and see what it is.*

Slowly and cautiously, he lifted the log with one hand, his other hand pressing on the knife, but as soon as he saw the animal dwelling there, he relaxed. It was a hare.

By now, he had learned to distinguish between a rabbit and a hare. The latter had longer ears and large legs, with a slit in the upper lip. The long ears were erect, like a pair of antennas, to detect sudden danger. Peter approached the hare and attempted to grab it, but it was faster. It stood up quickly on its long hind feet and bolted out of its hideout, dashing like the wind. He gave chase, although he was still sick. All he knew was that a hot meal was about to escape.

Peter ran after it, pulling his shoes from the snow. The rabbit ran fast, trying to avoid the snow, jumping at times from a broken branch to another, but Peter was at its tail. Finally it came by the creek, but the flooding bank made it hard for the hare to cross. It veered downstream and seemed to be looking for a place to hide. The hare could not jump, as it ran over a pile of drifting snow. Peter ran after it and was surprised when he found he was running faster than he imagined. The hare was about to jump from the snow to a broken branch when he seized it.

The hare was skinny, but Peter was happy to have the meat. Without hesitation, he slaughtered the hare. He then cut it to pieces and started roasting it over his fire in the shelter. He devoured about half of it and saved the other half for dinner. He was not sure whether he was going back to the village that day or waiting until the next day. He had all he needed now, the campfire and food.

Peter spent the rest of the day gathering more wood for the night. Once he had done that, he made up his mind to return to the village. But before he could do that, he had to find the unpaved road under the piles of snow. All he had to do was to look for a straight line devoid of trees and bushes. After some search, he located the unpaved road. It was not far from him.

The next morning, he was on the road heading for the Indian village. The hiking was less tiring than the day before. He had gotten plenty of rest, and his stomach was full. The road was covered with snow. The winds were stronger than the day before, which made it feel colder.

On both sides of the road, life was returning to the residents. The deer were getting out of the heart of the forest and coming to its edge, seeking water and food. He could see birds flying over the trees, singing and playing as though nothing had happened. The branches, heavily coated with ice and snow, had been recently liberated of that burden. Other trees had fallen, their branches broken.

It took him four hours before he reached the village. As he was marching in the foot-high snow, he thought of his rendezvous with death in the snowstorm, and he had to learn a lesson from it. *The lesson is that nature is a force to be reckoned with and respected*, he thought.

When he got to the house, he noticed that there was no smoke coming from the chimney. He knocked on the door, but no one answered. As he pushed the door vigorously, a big surprise was awaiting him. The cover over the well had been removed. Tracy and the beast were gone.

Peter went out and examined the footprints outside the house. They were mostly covered by the drifting snow, but he could still detect the huge footprints. He could not see Tracy's. Had the beast killed her? Peter did not even want to think of that possibility. Nevertheless, he went back to the house and searched every inch of it for any sign of Tracy, but he did not find anything.

Peter went back inside the house and examined the well. He wondered how the heavy sofa had fallen in the well. Had the beast convinced her to throw the sofa in or had Tracy removed the cover to give him food, and the sofa fallen by accident?

22

Peter woke up abruptly. He thought he heard something outside. His heart sank as the frightening image of the beast flashed into his mind. He crawled to the window and peeked outside. It was mostly dark. All he could see were shadows of a herd of deer running about a hundred yards away. They seemed to be chased by some predator, for they were racing toward the mountain at maximum speed.

Peter went back by the fireplace. The thought of the beast was robbing him of his sleep. *He knows where I am*, he thought. *Even if I find another place, he will find out about me from the smoke of the fireplace. Therefore, I cannot rest until he is gone. I must kill him. But how and when?*

Peter took another look outside and strained his ears. Everything was quiet. The view of his footprints in the snow obsessed him. He became prey to those thoughts. *Maybe I should remove the sofa from the well and see if I can trap him again. As soon as he falls in the well, I'll burn the house to the ground.*

But pulling a heavy sofa from the well was not easy. He was too tired to even think of that. He had survived so far and especially three days under blizzard conditions. He grew confident and the idea furnished him with the strength he needed. Even if the beast showed up, he'd manage somehow. With this thought, he slept.

When he woke up in the morning, he had a sore throat. It felt as if many knives were piercing his throat. *I wish I could have some orange juice and hot soup. If I were home, Aunt Pauline would have done everything to ease the cold. She would give me the medicine herself and would make sure I took it.*

Outside, it was sunny but cold and windy. Flurries flew in the air as though they were racing. He got up quickly and fed the fire with more logs, but he was very weak. He barely placed two logs on the fire when he felt weary and dizzy. He tried to sleep, but he could not.

Peter got up sluggishly and walked outside. As soon as he opened the door, a wave of icy air struck his face. He shivered and ran anyway to the creek and filled a jug of water.

When he came back, he was so exhausted that he fell near the fireplace, gasping for air. His coughing was returning, and his stomach was growling more and more.

Peter went outside and started looking for food. He remembered that he had seen the berry bushes next to the creek. He hurried there, and he could see the tiny scarlet berries still hanging indifferent to the cold and the winds. He ate some of them.

At the edge of the forest, he saw what appeared to be a carcass. He headed there at once, and it was the remains of a deer lying in the snow with its head bent back. The assailant must have been a bobcat, Peter thought. He had learned to distinguish between the several animal tracks. In addition to several pairs of two small toes of the deer showing in the snow, there was another set of tracks. He could see the bobcat's four toes in a circular print with no claws.

The back of the deer's neck was almost severed. Most of the meat was gone. Drops of frozen blood colored the snow. Peter took all the meaty bones and returned. Now he was ready for hot soup.

After he ate, his energy returned to him at once. His thoughts turned to Tracy, and he decided to go and see her.

Just before he got to the river, he noticed the hot springs. He was cold and decided to rest by one of them on top of the plateau. He was attracted by a geyser several hundred feet away from the creek. Once there, he noticed a small waterfall originating from the basin of a geyser. He approached it and noticed that the water was warm.

Peter went behind the falls and was surprised when he discovered an opening the size of a room behind the falls. The room was warm, thanks to the waterfalls. The only problem was the unbearable odor of sulphur. He thought that he could use that shelter in the future. The beast would never see any smoke.

Peter left the hidden shelter and came to the creek. He stopped by a beaver's lodge in the middle of the creek. He also watched the birds and chipmunks that appeared from nowhere. He was amazed at the life forms that were popping up out of nowhere after the sun came out. *I used to associate winter with stillness, darkness, and death*, he thought, *but it's full of life*.

Hiking to the cabin was not easy, as the snow was melting fast. Snow was getting inside his shoes. Above, white clouds floated over that endless ocean. When he passed by the waterfall, he smiled.

About an hour later, he arrived at the banks of the river. He stopped behind a curved boulder and surveyed the area around him. He expected to see the beast any second, but he was nowhere to be found. Peter continued advancing toward the cabin, looking in all directions. Every now and then, he stopped and strained his ears, but there was no unusual sound. All he could hear were the little waves of the river rushing downstream.

A half hour later, the cabin became visible. He came close to it, hiding behind a row of evergreen trees. There was no sound. It was close to noon now, and he hoped Tracy would be home. It was cold for her to venture outside unless it was terribly important. Peter got closer and hid behind a rock, examining the entrance. The wood door of the cabin was half open.

He waited for about ten minutes, puzzled at the silence. Finally, he took a rock and threw it in front of the cabin. Again there was no response. *Perhaps they both left*, he thought. *That's not bad, at any rate. I can at least go inside and eat some real food*. He advanced toward the door and peeked inside. When he heard nothing, he went inside. He had only advanced two steps when he stopped, horrified. Tracy lay on the floor motionless. There was no trace of the beast.

Peter hurried to her. She lay on the bed, her hands tied with a rope behind her back, her legs were tied to the bed itself. Peter called her and rubbed her cheeks. Tracy opened her eyes, glancing at Peter and closed them quickly but did not say a word. Peter cut the ropes, brought a blanket from a bed in the cabin, and covered her. He then grabbed a bag and filled it with food. He returned to Tracy and carried her outside. He knew his enemy would be coming soon.

Peter headed downstream. He wanted to get to the Indian village, but the mountainside was difficult since he had to carry Tracy. No sooner had he reached the river than he spotted the beast returning. Peter was so startled that he lost his grasp on Tracy and she fell. Her fall caused an audible thud. The beast stopped and looked for a minute in Peter's direction, then he continued his ascent toward the cabin. Peter picked up Tracy again and rushed away from the cabin. He figured it would be several minutes before the beast would realize what had happened. That should give him an edge. The natural barriers did not slow him. He figured that by the time the beast learned what happened, Peter and Tracy would be a quarter of a mile away.

He had crossed a hanging trunk by the riverbed when he observed the beast storming in his direction, like a genie who had just been released from the lamp. Peter continued his march, rolling the blanket around Tracy to protect her from winds. At this second she opened her eyes, and seeing Peter, she screamed and started scratching him on his neck, yelling, "Let me go, Billy beast."

"It's me, Tracy, Peter."

"Put me down, Billy. Put me down," she continued.

"But, Tracy, look at me. Open your eyes. It's me, Peter."

Tracy opened her eyes again and took a good look at Peter.

When she recognized him, she started and tried to free herself from him.

"Let me go, Peter," she cried. "I don't need your help."

Tracy ran and got away. He followed her and screamed at her, "Tracy, this is not the time to be stubborn. The beast is behind us."

Peter held her gently by her wrist and ran with her while she was trying to free herself of his grip.

"You and the beast are the same," she said. "You left me at his mercy. He could've killed me at any time."

"That's why I came back. I wouldn't have returned if it wasn't for you. We have to get rid of him before he kills us."

"You were supposed to come back with the police. You thought . . ."

"Don't say that. I survived by a miracle. I was buried alive under the snow. I'll tell you what happened to me later. Let's run now before the beast catches up with us."

Peter dragged her, and they both ran to the shelter behind the waterfall.

When they settled in the shelter, she told him what had happened.

"The beast convinced me to throw him some food. He told me that you were dead because you did not return. I believed him then because the snowstorm was terrible. When I tried to remove the sofa from the cover of the well, it fell inside. He climbed over it, came out, and beat me severely. He then took me to this cabin and tied me up. He said he would kill me someday soon."

"No, he won't. He won't be able to touch you again. We should be safe here. What do you think?"

"This is a warm shelter, but what are we going to eat here? We must leave to get food, and he'll see us."

"We've enough food for now."

Peter wrapped the blanket around her and opened the bag of food that he had taken from the beast.

23

Tracy could not eat any food, although she hadn't eaten for days. Her body was hot and Peter helped her to lie down on the blanket. His thoughts then turned to the beast. *If the beast discovers us, we're gone*, Peter thought. *In the early days, he would have probably spared Tracy, but now things were different. We are in a state of war, and Tracy has joined forces with me.*

The thunderous water prevented them from hearing clearly. Peter realized from the beginning that, since the beast had not discovered them quickly, they would be safe for a while. He concluded that the beast would go to look for them in the Indian village.

The problem, however, was how long they could survive in that sanctuary without food and a cozy bed. Peter could tell that Tracy was not enthused about the place. The roof was low and jagged, oozing water, and the floor was damp, bursting with rocks and pebbles. Peter, however, had learned to take one thing at a time.

He came out stealthily and climbed to the top of the falls. He hid behind a pine tree and surveyed the area to see the beast. He wanted to make sure the beast was heading toward the village because he had a plan. He climbed a cliff where he could see the beast a hundred yards away by the creek, pacing back and forth, looking in all directions. With his machete in his hand, his ragged clothes, and his huge size, he looked more frightening than ever. Peter watched him heading for the Indian village.

He went back into the room and told Tracy he was going back

to the cabin to get food from the beast while the latter was out looking for them. He figured he had a couple of hours since it would take the beast more than that to go to the village and discover that they were not there.

Wasting no time, he got out and crossed the field separating him from the little hill, then to the river. Once at the riverbed, he headed upstream. For the first time, Peter did not have to worry about the beast surprising him.

When he reached the cabin, Peter packed a box with all the food he could carry in addition to a blanket. He left briskly and returned to the shelter in no time.

Tracy was sleeping. He tried to wake her up, but she was sick and coughing now and then. He tried to give her some of the food he'd brought, but she would not eat. Peter was alarmed and touched her forehead. It was hot. He brought snow and rubbed her forehead with it, but she remained sleeping and feverish.

Peter realized that if the girl were to regain her health, he had to find a better shelter. The one behind the falls was safe, but it was deficient in other respects. The smell of the sulphur was intolerable. He knew he could get used to it, but Tracy found it obnoxious. Besides the smell, the thundering noise of the falls was deafening. They could not even hear each other, except if they screamed. Added to that, the humidity made them feel uncomfortable.

Peter could not take Tracy back to the village even if he chose another house there. Since he had to build a fire, the beast would notice the smoke. Building a campfire was a must, and it would continue to be necessary for several more months.

That night, Peter's eyelids did not close. His mind raced to find a healthy living quarters. A cave would have been ideal, he thought, but there was none around. He considered many options, but he rejected them as they were difficult to accomplish.

When he woke up in the morning, Tracy was still sleeping. Peter went out. The wilderness might give him an idea, he thought. He wanted to stay close to the hot springs so that if he built a fire, the springs would cover the smoke.

An important requirement for the new shelter was that it be not visible even if someone came close to it. He strolled up the hill, following a small frozen stream. A quarter a mile uphill, the stream parted into two. Peter followed the two streams visually and discovered that one of them disappeared in the mountain. He headed there and stopped where the stream disappeared in the mountain. He found that the water came out from a small opening about three feet in diameter.

Peter followed the water and went inside the mountain. The opening widened into a round room. He expected to see a lake inside the mountain, but instead the water was percolating from another opening at the ceiling of the round room. Patches of ice froze near the sides of the opening. He figured that once it rained, it would pour and thus he could not make the place his shelter. He looked inside for more rooms, but there were none. He sat on a boulder, enjoying the relatively warm climate, gazing at the blue sky showing from the water opening at the ceiling.

An idea occurred to him. If he could change the course of water from above, he would not only make the place fit for habitation, but he also could use the opening at the ceiling as the chimney.

Peter came out and turned around the steep mountain, looking for a way to mount the hill. It was vertical and not easy to climb. He walked around it. Not far from there was a small ravine. He followed it until he found a spot where he could climb to the top of the mountain. Once there, he was able to locate the opening. The creek, then, continued upstream until it further divided into several smaller streams and tiny frozen waterfalls. The stream was only several feet wide, and Peter figured that it would take several hours of hard work and a good axe to divert the stream.

Peter had to return to the shelter to check on Tracy. When he arrived, he found her lying on the floor, shaking and gasping for air. Peter hurried to her and covered her with the blanket, but she continued to shake violently.

"Tracy," Peter said. "What happened to you?"

"I'm sick. I think I'll die."

She barely opened her eyes. Peter got scared. He felt helpless. He could do a wide range of things, but he could not be a doctor.

"You'll be fine. I found a better shelter with a fireplace."

"It's too late."

Peter held her hands. They were hot, like burning pieces of charcoal. He gave her water, but she refused to drink and returned to sleep.

"Tracy, don't sleep, please."

There was no answer. He sat on the rough floor, thinking of his lamentable situation, his glances fixed at the rugged ceiling. *We are fugitives, being tracked by a ruthless beast. We are also at the mercy of an unfriendly nature*, he thought.

Envisioning the new place with its roomy fireplace and spacious chamber, his confidence returned. He figured that once they moved to the new home, Tracy's health would improve.

In the morning, Tracy was still feverish and refused to eat. He tried to talk to her, but she would not answer. The once-rosy cheeks were now pale and dry. The only clear features were her green eyes, which she could barely open. They still retained their lucidity despite the fever. Peter made her drink juice that he had squeezed from the berries.

He left to go to the cabin. He could not go to the village directly, knowing that the beast could be there. He got up at once and headed to the cabin.

Peter waited outside the cabin for a while until he saw the beast leaving upstream. That meant Peter did not have to worry about him for the entire day. He figured that the beast would not go to the village, at least not that day.

At the village, Peter made loud noises just in case there were animals there. Once everything seemed normal, he went to the house in which he had stayed for a few days with the old man. He would get some tools. But he was shocked when he got there. The house was burned to the ground. Peter reasoned that the beast had probably done that, thinking that he and Tracy were in the house.

Peter wasted no time and started looking for his tools. There were plenty of them. As he was looking, he came across wood boards. If he could somehow move them to the new shelter, he could build a complete room inside. There were also beds and other furniture. It would be nice to have a comfortable place to live.

Peter sat thinking of how to transport the furniture and the boards to the new shelter several miles away. He would require a big pickup to complete everything in one trip. That gave him an idea. *If I can make a cart, I can pull it myself. Otherwise, I can never bring the heavy furniture.*

Peter then looked for tires. He only needed two. He found them in a closed shop. It would be easier to pull and steer a two-tire cart. Peter spent the entire day building his new discovery. At the end of the day, he had a simple wagon with a straight surface as large as a bed. He loaded the cart with a mattress and various tools and headed for the shelter.

Peter spent the next day moving material and furniture to the new shelter. He had started by changing the course of the stream. Once that task was accomplished, he made sure the water returned in front of the new shelter so that there would always be a fresh supply of water.

As Peter was busy with his house, the animals were busy getting ready for the spring. Deer and sheep fought each other. Coyotes and wolves called. Birds soared to the sky whenever the weather permitted. Spring was on its way, and the whole animal kingdom was on the move, preparing itself and its next generation.

The next task was to build a fireplace. There were plenty of rocks, and Peter used mud to secure them together. As for the chimney, Peter covered the opening at the top with trunks and trees, leaving a small opening for smoke to escape.

The walls and the floor were the most difficult, but he had once seen a handyman building a deck and he followed the same procedure. At first, he filled the floor with sand and pebbles, then lay small boards on the floor vertically, securing them with rocks. He then lined the large boards horizontally. As to the walls, he secured boards to the floor. Two days later, he had what looked like a primitive deck inside the room.

The entrance to the shelter was narrow, but Peter wanted to have a door for protection against the animals and the cold winds. First, he had to build a frame, which he accomplished by connecting boards together, and the door was built.

During the several days he was busy building the house, Peter had seen the beast just one time. Peter was leaving the shelter behind the waterfalls when he saw the beast by the creek. He seemed to be examining the tracks left of Peter's makeshift cart. He had bolted suddenly and headed toward his cabin.

Tracy, in the meantime, was still sick. Peter would make her eat some food and drink liquids. He knew that if she did that, at least she would not die of dehydration.

On the third day, when Peter carried Tracy to the new shelter, she smiled when she went in, although she was still sick. There were two beds, a fireplace, and counters with utensils and most other things that a cook would want in a kitchen. Peter built a campfire at once and waited until it got strong. He left the shelter and went down by the stream. He smiled. He could not even see the smoke. That meant they would be safe.

They celebrated the new shelter by making a stew with the bird meat that Peter had caught the day before. He also had food that he had taken a few days earlier from the beast's cabin. Now all that Peter had to go was to get more food and keep Tracy healthy. He would do anything to keep her alive until he found a way to go home with her. Peter figured that by now it was probably February and that winter would soon end.

24

For the next several weeks, Tracy's health continued to deteriorate. Peter kept her alive by making sure she ate some food and drank some liquids. He rarely left the shelter. When she felt better, he would tell her about his parents, Mr. Jones, and some of his stories. He also told her about the life in town. Tracy would sit looking at Peter and listening attentively. She asked him about life in town, and she would remember things as he spoke. All her childhood memories were coming back. She also told him about the mother whom she had not seen for several months before she took the plane ride with her father. She would look for her once they got to town.

Peter told her that once they were back in town, he would make contacts to build a city there by the river. People would be attracted by the hot springs and the wonderful nature. He would make sure the new town was called Tracy. Once the town was built, he would make sure there was a sanctuary for the animals. These animals had been here for thousands of years. "A town may drive them away, so we'll make sure they will be happy, too," Peter said.

Tracy liked the idea, since she had lived in that part of the world for all her adolescent life. For Peter, it would be perfect since he would be living in a town without missing the wilderness that he had grown to love.

On the days when she felt sick, he spent most of the day hunting, getting firewood, and preparing wood. Peter had discovered a way to catch hares by seeking them under the snow. He also found a large amount of corn buried under the snow in several fields by the village.

The worst times were the long nights. He would sit alone as Tracy slept. The winter season persisted as though it was going to last forever, but the nights were getting shorter. He was worried all the time, not about the beast, but about Tracy. This helped him forget fear and worry about the beast. She had become weak at times, and he almost forced her to eat and drink. Peter hoped that the upcoming spring season would bring with it fresh flowers and other herbs that would cure her.

As for the beast, Peter was not overly worried about him. There was no way the beast would see the smoke from their camouflaged shelter as the smoke escaped through the hidden chimney to the top of the mountain. Even if the beast were to see the smoke, he would attribute it to the hot springs or he would not know its source. If, for any reason, the beast was to barge in, Peter had as a last resort dug a hole in front of the shelter even deeper than the one he had built in front of his shelter when he was staying by the river.

The days were getting longer and the weather getting warmer, though it was unpredictable most of the time. On one day it would be sunny and the temperature would reach fifty or even sixty. Then for a whole week it would snow continuously. Peter would take advantage of the sunny weather and gather firewood or go hunting.

He would take special care not to leave any tracks or footprints, especially near the shelter. He was also watchful, looking in every direction when he left the shelter or returned just in the event the beast was watching him.

These precautionary measures did not prevent a scary hour when on one afternoon, the beast seemed to be coming in the direction of the shelter. He had his machete in his hands. He seemed to be following some tracks in the snow. Peter had just returned from a trip to the village and headed directly inside to check on Tracy. He had only erased the tracks near the shelter, but those from where the creek parted to the main creek were visible. Peter could see the beast from an opening in the shelter. The giant creature walked along the tracks. He then looked up to figure out where the hidden shelter was.

For several long minutes, Peter watched the beast with horror. The door was covered with branches and would not arouse suspicion. The beast stood about fifty feet from the shelter and kept examining the area.

Tracy was sleeping and Peter did not wake her up. His plan was that if the beast came into the shelter, he would fall into the hole and Peter would have some time to escape and disappear behind the falls. If the beast did not fall in the pit, then Peter was planning to fight him with a wooden spear that he had made.

At one point, the beast went up to where the ravine was, then he came back, passing by the entrance. Peter squatted under the wood floor, his hands holding firmly to the spear. The beast stood just a few feet from him and seemed to be examining the top of the mountain. However, after several minutes of examining the area, the beast left. Peter was relieved and sighed deeply. He watched the beast stroll along the creek, then head to the river.

Peter wanted to follow him and destroy his shelter. He had been thinking of doing that for several days now. If he somehow burned the cabin, the beast would have no place to stay, but how would he burn the cabin?

Days were passing fast, and the snow was melting in the valley. Peter noticed that the days were getting longer and the sun did not set until late in the evening. The birds started to return to the area in large numbers. At first, they just appeared on top of the naked trees on sunny days. Then countless animals were becoming visible. There were chipmunks, muskrats, and squirrels as well as rabbits, deer, and elk.

The white scenery was gradually being replaced by a green one. At first, the patches of grass near the river turned green, then the small flowers started to pop out from under the ground, sometimes piercing the soft layer of the snow. The veiled nature, after the long winter months of swathing, was finally casting its veil aside to reveal its magical charm as it exploded with life in all its forms.

As the flowers and other plants were becoming abundant, Peter and Tracy were eating more and more of these fresh plants. Peter had also found a new source of delicious food. Eggs were becoming plentiful. Peter had discovered many nests of birds by the elm trees at the valley. The eggs were tiny and sometimes he would eat a dozen of them and still be hungry. Peter would boil the eggs in the hot waters of the geyser.

As the quality of food improved, Tracy's health also improved. The fresh flowers and plants were always available in the shelter, and Peter encouraged her to have a lot of them with the meals. Even the smell inside the shelter changed from a clammy one to that of a garden full of fresh flowers.

One evening, when Tracy was sitting on the bed, Peter approached her and held her hands. The weather outside had been sunny all day. The snow had been melting fast in the last several days. The night was quiet but cold. The creek outside was flowing rapidly, emanating pleasant gurgling sounds. They listened for a while, then Peter broke the silence and told her that since the snow had melted, they would be going home soon.

"But how about the beast?" she asked.

"You're right. I can't imagine him leaving us alone."

"So what are you gonna do?"

"I don't know. He is a vicious creature, and sooner or later we'll have to confront him."

"With what?" asked Tracy.

Peter fetched his spear and waved it in the air. "With this," he said, pointing to the spear. "I'll have to do it if we're gonna leave this wilderness."

"Couldn't we find a way to go home without having to fight

him?" She fixed her large green eyes on him and then went on examining the flames.

"We are here stranded in the wilderness full of animals. But we could survive, if it weren't for the beast. I wish there was a way to leave this wilderness without having to confront him."

"We can't do that either, Tracy," he added.

"Why not?"

"Because he'll continue to rob and kill people in the neighboring towns."

Tracy got up and went to the fireplace. Peter was thinking of his last sentence, of the neighboring towns that the beast would continue to rob and kill. His blue eyes fixed on the top of the chimney. After a couple of minutes, he looked at her with a big smile. "I think I've got it, Tracy. Here is a sure way to go home without fighting the beast."

"What is that?"

"I'll follow the beast to the town."

"What do you mean?"

"He goes to the town every once in a while to steal food and rob, right?"

"Yes, but how would you know when he will go next?"

"Easy. When he runs out of food."

"And how will you know he's run out of food?"

"He won't have any food left tomorrow."

"How do you know that? Were you at his cabin today?"

"No, but I will be there tomorrow. As soon as the beast leaves, I'll take all his food. Any food that I can't carry, I'll destroy. When he comes back and finds he has no food, he will have no choice but to go to the town and restock his groceries, and I'll follow him." Peter watched as Tracy's eyes opened wide with wonder. He was proud of himself.

The next morning, the sun shone. The snow had melted, except on top of the mountains. Patches of snow also remained in the shadows and in the ditches. Before he left, Peter made sure the beast did not see him.

"Listen, Tracy. As soon as I get to town, I'll head to the police and I'll return to get you."

"But I'll worry a lot about you."

"If I don't return in a few days, you should proceed immediately to where the old man told me to go. There is a gas station by the road. You will find it if you look hard."

Peter followed the creek down until he reached the main creek in the valley. The water was rushing downstream everywhere, creating little waterfalls here and there. All types of flowers were adorning the nature that just was born of the long winter. Some plants had flowered, but the trees still had no leaves. The buds, however, were conspicuous on the branches. The birds soared to the skies, celebrating the advent of the spring. Peter, however, was watching the area for any trace of the beast. He was now nearing the cabin. It was still early morning. Peter hid behind a boulder and watched the beast's house.

An hour later, the beast came out. He had his machete in his hand as usual. Peter had not seen him for a while, but he looked even uglier than ever. He was barefoot and wearing the same torn clothes. Even the hole in his forehead seemed to be getting deeper. The beast left in the upstream direction. Peter waited for five minutes and went into the cabin.

In less than ten minutes, he was out with all the food. After taking some for himself, Peter placed the food in a box, secured it firmly, and hid it near the river under a tree so that the animals would not get it. He then returned and searched for a place to watch the beast. He decided to stay at the grotto above the cabin. It would allow him to see the cabin at all times without being seen.

The day was warm, but it got colder at night. Peter recalled the frigid weather when he had to remain in the grotto in the winter months. It was not a bad experience if he emerged safe, he thought. He was cured of his disease and had won a dear friend, Tracy.

Later at night, Peter saw a fire inside the cabin. He knew the beast was back. Peter could imagine the beast getting furious upon discovering the absence of the food.

Peter woke up early and proceeded to a point where he could see the beast if he left. For several hours, there was no sign that he was leaving the cabin. Peter got worried, for he thought the beast might have gone without Peter seeing him. Around noon, the beast left, proceeding in the upstream direction of the river. Peter followed him as the beast was forcing his way to the riverbank.

As he passed by his first shelter, Peter realized that the beast was not going to any town. He was probably just going hunting, for Peter had surveyed all this area and there was no human settlement in that vicinity. Peter thought of going back to preserve his strength for the time when he would have to hike to the town with the beast. When Peter got to the forest that he had witnessed burning in the fall, a flood of memories came sweeping back.

In a couple of hours, Peter was at the cabin. He first checked to see if he had forgotten any food at the cabin, but there was nothing. Peter left, went to the grotto, and waited again. He figured that the beast would leave at night. Peter was right. The beast was back soon, and after he rested for an hour, left again. But this time he proceeded downstream. Peter followed him, keeping a good distance between them.

When the beast got to the hot springs area, he veered to the left, climbing a series of hills. By now it was becoming dark. Peter could only see the top of the mountains. He could no longer see the beast, but he could hear his footsteps.

The beast climbed the mountainous series that stood erect like a huge wall. Peter had not thought of climbing them before because he'd thought they were a continuation of the range by the crashed plane. His heart pounded as he hoped to see towns on the other side of the mountain.

By the time they got to the top of the mountain range, it was dark. Only the top of the mountain range could be seen. The monotonous sounds of the insects had started and soon became loud, providing Peter with something to get busy with. The night was cold, and the winds became colder and gusty once on the top. Peter felt that it was about to snow.

The beast proceeded down the mountain, but Peter positioned himself behind a boulder as there were no trees to hide himself. He waited until the beast was at a safe distance, then he took a look at the dark valley below. At first he did not see anything. It was merely another dark endless page. Then suddenly, he was overwhelmed with joy when he saw faint lights moving. There were red moving lights down below. "It is a road," Peter whispered. There was finally a real road with cars.

Peter did not know how long he stood there motionless, his eyes glued to the red-and-yellow lights moving at a turtle's pace, when he noticed that the beast was gone. Peter wanted to follow him, but an idea occurred to him. Why not just remain where he was until daybreak; then he would go to the road and then to the nearest town? Let the beast do whatever he was about to do. But he saw himself getting up and walking slowly in the direction of the beast's footprints; he wanted to know what he was up to. He was sure he was going to go to the nearest town to rob and steal.

Peter was trying to decide what to do. He did not want to take any unnecessary risks. Tracy was still sick, and she needed him. On the other hand, he could just go to the road until he saw people and they would take him to where he wanted to go. Or he could warn the people about the beast and he would be arrested soon.

Peter wasted no time and hurried down in the beast's direction. At least he would warn his victims. After a minute of running, he stopped. He noticed that the beast's footsteps had also halted. Peter stopped and listened. For the next minute, silence prevailed. Peter imagined the beast waiting to pounce on him.

A minute later, Peter could hear the beast advancing toward him. Peter did not know what to do. He could stay where he was and hope he was wrong, but the beast continued walking in Peter's direction, as though he knew where he was hiding. Peter had to make a quick decision or it might be too late. The heavy footsteps stopped for a second, then continued. Through the top of the boulder where Peter was hiding, he could see the shadow of the machete in the beast's hand.

Peter jumped up and raced down the mountain. The beast might decide to resume his original plan of getting food from the town and leave him alone. But he was wrong. The beast was at his heels. Peter decided to go to the river's area. It was easier to hide there, he thought. Besides, he could always use the waterfall shelter.

The night provided a good cover for Peter. He continued running without halting to rest. He fell several times on the way, but he got up as soon as he fell. The heavy footsteps behind him would not let him stop or even slow down. The beast was crying every now and then, "I'll get you, boy. I kill you now. I've got you now for sure."

About half an hour later, Peter was by the river. He had to cross it to get to the creek and then go to the waterfall. In the past, he would have used the long fallen trees to form bridges over the river, but it was dark now and it would be difficult for him to find anything. Peter continued looking for a long fallen tree to span the river. At some distance he saw what looked like a tree over the river. He climbed a branch protruding from the riverbank. As he came on top of it, the branch collapsed and Peter fell in the water. He was, however, near the bank, and he forced his way to the trees guarding the river. Soon he was walking along the water surrounded by a vertical wall.

The threatening curses of the beast thundered in the quiet night. Peter did not pay attention to them and kept moving. Minutes later, he came to a cavity by the water. He went there and lay on its floor. He would not be discovered easily. The only way for someone to find him was to sail down the river. Peter heard the beast, screaming and threatening that he would kill him.

An hour later, the thundering of the beast stopped, and Peter finally calmed down. He started to put together a plan of action for tomorrow. He would take Tracy and go to that road he saw that night. It was a sure thing this time.

That night Peter had a dream. He was home with both his parents. Peter introduced Tracy to them. He and Tracy were telling them their story in the wilderness. The only person missing was Aunt Pauline.

25

The singing of the birds awakened him early. Still half asleep, he kept listening to their singing. There were innumerable kinds of singing sounds. Some were continuous tunes that would stop suddenly, then resume with a different pace, and others were intermittent melodies, which slowed or gained speed as they commingled with other bird sounds. There were chants and carols that would start suddenly and continue for a while, then become more intense with one sound dominating the others. Moreover, the chants ranged from almost inaudible singing to loud incessant shrieks as though the birds were fighting.

That morning Peter heard more bird singing than on any previous day. Before venturing into the wilderness, he had thought that all bird singing was the same. Throughout his journey, he had noticed some other kinds. But today, he realized that there were as many bird sounds as the number of birds.

As he was prepared to leave, he remembered the dream. He was surprised that he saw his mother, although she has been dead for years. He started to imagine his house. He imagined his father back in town and he and his father becoming friends again. Peter would have stayed longer and given free reign to his imagination while listening to the birds, but he wanted to get Tracy and go home.

I can't believe it. We can be home today. Peter then imagined himself in the town surrounded by Aunt Pauline, Mr. Jones, and the other people that he knew. *I'd better go now and take advantage of the daylight.*

Peter left the cavity quietly, after looking in all directions. The beast could still be there, waiting for him to make the first move, he thought. At first, he looked for a place to cross the river. He preferred to swim across the river, but the water was icy cold.

Not far from where he was, he saw a number of fallen trees forming a half bridge over the river. When he got to the end of the trunk, he was only halfway through. There was a distance of more than fifteen feet left. He looked around and saw a branch dangling from a huge tree. He grabbed it and pushed himself. He glided smoothly over the water and landed at the river but only a couple feet from the other side. He quickly got up and got out of the freezing water, rubbing his hands for warmth.

Peter climbed a bluff and looked for any suspicious sign. Everything was quiet. There was no trace of the beast. He then headed directly to the mountain shelter. As he got close to the entrance, he smiled and looked forward to telling Tracy what he had found. *I wonder what Aunt Pauline will think about this adventure?* She might think he was crazy, but she would be surely happy to see him.

Peter was just a few steps from the shelter when he heard heavy footsteps behind him. His heart sank as he turned around and looked. *Disaster has struck*, Peter thought. The beast was fifty yards away. Peter stood still for a second, but he was able to regain his self-control. It was too late for him to change his course and go elsewhere, for the beast knew by now where the hidden shelter was.

Peter rushed in and in no time removed the branches from the shelter's entrance. Tracy was still sleeping. Peter carried her and hid her at the side of the shelter under the wood floor. No sooner had he settled in his hideout than the beast burst in. Peter could not see him, but he could hear his heavy footsteps on the elevated wood floor. Peter got his spear ready. He could hear the beast advancing slowly. *I could surprise him and stab him with my spear, but it may break and then we're gone.* Peter waited, hoping the beast would fall in the pit.

As he crouched, thinking what to do, he heard a clamorous sound as the beast fell in the pit. Peter wasted no time. The noisy fall had awakened Tracy, who opened her big green eyes and glanced at Peter, then closed them again. He carried her and left the shelter. Peter figured that it would be a full minute before the beast could get out. By then, he would be safe elsewhere.

Peter and Tracy, now awake, ran down the mountain, but there was no trace of the beast. It wasn't until they got to the creek that they saw him at the entrance of the shelter, limping and holding his forehead. He seemed to be looking for them. After standing there for several minutes, the beast went inside the mountain shelter. Peter hurried and pushed Tracy gently in the shelter behind the waterfall. When he came out to check on the beast, the mountain shelter was burning. *The wicked beast set it on fire*, Peter thought. *Now I'm going to do the same thing to his cabin.*

The beast then came down and stood by the waterfall where he had last seen them. He seemed to know the general area of their whereabouts but not the exact place. Peter was watching him from behind the rocks.

Peter went inside the waterfall shelter, assured Tracy that they were safe, and told her about the road he had found.

"Was it a real road with people and everything?"

"It was so dark that I didn't see the people, but I saw lights from the passing cars."

"Did you see a town, Peter?"

"No, but all we have to do is go there and wait for a police car to pass."

"Then go where?"

"Then we can go home and stay with my aunt. You would not have to worry about anything. You can go to school and even work, if you want."

Peter then gazed at her and looked at the door. "But first, we have to get out of here. Even if the beast is gone, how do I know he is not waiting for me to leave, just like he did when I crossed the river and went to our shelter?"

About an hour later, Peter came out of the shelter, but the beast was still there. The beast had chosen a spot on a small hill about fifty yards from the falls so that he could see any of their movements.

We are trapped, thought Peter. If he remained in his position, there would be no way out. *We'll be dead. We are prisoners. And worse, we have no food here. I think I'll wait until night falls; then I'll leave quietly.*

Peter, however, was becoming restless. He had thought of a way to get at the beast, but he had to leave without being seen if his plan was to succeed. But how would he leave? The beast would surely see him. In order for Peter to leave safely, he would have to pass the treeless field before getting to the small elevation, then to the river.

I have to leave now, Peter thought. *At least I know where the beast is. But if he hides himself, then I won't know where he is until he surprises me.*

Peter spent the rest of the day thinking of a way out, but there was no safe way. Before they slept that day, he was hoping that the beast would be gone in the morning, thinking that they were elsewhere.

When they awoke in the morning, Peter went up and looked. The beast was there. *He has apparently spent the whole night there*, Peter thought. *I have to figure a way out.*

He went down to the falls and started to explore all the possible ways to leave. One alternative was to simply get out and run. The beast would have to follow him, but Peter did not like the idea, since it was possible for the beast to catch up with him. The other possibility was for Peter to sneak quietly until he got to the river, but he would run the risk of being seen. He also thought of other ways, but he rejected them all.

Peter explained his dilemma to Tracy and asked for her help.

"What are you going to do when you get out?" she asked.

"I'll have a surprise for the beast."

"So you're not going to that road to get help."

"This will be the second thing I'll do, but first I want to give the beast the surprise of his life."

"Aren't you going to tell me?"

Peter whispered his idea to her as though he was afraid the beast would hear him. Tracy was amused and hugged him.

"Tracy, think of a way so that I can leave without him seeing me."

"I can't believe you ran out of ideas yourself."

"Well, I do have some ideas, but you know I can't fight a monster."

"But you're smarter than he is."

"You're smart, too. Why don't you think of something?"

Tracy seemed to be thinking intensely. Finally she looked at Peter. "Why not make a bow and arrow to shoot the beast? Didn't you create the first fire with that?"

Peter liked the idea since the arrow would be more precise, but he did not have the tools in his shelter.

"Maybe I'll find something to make a bow from here in the shelter."

Peter then got his knife and chopped a thick stick that he found by the falls. He walked by the edge of the falls and examined the currents of water plunging down below.

"Do you know, Tracy, where this water is going to?"

"Of course. It's going to the creek."

"Exactly. And from the creek, where does it go?"

"To the river."

"Precisely," said Peter.

"What are you getting at?"

"I thought of something. If we had a sheet of paper and a plastic bottle, we could send a message. You see, this river eventually grows and passes by numerous cities until it reaches the Mississippi and eventually the Gulf of Mexico. And if we send a message, someone will eventually see it."

"But it may take months until the message reaches there."

"No. If we had the bottle, it could be there in hours, but there is no use. We have no bottle. We must think of another solution."

"Well, I feel strong now and I can run fast. Let's just run together."

Peter did not hear her. He was walking back and forth in the sanctuary, looking in all directions. He finally stopped at a tall round bush by the edge of the falls.

"Here is the solution, Tracy," he said, pointing to the bush.

"What do you mean, Peter? Are you going to make a bow from the bush?"

"No, I'll use it as an umbrella."

"Umbrella? I don't understand."

"I'll use the bush to cover me."

Tracy still did not understand. Peter cut the bush from the bottom. It was about six feet high with thick branches and a lot of leaves. Once he cut it, he cut some bottom branches in a way so that the tree would cover him well. He then carried it like an umbrella and placed it on his head. He lowered it until he disappeared and walked in the small chamber.

"Can you see me now, Tracy?"

"Not at all."

"But I can see you through the branches."

Peter put the bush aside and prepared to leave. "I will be back soon."

"Wait a minute. How about me?"

"I'll come soon to get you."

"Why don't you want to take me along?"

"Two reasons. First, there is no room for both of us to hide in the bush; and second, if he discovered the trick, it would be easier for me to run if I'm alone."

Peter sneaked out and the beast was still there. He was not disappointed. At least he knew where the beast was.

In the next few minutes, a slowly moving bush emerged outside the waterfalls. The beast did not pay any attention to it. Peter could see the beast sitting on the little hill, looking in all directions. Peter moved a few yards and remained in his position until the beast turned his glance away from the bush. He then moved a few more feet and stopped. The beast was looking at the other side.

Peter continued this process of moving and stopping until he was more than twenty yards from the falls. Now he had to cross the field, which was about one hundred yards before he would disappear behind a cliff near the river front, then he would not need any cover.

Peter wanted to continue his gradual advancement, but he changed his mind when he saw the beast coming his way. Peter had moved several more yards in the last minute when the beast saw him. The beast advanced several steps, examining the bush and then returning to his position. The beast then came down the little hill from the other direction. Peter took advantage of this and moved closer to the river where a boulder stood erect. He looked at the falls, and he could see Tracy's eyes glaring at him.

When the beast returned and noticed the bush in the center of the field, his glance froze. The beast came down off the hill and went to the bush. He was advancing slowly to it, his machete in his hand. When he got to the bush, he moved it around, but there was no one there. He went around the boulder and looked in the immediate area, but he could not find anything.

Meanwhile, Peter had taken advantage of the beast's brief disappearance and darted to the river, fixing the bush by the boulder. Peter was watching the whole episode with enjoyment, but he was preparing something more serious for the beast.

Peter went to the river and headed upstream. He walked fast, for he wanted to get to the cabin and then go to the crashed plane.

He would need the plane for his plan. Once at the cabin, he took a container that would hold a gallon of fuel and headed for the plane. He had become familiar with the area, and in less than an hour, he was at the plane. It sat there as before unaffected by time. It was probably noon or one o'clock in the afternoon, Peter thought.

He looked for the fuel tank of the plane but did not know where to start. He climbed the cabin and started looking for an extra fuel container. Under the backseats of the plane was a sheet of the floor that could be lifted. When he did that, he found the lower floor of the plane where luggage was kept, but Peter did not find anything. He jumped inside and started looking for fuel. He did not find any fuel, but he saw some tools.

Peter examined every inch of the plane. Finally he saw a small door beneath the left wing. When he broke it open, he found a little round lid of the fuel tank, but he could not open it. He used some of the tools that he got from the plane to break the cap. After a struggle, the cap of the fuel tank broke open. Peter wanted to know if there was fuel in the tank, so he threw a pebble in the opening and strained his ears. He could hear the bubbling sound of the pebble settling at the bottom of the tank.

Now, Peter needed a hose to get the fuel from the plane tank to his container. He went up in the cabin again and found the fire extinguisher. He cut the hose, and in a matter of a few minutes, the container was full of gas.

When Peter carried the container to the beast's cabin, he was filled with excitement. In minutes, the cabin would be reduced to ashes, he promised himself. He would set it ablaze with the fuel, burn it to the ground, and the beast would be homeless.

When Peter returned to the beast's cabin, he knocked at the door several times, just to make sure the beast had not returned, but there was no one there. He spilled the fuel inside and outside the cabin, over the wood furniture and around the walls. When he was through, he lit a small piece of wood, threw it on the fuel, and ran outside. He had barely made it to the boulder outside the cabin, when the entire cabin was ablaze. The fire consumed the cabin so fast that it was literally melting and disappearing.

26

Peter sat on the nearby boulder and thought of how to get Tracy and go to the new road. He thought of going and enticing the beast to the remains of his cabin.

Once the beast comes here and sees his home gone, he'll know that I am not hiding by the waterfall area and he'll quit watching it, he thought. *But that requires me going there and showing myself to him.*

After thinking of all possible solutions, he was unable to come up with any satisfactory alternatives. Once night fell, the beast would see the fire or the smoke and he might quit his watching post to investigate the fire. But Peter could not wait until night. It would be several hours before night came.

I think I'll just go to that road now and bring help. Tracy should be fine, even if help does not arrive until tomorrow. I should be there in a few hours. Nothing will stop me this time. There is not going to be another blizzard in May to trap me.

Having made up his mind, he headed downstream to reach the area where he would have to veer to the hidden mountain and then to the road. As he was by the grassy riverbed, he hoped someone had seen the fire so that he wouldn't have to do anything further. If the fire could be seen, firemen could be here in an hour. But no one had come to extinguish the wildfire last year and none would come this time either.

Peter was gone for just a few minutes, when he heard footsteps coming from the downstream side. He clambered up a tree and took a position where he could survey the area without being seen. Perhaps it was a ranger or a hunter, Peter hoped. After a while the comer emerged. It was the beast storming in his direction. He must have seen the smoke or smelled the fire, Peter thought. He remained in his position, watching the beast moving swiftly toward his cabin. Peter wanted to continue his hike, but this time, he would take Tracy, he thought.

But a thought occurred to him. The beast might see the cabin in flames and return to the waterfall area. *Then I must stay and see what he is going to do once he sees the charred remains of the cabin.*

Peter came down from the tree and followed the beast. Although he could not see the cabin, the smoke was visible, rising in the blue sky like a black column. In a few minutes, Peter had moved to where he could see the cabin's area. He could see the beast stopping just a few feet from the structure, which was still in flames. The roof and most of the walls were gone.

The beast seemed to want to go inside, but he was repelled by the flames. He tried with his bare foot to extinguish the fire, but he burned one of his feet badly. He then took his machete and started to fight the fire with it, as though it were an animal. The machine fell into the fire, but the beast soon retrieved it. He threw it on the ground by the boulder and returned to extinguish the fire with his bare hands. After a minute of struggling with the flames, he seemed to be giving up. Peter could see him just standing there, crying like a baby. The beast, then, went to the boulder where Peter had stood a few minutes ago and watched the fire. His weeping soon changed to mumbling. It then changed to a shrill and thunderous laughter. Peter was scared. *The beast is losing his mind*, Peter thought. He was laughing and turning around the boulder with the machete in his hand. He turned to the woods where Peter was hiding and started talking.

"Peter, you make my life miserable since you come. I know you here. You all over. Like there ten of you. I know you hear me. But I get you soon, boy, and I kill you and burn you. I know you and Tracy hid near waterfall. How you escape?"

Peter was frightened. He thought the beast knew where he was hiding. He froze in his position and made sure that he breathed without a sound.

By now, most of the cabin was gone. The wind blew the fire, and Peter was almost suffocated by the smoke. At times, he could not stand the heat and the smell. The fire was rapidly turning the cabin into a pile of charred lumber. *The beast not only has no food now, he has no place to sleep either*, Peter was thinking. *But he won't be needing it, since he is going to be in police custody soon.*

Peter decided that since the beast had given up, the best thing was to leave now. He would get Tracy from the shelter and head to the road at once. He quietly came down out of his hideout and started heading downstream. At this moment he heard footsteps in the woods. Peter thought the beast had started to follow him. He looked through the trees, and the beast was still sitting on the boulder, but the footsteps continued. Peter was baffled. He was sure the footsteps were those of a human. Who could the person be? Instead of being happy, he was frightened.

Peter mounted a tree and looked to see who the person was. As soon as he did that, he jumped again from the tree to the ground and hurried to that person. It was Tracy. Peter wanted to warn her that the beast was there, but it was too late. The beast had also heard the footsteps, for he got up and headed to where Tracy was coming from.

As the beast tried to run to her, he was limping even more than before. It became clear to Peter that his feet and hands were burned. The beast slowed down and looked. Peter and Tracy made no movement. The beast went back to pick up the machete, but he threw it away as it was still hot. He then returned to where he heard the footsteps and started surveying the area. Peter's courage returned, especially when he saw him approaching without the machete. As he was trying to decide what to do, Tracy ran and disappeared behind some trees. A minute later, Peter saw her by the burning cabin. She snatched the machete and threw it inside the burning structure. In no time, she came back and tried to join Peter.

The beast, however, was faster and tried to grab her. Peter immediately came out and screamed at the beast, "Leave her alone, stupid beast." The beast, upon seeing Peter, became infuriated and charged him. He carried Peter and attempted to throw him into the burning cabin, but his burnt hands would not allow him and he eventually threw Peter on the ground.

"You not escape now, boy. I burn you." He then came again and attempted to grab Peter.

"Not on your life, monster," said Tracy.

The beast grabbed Peter, lifted him, and tried to throw him. At this point, Tracy jumped on the beast and clung to his neck, scratching his face with her nails. He turned around to shake off Tracy's grasp, but he could not use his hand without considerable pain.

After freeing himself from Tracy, he reached again for Peter, who was still on the ground. Tracy again clung to the beast's shoulders. When he wanted to remove her, she bit him on his hand. The beast threw her to the ground, cussing her, "You bad girl. I kill you too and throw both of you in fire."

Peter by now had gotten up. He was in pain, for he was moving slowly. But seeing the beast throwing Tracy to the ground, Peter threw a stone at the beast, which hit him at the head. The beast then left Tracy and came to Peter.

Peter moved fast from his path and signaled to Tracy to leave. They both ran downstream, but soon the beast caught up with them. He seized Peter and threw him in the water. Tracy again came at him and grabbed his hands. He was trying to remove her, but she locked her hands around his neck. By now Peter was out of the water.

The beast was trying hard to detach Tracy, but she had become a piece of him. His hands were becoming weaker. At one point, the beast grabbed a stick from the ground and tried to strike Peter on the head. Peter moved fast but struck his head on a boulder. He was hurt and blood poured from his forehead.

The beast was about to hit him again when Tracy suddenly struck the beast's head with a rock the size of a man's fist. The beast stumbled for a second and seemed to be falling, but he regained his control. Peter, however, did not wait and struck another rock at the upper part of the beast's head. The beast staggered and fell to the ground.

Peter walked slowly to where the beast lay motionless. He took an examining look at his body, but there was no movement at all.

"I think he's dead," said Peter.

"Are you sure?"

Peter listened to his heart, and he lifted one of the beast's hands. When he let the hand go, it dropped to the ground.

"Yes, he is dead."

Peter collapsed to the ground. Tracy came to his assistance and examined him. He had numerous bruises, in addition to a deep cut to his head. His body was hurting all over.

"Just lie down here, Peter."

Peter held Tracy's hands and pressed them tenderly, looking her in the eyes.

"Thank you, Tracy. You saved my life."

"I can't believe I did what I did."

He hugged her. "You were great, sweetheart."

"You too, Peter. I feel invincible when I'm with you."

"We'll have to sleep here tonight," said Peter.

The wind was getting cold, as though it was getting ready to snow, and it was becoming dark.

"I'll get the campfire ready," said Tracy. "Let's move downstream, Peter. I don't want to sleep near him."

"How about his body?"

"The police will come tomorrow and bury him. I can't do it myself."

Peter was able to walk a few yards so that he wouldn't see

the beast's body. Tracy walked to the burning cabin and brought a piece of burning wood. She used that to build the fire. Peter lay down next to it.

"You know, Tracy, I'm sick and exhausted, but I can't fall asleep."

"That is because you're hungry. We're both hungry."

"Don't even remind me. I'm starved. We both spent two terrible days without anything to eat."

"But there is nothing."

Peter got up. He remembered that he had some food hidden nearby.

He went to the place where he had concealed the remainder of the food he had stolen from the beast, but the food was gone. Only the cloth in which he had wrapped the food remained. Raccoons must have eaten it. He went back with a dismal look on his face. He was shaking due to hunger. He told Tracy what had happened.

"Let me see what I can do."

Tracy proceeded to a tree by the river. Peter closed his eyes and tried to sleep. He smelled the odor of wood burning. *But I don't have to put up with it for long*, he thought. His craving for food was stronger and made him forget the obnoxious smell. Even the singing of the insects had stopped that night. They must have been repelled by the smoke, but it was also the cold weather that made the insects vanish. He looked in the direction of Tracy near the river. *If she is lucky and finds something to eat, then I can sleep. Otherwise, I probably will just stay awake all night*. But he wanted to eat something so bad. Besides, they had a long way to go tomorrow.

In a few minutes, Tracy was back. She was carrying a dozen birds' eggs and some wild plants that resembled romaine lettuce.

"Where did you get them from?"

"I got the eggs from some nests by the hill and the vegetables from the riverbank. I get a lot of eggs every year, and we used to eat the plants as vegetables. I used to do that every spring."

Tracy was talking with pride. Peter realized that Tracy had come a long way. She had saved him twice that day. He held her hand so as to show her his gratitude. They placed the eggs near the fire and watched with enjoyment as the eggs cooked. Soon they were eating the eggs with the wild lettuce. When they were done eating, their hunger was allayed. They lay down near the fire and slept.

27

Peter woke up the next morning to the sound of something falling in the river. But he did not pay any attention to it and continued listening to the birds singing. It was cold and he put his arms around Tracy, getting closer to her. He looked at the campfire, but it was gone. The few logs that remained solid were rapidly turning into ashes. He got up and fed the campfire with small pieces of broken branches. Smoke flooded the place. He kept blowing at the fire until it started blazing. He placed more logs since it was early, and he figured they would be there for another hour. He lay down again next to Tracy and waited for her to awaken.

Tracy opened her eyes and looked at Peter next to her. He noticed that she closed her eyes at once and brought her face closer to his. Peter smiled and closed his eyes, as though he was in a dream and did not want the dream to end.

No longer had he closed his eyes than he heard the sound by the river again. It was coming from the river, which was about fifty feet away. Peter got up and listened carefully. The sound stopped, but Peter had become an expert in the sounds, footsteps, and other voices in the forest. His senses told him that there was someone or something there by the river. Could it be a bear or a mountain lion? Or could it be the beast?

"But that's impossible. He is dead," he whispered to himself.

At this minute, he heard a splash in the river. He stood up and looked, but he could not see anything.

It's an animal, Peter thought. *The fire will scare him away*. He looked again and tried to sleep, but he could not fall asleep anew.

Tracy seemed to be sleeping like a baby. He covered her with his coat and sat listening to the melodies of the birds.

Soon, the sun came out. He first saw it as it reflected in the snowcapped mountains gleaming under the sun as though they were sheets of glass. The last spring snow had melted by the valley in the warmth of the last several days. Wildflowers in amber, pale-purple, and crimson colors filled the riverbed and the low slopes.

Very soon we will be gone and there will be no one to enjoy them, thought Peter. *What a waste.* He recalled the town that he wanted to help build there in the future. He imagined the road that would be built along the river, which would have several bridges. There would be houses on the hills and at the foot of the mountains. He'd make sure all the shelters he and Tracy stayed at would be preserved.

Peter started to go over important events that had occurred to him in the last nine months in the wilderness. "Yes, nine months," he whispered. "That's what it takes a woman to give life to a baby. This wilderness is the mother that gave me a new life when it cured me of that disease. This is the same wilderness that gave millions of first settlers before me a first crack at life before there was any civilization. I'm a continuation of these pioneers and I proved that nature is still generous."

A soft sound brought him back to reality. He thought he saw a shadow coming from the river toward them. He looked in that direction and his heart sank. It was the beast in wet slacks. He was carrying a big rock, oozing with water. The rock was about two cubic feet long. The beast threw the rock at Peter and Tracy. Peter swiftly moved and pushed Tracy aside. The huge stone missed them and landed in the middle of the campfire.

The beast then came to Peter and tried to lift him, but he seemed to be weak. His fist would not hold Peter firmly, due to the fire injury. Peter slipped from his hands easily. He led Tracy, who had just awakened, and ran. To his surprise, the beast did not follow them. Peter ran for about a hundred feet and stopped, looking at the beast.

Tracy was shaking violently. She kept looking at the beast as though she were seeing a zombie. She glanced at Peter, demanding an explanation. "I thought he was dead," she said.

"He was just unconscious. We should've finished him off last night."

"He almost killed us. Let's get out of here."

"I think he's gonna be harmless for a few days until his hands and feet heal."

The beast continued to sit by the campfire, getting warmth from the blaze. He did not pay any attention to them.

"What happened though, Peter?"

"I heard a sound by the river. It was the beast getting the large stone from the water."

Peter came a few feet closer to the beast and watched him. He was hugging the flame with his hands. The wet stone was still in the middle of the fire, and it had already turned black from flames.

"I think we can now leave safely," he said.

Peter was returning to Tracy, when an explosion shook the forest. It came from the beast's direction. Peter looked and saw the beast on his side, bleeding. Peter and Tracy ran to where the beast lay motionless. The wet boulder, in the middle of the fire, had exploded and scattered into pieces.

"Look, Peter. He wanted to kill us with the stone, and now the stone killed him."

"But he is not dead," said Peter. "Look, Tracy. He is moving."

They came closer to the beast. He was bleeding from his head and his chest. Blood oozed from his body and created a small pool on the grass. The beast looked at them with submission and closed his eyes. Peter came a step closer and lifted the beast's hand, but it fell to the ground. The beast was finally dead.

"Let's go, Tracy."

Peter led Tracy downstream. They continued hiking without looking behind them. They were both walking quietly. Peter's mind was now a stage with many competing thoughts, the scene of the beast trying to kill them, the scene of the first town, and the scene of Aunt Pauline hugging him.

In an hour they were at the hill leading to the high range abutting the road. Peter was tired from yesterday, but he felt a sudden energy. He and Tracy climbed the hill, resting every now and then, but they did not stop to look for food. They were hoping to find a hot meal soon.

It was late morning when they got to the top of the mountain. Peter collapsed on the ground. His wounds and bruises were causing him excruciating pain. Tracy and Peter looked at the other side of the range, and they both froze in their position without saying a word. There was a town at the end of the road. Peter had seen this place at night, but he could not see the town at that time.

They sat on a tree trunk forming a natural bridge and examined the panoramic view surrounding them. On the one side of the mountains was the civilization with all that created to make life a bit easier. On the other side was the virgin wilderness. The wilderness had its own stillness and reverence, a feeling of isolation and remoteness born of the vast spaces and monstrous mountains. Peter thought that he might never experience that sort of beauty again, beauty in slopes painted with rows of evergreen pines on top and a rainbow of the flowering early summer colors down below, beauty in the grassy ground adorned with strange flowers, cactus, blossoms, mosses, and lichens. Added to that, the tranquility and serenity were a domain for his restless soul. All noises of the town and of all that man calls civilization were on the other side of the mountain. All he could hear was the natural music and singing of the wild. And the important thing was that he was in the center of it. He was a part of every robin who sang, every eagle that soared to the skies, and every squirrel that rushed to its hole. It all belonged to him without a rival. But now he was leaving it.

Days ago, he would have paid anything to leave the wilderness. Now he felt he was missing something vital by leaving it. He was sad, and for a while forgot where he was going.

They rested for some time, then they started descending. The elevation was not very steep. They were hiking together as though they were one piece. In about half an hour, they were at the road. But they stayed some hundred yards from the road, so as not to attract attention to their torn clothes. After a half an hour of hiking, they reached a telephone booth. Peter was overly excited. *Soon Aunt Pauline will be here. She will ask me to remain by the road until she gets here. She may only be a short distance.* Peter hurried to the phone, and he placed a call to his Aunt Pauline, after convincing the operator it was an emergency call. A man answered the phone.

"Can I speak to Pauline? . . . What do you mean she is no longer there? . . . Me? I'm her nephew, Peter. Who are you? . . . What? She died? . . . When? . . . "

Peter hung up the receiver and collapsed on the floor. He was crying quietly. Tracy came to him and asked him what had happened.

"My only aunt is dead."

"When did she die?"

"Six months ago."

"I'm sorry, Peter. Now both of us are without any relatives."

"Yes, without home and without a family."

Tracy hugged him as he sat by the phone booth. "At least we have each other," she said.

Peter stopped crying and got up. He went to the phone booth again and called the sheriff's department. Peter told the officer who answered the phone that he had some information about the beast. He figured that it was better to start that way than to explain to them what happened. The officer then asked him to stay where he was. Peter did not know where he was and gave them a physical description of the area around him.

In ten minutes, a sheriff's car stopped by the phone booth. Peter and Tracy were taken to the sheriff's station where they met the sheriff and briefly told him their story. He ordered lunch and asked them to give him more details. Peter and Tracy enjoyed their first real meal in a long time. The sheriff then ordered a helicopter. He wanted to take an army of men with him, but Peter assured him that the beast had become harmless due to the fire and the explosion. The sheriff took three strong men with him, and they all flew to the site of the beast.

From the plane, Peter could see all the places where he had spent almost a full year. He could see the river where it started and continued until as far as he could see. In a matter of minutes, they were at the beast's cabin, which was now reduced to ashes. Peter told them to go a little farther, where they saw the beast lying motionless. The sheriff asked Peter and Tracy to remain in the plane for their safety while he and his men came out. They advanced cautiously toward the beast, yelling at him to put his hands behind his back. There was no answer.

After several fruitless attempts to get his attention, the sheriff approached the beast with a gun in his hand. When he got to him, he kicked him with his foot. The beast did not move. One of the men checked his heart.

"He's dead. He just bled to death."

Peter and Tracy came down and approached the beast. This was the first time that Peter was looking at the beast without being scared. This huge creature was finally harmless.

"But how did this explosion happen?"

"He threw a wet stone at us, and the stone landed in the campfire."

"Now it makes sense," said the sheriff. "Once the wet stone was in the middle of the campfire, the water inside its pores expanded and the rock exploded."

The sheriff then called his headquarters and asked them to send a medical team. They all then went back in the plane. Just when the plane was ready to take off, Peter stopped the pilot. "I almost forgot, Sheriff."

"What is it, young man?"

"The crashed plane?"

They flew again to the site. The sheriff had radioed to his department for more help.

On their way to town, Peter leaned over to Tracy. "You know, we have to start from zero. It is a different kind of battle here."

Tracy did not answer. She just smiled.

As Peter and Tracy were being driven to the bus station, the sheriff stopped them.

"I almost forgot. Stop at the accounting office and get your check."

Peter and Tracy looked at each other, perplexed.

"Our check?" they inquired together.

"Yes, there is a reward in the amount of ten thousand dollars for whoever provides information leading to the arrest of the beast. It's yours. Good luck, guys."